I0788861

ALSO BY ROB NETO

Fiction

Beyond the Grate
Into the Darkness Beyond

Adventure series

Beneath the Jungle of Cozumel: Connecting the Crowns

Non-fiction

Sidemount Diving The Almost *Comprehensive Guide 2ⁿᵈ edition*
Available in English, Dutch, German, and Spanish

BEYOND HOPE

ROB NETO

Published by Chipola Publishing, LLC,
Greenwood, Florida 32443, U.S.A.
www.chipolapublishing.com

Excerpt from *Beyond the End of the Line* © Rob Neto, 2024

Cover photography by Laurent Miroult; Artwork & design by Rob Neto

Author photography by Jen Neto

Printed in the United States of America

PUBLISHER'S NOTE

This is a work of fiction. Names, characters, places, and incidents either are the product of the author's imagination or are used fictitiously, and any resemblance to actual persons, living or dead, business establishments, events, or locales is entirely coincidental. While the names of certain locales, such as the International Hospital, Cozumel, and Marianna, are used to add depth and reality to the story, they are in no way meant to disparage such locales or past or present ownership of such establishments.

ISBN: 9781961612082

DEDICATION

This book is dedicated to the memory of Brendan Napier. A life taken too soon.

Analyze every tank every time without exception – Brendan's Law

ACKNOWLEDGMENTS

I'd like to thank the readers of my first two novels, *Beyond the Grate* and *Into the Darkness Beyond*. Those novels have been a success because of you. I keep writing for myself, but also for my readers. I especially thank those who have left reviews. I read every review and use the comments to improve my writing. I sincerely believe *Into the Darkness Beyond* is a better book than *Beyond the Grate,* and *Beyond Hope* is better than both. That's because of the reviews I've received on the first two books.

I would also like to thank all the other authors I have been reading over the past year. Your words and writing styles have certainly had an influence on my writing. I no longer read simply for entertainment. I now read as a way of research so I can incorporate styles that I see into my writing. This has even made my reading more enjoyable. While this book is short on dialogue, mainly because it all takes place underwater, I have incorporated more dialogue into my stories because of you. I have also incorporated other techniques and styles that I have encountered. I would name you individually, but I'm afraid I would leave someone out.

I would like to acknowledge Brendan Napier. He died too soon and due to an avoidable issue. Because of Brendan, I have since analyzed every single tank of air and nitrox from which I breathe. Carbon monoxide is an odorless and tasteless gas. The only way to know if it's in your tanks is by using an analyzer to test the air in them. At the time of this publication, a carbon monoxide analyzer cost about $150 and lasts about two years. It's a small price to pay for the peace of mind in knowing the gas you're breathing isn't going to get you killed.

Finally, I would like to thank my wife for supporting me throughout the writing of this third novel. I embarked on this writing journey many years ago but only recently began to devote more time to it. This is my third book to be published over the course of a year. She has not only had to be a sounding board to ideas I've had, but she's also been my first and last editor for each novel that I've written. That means she's read each novel at least twice. Her suggestions and advice have been invaluable to me.

FOREWORD

The idea for *Beyond Hope* came to me after a dive I did in Cozumel with a very good friend. We had discussed and agreed upon a dive plan, but the plan was not precisely followed. We ended up separated during the dive, and I spent about an hour looking for my friend, never able to find him.

The thoughts that ran through my head during the time I was looking for him kept getting more desperate. I wondered what had happened to him. I had lost a friend to carbon monoxide in Cozumel during my first visit there. Did the carbon monoxide analyzer fail? Was there carbon monoxide in his tanks and did he succumb to its effects? Did he have a medical event? He's in good shape, works out, eats right, but we hear of young kids passing out on basketball courts or football fields all too often. Was he stuck in some restriction unable to get himself free?

I also found myself wondering how I was going to tell his mother and fiancée that he had died while cave diving. And worse yet, I hadn't found his body. I wondered how I would be able to go back into the cave the next day to look for his body. Would I be able to set aside the emotions I was feeling to do what needed to be done. To add to that, the cave has more than five miles of tunnels in it. The area where we had been diving had about two miles of tunnels. I was thoroughly familiar with this cave, having been in every known part of it, surveyed every tunnel, and created my own map. It would likely still take several dives to locate his body, if it could be found.

When I finally surfaced because my air reserves were getting low, I retrieved my phone and called my wife. She was also a cave diver and knew the risks involved. She was just about to get in the car to come to the dive site when I saw a light coming out of the cave opening into the cenote. It was my friend, more than an hour behind schedule.

He had a decompression obligation, so I sat on the surface throwing rocks in the water right above his head. He spent a bit of his decompression dodging falling rocks. Once he cleared his decompression obligation and exited the water, I gave him a big hug. Then I yelled at him for diverging from the dive plan. He tried to talk his way out of it, but he knew he had not followed the plan. Lesson learned. No one was hurt. No one died. It was the first dive of the trip, and the rest of the dives went as planned with no further issues.

While some of the underwater incidents described in this book did occur, such as the main premise of the book, only the ideas were used. The tunnels described are real. Anyone who has been in them should recognize the descriptions in the story. The details in the story are products of the author's imagination. The incident was incorporated as a foundation, but imagination dictated the rest.

There are incidents in this book which are true. The story of Brendan, for example. I've included it because it serves as an important lesson for all divers, both cave divers and open water divers. I've also included references to other cave diving fatalities that happened in Florida and Mexico. These are all real. They did occur. This is all done to add to the story and make it more realistic. See if you can pick them out.

I've included parts about getting stuck in small restrictions. This happens from time to time to any cave explorer who is willing to go into such tight spaces. Some people might disagree with this. I don't include these scenes to encourage anyone to go into restrictions or to make contact with the cave. I include them because they are a part of reality. This is what happens in exploration. It's always happened in exploration.

In no way is this story or any of the scenes included in it intended to disparage the reputation of any living or dead person. The story is fictional from beginning to end with only snippets of real events inserted to add a sense of reality. The characters are not real. The actual divers involved in the incidents are not a part of this story and nothing in this story is meant to be applied to them or how they handled their own situations.

* * *

The story about Brendan Napier is true. I was a member of that dive and I helped bring his body out of the cave and assisted with resuscitation efforts. It was a horrible experience. For about a year after that incident, whenever I was diving with someone else, if they stopped moving for a few seconds I had flashbacks to that dive with Brendan. I still have the occasional flashback even after more than a decade. To this day, I still analyze every single tank I breathe from for carbon monoxide. I've found it in four tanks while away on a dive vacation. The levels were within acceptable limits, but still unacceptable for me. I advised the dive operator and the issue was corrected that day.

* * *

This book is a work of fiction. The characters, incidents, and dialogue are drawn from the author's imagination and are not to be construed as real. Any resemblance to actual events or persons, living or dead, is entirely coincidental. This story is simply one in which the author creates a story based on his imagination of what could have happened. The snippets of fact embedded in the story are included to give the story more depth and reality. They are by no means implicated in any wrongdoing by anyone.

There is no Joey Simmons. There is no Lindsey Carter. There is no Gary. These characters, as well as the other characters in the book, are all imaginative creations. This work of fiction simply takes an incident that occurred and creates a different version of fictional events to tell a story.

1

Joey

Well, this lead didn't pan out. It was two hundred feet long, maybe a bit longer. Not the one thousand plus feet I was hoping for. I still had to survey the line on the way out to know the exact length. First, I had to get out.

The tunnel was a decent size…initially. I was swimming along quickly, listening to the whirring sound coming from my large explorer reel as the spool spun rapidly feeding out line. I bought the explorer reel just for this trip. It held more than one thousand feet of cave line on its spool. I had high hopes that I would get to empty all the line from it into unexplored, virgin cave passage at least once during our weeklong vacation.

This was the third day of the trip. We had two more days of cave diving. We had been doing two dives a day. The first two days were duds. I was disappointed that I hadn't had the opportunity to use the explorer reel.

The first dive was our orientation dive with Jose. He was the local cave diver we met during our last trip who told us there were caves beneath the jungle of Cozumel. If it hadn't been for him, we'd never have even known they existed. He took us into the cave the first day to show us how to get to the guideline and give us a tour of the main attractions. Then he left us to our own devices. We did another dive after lunch that day and returned yesterday. Four dives and no leads. There were even tunnels not on the map that had line in them. Disappointed was an understatement.

Then today happened.

This was my first virgin cave passage. A passage that no other cave diver had ever found and been in. I was in a place on this earth - actually in this earth - where no other person had ever been. The first person there, and maybe the only person that will ever enter this tunnel. The excitement of finding and venturing into it was almost too much to bear.

Lindsey and Gary stayed behind in the tunnel leading to this one. I wasn't sure why they didn't follow. A little sad that they didn't follow, but at the same time, happy they hadn't. While it would have been nice to share the excitement of finding and seeing the virgin cave passage, I was happy to be able to lay claim to it by myself. Happy to be able to tell others I *had boldly gone where no man has gone before*. Yeah, I'm a little bit of a Trekkie. I wouldn't have been able to claim that if they had followed. The going where no man has gone before part, not the Trekkie part.

After about one hundred feet, the tunnel started to get smaller. Before the trip to Cozumel, I tied knots every ten feet on the cave line that was wrapped around the explorer reel. What a mess that was! First, unspooling the eight hundred feet of line that came on it. Then tying the knots as I spooled it back on. And of course, it got all tangled up…several times! Zoe, our cat loved it, but she only made things worse by getting tangled up in the line. The additional two hundred feet of line I put on it was so much easier to knot and spool on. If I ever buy another explorer reel, I'll try to order it without the line already spooled onto it.

Anyway, as I got farther into this new tunnel, I was sure I had counted ten knots. Kind of sure. In the excitement of the moment, I may have lost count.

Ten knots! One tenth of the line on my explorer reel!

The tunnel continued to get smaller. The walls got closer to each other. The ceiling dropped. But it wasn't too small for me to continue. So I continued forward hoping it would open up and get bigger again around the next corner.

It didn't. It kept getting smaller and smaller until I couldn't go any farther. I was sandwiched between the floor and ceiling of the cave, snuggled in between the walls. I almost couldn't take a full breath. As my lungs filled with air, I could feel the floor and the ceiling squeezing my torso. Some might get claustrophobic from being in such a place. Not me. It felt comfortable. Cozy.

I aimed my light beam straight ahead. I swear it looked like it opened up twenty feet farther in. If only I could get through the restriction between me and where it gets bigger. I grabbed the floor in front of me and tried pulling myself in. I gained maybe an inch. I anchored my heels on the ceiling and tried pushing myself in. I exhaled the air from my lungs trying to diminish my size. I pushed myself forward and felt myself move. I stopped. I had second thoughts about what I was doing. What if I got stuck and couldn't expand my lungs enough to take in a breath? There was cozy and there was crazy.

I quickly pushed back before I did get stuck in a tighter spot and I inhaled until my lungs were full, relieved I was able to do so. I lay there in my cozy cocoon, slowly breathing from my regulator, contemplating my situation. It was no use. The tunnel in front of me was too small.

Resigned to the fact that this tunnel wasn't going anywhere, at least not where I could fit, I secured the cave line I had just deployed around a small protrusion sticking out of the floor about a foot in front of my head. I wrapped the line around a few times before pulling my line cutter out of the sheath on my forearm and slicing the line about a foot and a half out from the wrap. I tied off the line and formed a loop on the end of it, hopeful that I would be able to use it sometime soon. Preferably the next day or two.

The loop was a thing I learned from an old-time cave diver and explorer back in Marianna, Florida where I did most of my cave diving. I was diving at Jackson Blue one day when this guy saw my explorer reel and approached me.

"Find any virgin passage in here?"

I looked at him, wondering what made him ask that question. Before I could answer, he continued.

"That's a lot of knotted line on that big reel. Looks like you're expecting to find a whole new section in here."

"Oh," I replied, a bit embarrassed. "No, I just got this and I'm bringing it with me to test the weight and balance. I'm heading to Mexico in a couple of weeks and I'm hoping to find some virgin cave down there."

He stood there nodding his head and smiling at me. I was thankful he didn't laugh at me, although I felt like he was probably holding back a laugh.

"Well, here's a little trick for you. Whenever you put line in the cave, leave a loop at the end so it's easier to connect the line from the reel to the loop when you return to continue pushing farther into unexplored territory. Much easier than tying the line around the end of the line or around a formation."

"Wow! Thanks for the tip!"

"Good luck in Mexico."

We both went back to setting up for our dives in Jackson Blue. I didn't know who this guy was, but I had a feeling he had put a lot of the line in the caves on Merritt's Mill Pond.

Here I was using that bit of information for the first time. I wasn't too sure why. I had no luck getting through the restriction. What made me think the next day would be different? Maybe it would. I could always eat one less taco at dinner. Always the optimist, Lindsey would say.

I placed a line arrow on the line pointing back the way I had come. The arrow had my initials on it – JS. If anyone ever ventured into this small tunnel, they would see it and know I was the one to have found it. I hoped to leave many more arrows in this cave.

I formed a loop large enough for my fist to pass through on the end of the line coming from the reel and tied the loose end back on itself. I then reeled the loop in until there were just a few inches of it sticking out of the line guide on the reel. Placing the loop over the stop screw I pulled in the line and rotated the stop screw clockwise until it was snug enough to prevent the spool from turning.

I tried to swing my arm around toward my back to secure the reel to a D ring. The problem was the reel was too big to fit back there in the small tunnel I was in. I clipped the reel to my left chest D ring instead, at least until I could back up enough to relocate it out of the way.

I tried to back up.

I didn't move.

I couldn't move.

I was stuck.

Flashbacks to my dive in Jackson Blue a year and a half earlier flew through my mind. It wasn't exactly the same. At least in this cave I could still see. There was no silt in this tunnel so nothing to obscure the visibility. In Jackson Blue I was squeezed in by the wall on the right and the ceiling dropping down to the floor on the left. There had still been a bit of vertical space.

Here, in this cave in Mexico, I was squeezed in between the floor and the ceiling as well. But instead of the smooth limestone of the Florida caves, the floor and ceiling of this tunnel were anything but smooth. It was like the cave had hundreds of fingers that were reaching out and grabbing me and holding me in place. I could almost feel the fingers wiggling to get a better grip on me.

The calm relaxed feeling I had started to slip away as I felt my breathing rate increase. My heart started to race. I closed my eyes momentarily to try to calm down before the anxiety got the best of me and I panicked. Panic wouldn't do me any good. Especially in this tight coffin I had gotten myself stuck in.

Okay, maybe not the best analogy to help calm my nerves.

Think cozy thoughts again.

Wait! Lindsey might still be able to see me. I shielded the beam of the light mounted on the back of my left hand with my right palm and looked for the illumination of her light. I could see a light coming from behind me, but it wasn't very bright, meaning she was likely pretty far away. Hopefully she was looking toward me.

I crossed my fins, the cave diving signal for *I'M STUCK!!!!* I waited to feel Lindsey tug the fins to let me know she was there and ready to help. I didn't feel anything. Nothing happened.

I shielded my light beam again. I still saw light coming from behind me. Lindsey must have been looking somewhere else and hadn't noticed my crossed fins. I moved my left hand back and aimed the beam behind me. I then wiggled my hand back and forth in a slow rhythmic pattern trying to get her attention.

I pushed the light head in toward my thigh to shield it and waited. Several seconds passed. Maybe a minute. It seemed so much longer. Still nothing. Why wasn't she responding to my light signal??

I wiggled my left hand frantically back and forth this time. A slow back and forth was meant to get the attention of the other diver on your team. A frantic movement was the signal for out of air. And there was only one way to respond to that.

There was still no response. There was no second stage regulator shoved in front of my face for me to breathe from. Lindsey must not have been able to see me.

I pulled my left hand back in front of my head and tried once again to free myself. I wiggled my body side to side and back and forth. I couldn't move forward because the tunnel was too tight to go any farther. And something was holding onto me around the front of my waist preventing me from moving backwards. Something was digging into my belly.

I brought my right hand down and tried squeezing it between the floor and my abdomen. It was too tight, though. I couldn't get my hand quite far enough to feel for what was grabbing me. Something else was grabbing at my arm. The cave had too many fingers trying to hold me in place. I lay there imagining thousands of fingers all over my body, grabbing it, and preventing me from moving. I could almost feel them moving.

The panic began to return.

Eyes closed, I concentrated on my breathing again. Slow deep breath in, count to five, slow exhale. I did this for a full minute, maybe longer.

With my breathing back under control and the panic abated for the time being, I returned my focus to my present situation. I had done a good job of sandwiching myself in this tight space.

Pulling my hand back in front of me, I noticed the dive computer on my wrist. Maybe that was the thing preventing my hand from reaching my waist. I slipped the dive computer up my forearm toward my elbow, stretching the bungee cord holding it in place. I brought my right hand back down along my body. I reached in between my abdomen and the floor again, feeling the hard, rough, uneven surface of the cave on the back of my hand. My fingertips brushed against the hard straight edge of something metallic. My harness buckle! One of the fingers sticking up out of the floor had grabbed the bottom edge of the buckle and was angling it up. I had to get the buckle over that finger. Then I should be able to back up.

Pushing off the ceiling with my feet again, I tried moving myself forward enough to get the buckle to lie flat against my belly. If I could do that, I should be able to suck my gut in and move backwards, clearing whatever it was that was catching onto the buckle. Damn all the tasty Mexican food! Especially the Mr. Chelato ice cream every evening!

The buckle fell flat against my belly. I exhaled, letting out as much air from my lungs as I could, allowing my diaphragm to move out of the way so I could suck in my gut. As I pushed myself backwards, I felt the buckle slide over something below me as it pushed deeper into my belly. I continued to push backwards until I felt the buckle ease off the pressure it had been exerting just below my belly button. Relaxing for a moment, I took a deep breath, released it, and continued to push myself backwards. Then something stopped me again.

I had only moved a few inches.

2

Lindsey

Where the hell was he going now? That boy! Always running off, or rather, swimming off to check out dark holes. Let him do this one on his own. I'm hanging back here with Gary.

Speaking of…

Dammit! Where was Gary off to?? Diving with these two was like trying to corral wild horses. They were always swimming off in different directions to check what might be some tunnel they think the previous explorers somehow missed.

The past two days diving with them had not been all that much fun. It was almost exhausting. I just wanted to see the cave. I wanted to take in the beauty of the passages and the formations in them. The caves in Mexico were very different from the caves in Florida. The formations that formed while the caves were still exposed to air twelve thousand years earlier held their own beauty that couldn't be found in many other places.

And the haloclines! Where freshwater and saltwater met each other. Swimming below the halocline in the saltwater layer gave the appearance that we were swimming just below the surface. Swimming above it in the freshwater layer made it feel like we were soaring through the air just above the surface of Merritt's Mill Pond like a heron looking for its next meal. There were no haloclines in Florida.

The layers were so distinct. You could see the line where they met and remained separated from each other. That is until they were disturbed. Then the different layers mixed with each other and blurred the visibility. The first time we came across a halocline, Joey and Gary practically spent the entire dive poking their fingers into the line and swirling the two types of water around, purposefully making it blurry. And I was stuck behind them, watching them ruin the visibility so I couldn't see a thing!

Fortunately, that fascination quickly wore off, but now all these idiots thought about was finding some tunnel that didn't have cave line in it yet. I didn't get it. Did they really think there was any virgin passage in this cave? Were they not seeing the beauty of these caves? Beauty unlike what any of us has experienced in the Florida caves. Don't get me wrong, the Florida caves hold their own beauty. But we live there and see them every day. We only get to see these caves once a year if we're lucky. Why couldn't they just enjoy the view?

Sure, this wasn't a cave that saw a lot of traffic. But it was thoroughly explored thirty years earlier. And others had been diving it looking for more virgin passage since. What made Joey and Gary think the two of them, who had only been cave diving for three years, and had only been in this cave four times before this dive, were going to find something that cave divers with decades of experience and hundreds of dives in here hadn't found?

I just wanted to swim through the cave and enjoy the magic.

Well, I'll be damned! It looks like Joey may have found something after all.

It probably wasn't much. I doubted it would go very far, but if it made him happy to lay some line in it, so be it.

I better check on Gary. Where did Gary go? I just saw his ridiculous yellow fins thirty feet in front of me a minute ago as he was swimming farther into the cave. This wasn't good. The three of us shouldn't be completely separated from each other like this. That wasn't the plan.

I glanced back into the tunnel Joey had reeled line into but couldn't see him. I looked back toward where I had last seen Gary. Nothing but darkness. Here I was left alone in the cave.

I decided to check on Joey first. I placed a line marker next to Joey's on the exit side of the line coming from Joey's ridiculously big explorer reel. This way Gary would know Joey and I both went into this new offshoot if he got back before we returned. Gary hadn't bothered to put his own marker on the line. To be fair, he was on the other side of it when Joey created this new intersection of lines.

I started into the tunnel following Joey's line. A couple minutes later I saw Joey's light. The ceiling was getting really low. Too low for my comfort, especially for two divers to be in it at the same time. I wasn't even sure two divers could fit in there. I doubted Joey would be able to go much farther so I turned around before getting into the really tight area, and I headed back to where Joey's line formed a T with the permanent line. I saw our markers lined up on the permanent line. I didn't see Gary.

A minute later, back on the permanent line, I looked for Gary both ways on the main tunnel we had come in on. No sign of him anywhere. I left my line marker in place and began swimming farther into the cave toward where I had last seen him swimming into the darkness. It was only a few minutes since I had seen him. He couldn't have gone very far. I swam slowly along the cave passage sweeping my light back and forth along both walls looking for a hole that might have enticed Gary to go explore it.

Gary should have left a line marker and should have deployed the line from his explorer reel before leaving the permanent guideline in the tunnel we were in. Too many should haves. The problem was I had already caught both Gary and Joey swimming off the line a few dozen feet to look at what they thought might be a lead. I had lectured them both about not doing this, but they always got so excited and forgot the rules when they saw something. They really thought they were going to find a lead to some huge new section that no one had found before.

"Come on, guys! This has to stop! Y'all need to run a line from the main line whenever you get more than ten feet away from it. What y'all are doing is dangerous!" I told the boys as we sat waiting for our food in the taqueria where we were for dinner.

"Oh, com'on, Linds, it's not dangerous!" Joey replied. "Every time I swim off the line to check something out, I make sure I can see yours or Gary's light. I always stop before you get out of view."

"And what if something happens and the visibility gets silted out? Then what will you do?"

"There's hardly any silt in this cave. At least not where we've been looking."

"Yet… Joey, you know better. Would you do this back home in Florida?"

"Well, I guess not. But those caves are different."

"How so? It's still an underwater cave. And we've only done four dives in it so far. You don't even know this cave. Every dive we do is in a new section so how do you know you won't encounter any silt?"

"Com'on, Gary! Help me out here," Joey pleaded.

Gary put his hands up in surrender. "I'm staying out of this. This is between you two lovebirds. My partner isn't here so I'm free to do as I please," he said with a big grin on his face.

"Oh, yeah, mister! Let's just see what Jim thinks about that!"

I grabbed my phone and started to dial Jim's number.

"Okay, okay, okay!" Gary yelled as he grabbed my phone out of my hand. "I'll be better. I won't stray off the line unless I tie a jump spool onto it first."

"Joseph…"

Joey dropped his head and muttered, "Yes ma'am."

"What does that mean?"

"I'll be better too. No more wandering off without a line."

Apparently, that part had stuck with them. At least with Joey. This time he was using his explorer reel. Now, if I could only find Gary and make sure he was keeping his word.

After swimming for about five minutes, I still hadn't seen any sign of Gary. No lights. No bubbles. No silt. Nothing. And I hadn't seen any leads off this tunnel either. Would he have continued swimming farther into the cave?

We had discussed not wandering off the permanent guideline without deploying a line from one of their spools or reels, but I didn't think of the possibility of one of them continuing to swim along the permanent guideline without the other two. Neither of them had done that yet. Until now. *Damn you, Gary!*

We had plenty of air in our tanks. Probably enough to swim around in the cave another half hour before turning to begin our long swim back to the cenote where we had started. I didn't want to spend that half hour swimming around trying to keep these boys corralled. It was bad enough I had to do it at all. I decided to swim another five minutes to look for Gary. Even if Joey turned around right after I turned back and started looking for Gary, it would take him a while to be back at the line intersection. Joey already went far enough that he would want to get survey data of the line he placed.

I thought about the cave survey class Joey took right before this dive trip. He hadn't had time to practice his new skills much before we came down. He did survey that one line in the area we visited the day before and that took him a while. This would be only his second time doing this outside of class. It would take him several minutes, so I had some time to look for Gary.

Sweeping the light back and forth, I still didn't see anything. This was a dark cave. The walls were almost black. If not for the light gray color of the dive tanks we were using, we would probably blend right into the background. Well, except for Gary's yellow fins.

I occasionally covered the front of my dive light to shield the light beam and looked for illumination from Gary's dive light, but other than the soft glow of the numbers and letters on my dive computer displays, it was completely dark every time I shielded it.

Where the hell did he go?

Glancing at my dive computer, I saw I'd been swimming nine minutes since leaving the line intersection. Close enough. I shielded my light one last time and looked into the darkness for any signs of Gary's dive light. I uncovered my light and swept the beam around the passage looking for visual signs, such as bubbles rushing along the ceiling or silt hanging in the water column that our exhalation bubbles had caused to percolate off the ceiling. Still nothing. Unfortunately, we were too deep for the halocline to be in this tunnel so I couldn't look for disturbance in the layers. Either Gary hadn't come this way, or it had been long enough since he had that there was no evidence to indicate he had been through the area.

I turned around and began swimming back to meet with Joey. Joey had been diving with Gary a lot more than I had. Maybe he would have an idea where Gary might have gone.

I looked at my dive computer. Twelve minutes since I left the line intersection where I had left my marker next to Joey's. Suddenly a feeling of anxiety came over me and I felt a slight tightness in my chest. It felt like someone had put a belt around it and cinched it up. My breathing came in short, shallow bursts. I tried to take a deep breath, but that belt wouldn't allow it. I began to kick my fins more quickly. I had already been separated from Joey for twelve minutes and had another eight minutes before getting back to him. Twenty minutes. That was a long time when it came to being underwater on a limited air supply. It was plenty of time for him to survey any line he placed in that tunnel and take off looking for another lead. Plenty of time for him to remain separated from me and Gary.

I hastened my pace even more while at the same time concentrating on controlling my breathing. I had to get there before he took off to Lord knows where.

3

Joey

I felt the anxiety creeping up inside. My breathing was a little faster. My heart was thumping like the leg of my parent's dog, Ramp, when you scratched his side. I pictured the big, goofy red Golden thumping in response to being tickled. It calmed me but only momentarily. My breathing rate increased again. I felt my arms and legs starting to tingle. I immediately closed my eyes and tried to think good thoughts. Calming thoughts.

The panic started to ease. I would get through this. I focused my attention on the situation I was in. I couldn't believe I was stuck again. And not again as in on this one dive. This was my first time getting stuck in this cave. But I was probably farther inside this cave than I had been when I got stuck in Jackson Blue the year before.

We had been on this dive for forty-five minutes before finding the lead. Forty-five minutes of swimming meant about twenty-two hundred feet of penetration into the cave. Probably more. The current in that one section of tunnel seemed to be pushing us in rather than working against us. I also swam a little faster when I was excited about the dive.

Okay, a lot faster.

Lindsey was always signaling me from behind to slow down. Today was no different. I slowed down every time she signaled me. But a few minutes later she signaled me again because my pace had quickened.

At least I had depth on my side in this cave. Jackson Blue averaged eighty-five feet of depth. This cave only averaged twenty-five feet of depth the first one thousand feet we had traveled and then fifty feet of depth in the passage we were currently in. That meant my air should last a bit longer. As long as I kept my breathing rate under control.

I also had my stage tank clipped onto the permanent line back in the larger tunnel rather than clipped onto me. So I wouldn't have to leave that behind this time. That would be difficult to explain to Jose.

"You're short one tank."

"Ummm, yeah, about that."

"The fill station will not be happy there is a tank missing."

"We'll get it back. I know exactly where it is. I just have to try to get back in that tight tunnel to get it."

"You better! Or else the fill station will want $200 US to pay for it."

That wouldn't be a fun conversation. Good thing the stage tank wasn't with me.

I was still stuck, though.

There was another difference between this situation and the one in Jackson Blue. I was able to see. There was no silt in this tunnel to obscure the visibility. I could see everything clearly. Well, everything in front of me. It was too small and tight to look back and see how I was stuck. Closing my eyes had helped me deal with the anxiety when the visibility was nonexistent. Maybe it would help now as well.

I closed my eyes and tried to relax. I concentrated on my breathing. Deep breath in. Count to five. Slowly exhale. Repeat. I did this about five times, and it seemed to be helping. I felt myself calm down even more. I could almost fall asleep. Almost.

I began analyzing the situation. It seemed to be the harness buckle that kept getting grabbed by the fingers coming out of the floor as I tried to back out. I tried reaching in between my abdomen and the floor to undo the buckle but the space was too tight. I could fit my hand in between but there wasn't enough room to open the buckle and slide the webbing out of it. I would have to keep chipping away at the distance slowly, inch by inch.

Opening my eyes, I looked around the tunnel I was in. It was still too narrow for me to turn around so I could be moving forward rather than backwards. Feet first it was. I'd have to do this blind.

I had been able to move forward the last time without having to push off with my heels on the ceiling of the cave. I moved forward until I felt the tension on the buckle release. I then exhaled until my lungs were as empty as I could get them, sucked in my gut, and pushed back again. This time I moved about a foot before another finger caught my buckle.

Shielding my light, I looked for Lindsey's light behind me again. I saw a faint glow. I could finally move my head and twist my body enough to actually look behind me this time, not just use my peripheral vision to detect light. No wonder Lindsey hadn't responded to my light signals earlier! I brought my hand back toward my legs and squeezed it in between my body and the scuba tank clipped to my side. I found the flap to my thigh pocket, ripped it off the Velcro closure, and stuck my hand inside. I moved my fingers around until I felt the knurled body of my backup dive light. I grabbed the light and pulled it out of the pocket. It was powered on and bright as could be. Somehow, as I was making my way into this tunnel, the switch on my backup dive light had been depressed. The glow I had seen was the beam of my own backup dive light piercing through the mesh bottom of the pocket.

Where was Lindsey?

It didn't matter. It was too tight in this tunnel for her to be of any help anyway. I doubted she would be able to pull me out by my feet. I wasn't sure she would even be willing to come in after me. She wasn't a fan of tight spaces. I pressed the button on my backup light to turn it off and shoved it back into my thigh pocket, making sure the bolt snap attached to the dive light was still clipped to the small D ring inside the pocket.

I felt my wetnotes inside my pocket and remembered my survey notes were tucked in there. I started to pull them out so I could begin to survey the line I had just placed.

Maybe that wasn't such a good idea. I was still stuck, unable to move very far. I'd survey from the permanent line once I got back to it. I would just count knots for now. I pushed the notes back into the pocket and folded the pocket flap back down, pressing on it to make sure the hooks and loops grabbed hold of each other.

Turning my attention back to the issue at hand – me being stuck – I concentrated on getting myself out of this tight spot I had gotten myself into. I chuckled at my own joke. At least I could still laugh about it. I shielded my light beam. The only light I saw came from my dive computer displays. Nothing behind me this time. I pulled my hand away from my light beam and set it in between a couple of the cave's fingers that were sticking out of the floor in front of me, probably the same ones that had grabbed my buckle a moment ago. I exhaled, sucked in my gut, and pushed back. I was moving!

Until I wasn't. Well, at least this time I made it more than a foot. Judging by the line I had just laid in the passage it looked like I had managed to move back about five feet before getting stuck again. Progress!

4

Lindsey

I was breathing the fastest I'd ever breathed on a dive. That wasn't good. That wasn't like me. I couldn't remember ever feeling this way underwater before. I needed to get it under control. I needed to conserve my air.

The three of us were separated. I was probably going to have to spend the rest of my dive looking for one or both of my dive buddies. I needed air in my scuba tanks to do that. And what if either one was low on air? I would need to share that air.

Slow down.

Breathe deeply.

Hold.

Slowly exhale.

I slowed my pace and focused on controlling my breathing rate. Nice easy breaths, in and out. I used just the tips of my fins to propel myself through the water. Small muscles required less oxygen. Using the bigger muscles meant I'd have to breathe more. I looked at my dive computer and saw that seventeen minutes had passed since I had left Joey. He should have gotten out of that tunnel by this time, and I should be able to see the beam of his dive light at any moment.

My breathing rate started to creep up again. Concentrate! Deep breath in. Hold for a few seconds. Slowly exhale.

I continued to sweep my light beam from left to right, still searching for Gary as I made my way back to Joey. Maybe I had missed him earlier when I was swimming along this tunnel. Maybe he had gone off looking at some lead without using his explorer reel even though he had agreed not to do that. Lots of maybes.

No such luck. I was back at the line intersection. Both Joey and my markers were on the permanent line. Joey's stage tank was there too. I really wished he hadn't taken the stage tank off before going into that tunnel. It would have at least prevented him from going so far into it.

He should have been back out already. If that child went off looking for another lead and left his stage tank here! I decided to follow his line again to check on him. I couldn't imagine him still being in there but maybe he managed to find a way to keep going. I swam next to the line he had spooled out heading in the direction where I had last seen him. I didn't know if I'd be able to follow him beyond that point. It was already getting too small for my comfort where I turned around last time.

I went around a corner and saw a light ahead. I felt a sense of relief envelope me. I swam into the tunnel a little farther until I saw blue fins. Joey's fins.

Wait! Why was I seeing fins? I'd been gone for more than twenty minutes. He should be coming back out, not heading in!

My heart sank in my chest. I picked up my pace and closed the distance between us. Joey was motionless. He should be moving.

5

Joey

Getting stuck was more tiring than swimming against current. I had only moved about ten feet from the end of the line. Progress was slow. I decided I might as well get some survey data while taking a break from trying to get myself unstuck. Maybe focusing on that would help me clear my mind and figure out how to get myself out of this place.

I reached down and pulled open the Velcroed pocket flap. I felt for the wetnotes, grabbed them, and pulled them out. After bringing them back up and balancing them on three of the fingers jutting out of the floor in front of me, I reached back down and made sure none of the other pocket contents got pulled out when I grabbed the wetnotes. I could feel the dive light and line markers still in the pocket. I resecured the flap.

I grabbed the wetnotes and opened them to the page with my survey notes table. There was paper made and sold with all the lines printed on it specifically for cave survey, but it was expensive. More than a dollar a sheet! After my survey class I took a ruler and made the necessary lines to create the table. I did this with fifty sheets of paper. It took some time but saved a lot of money. At the rate I was going this week, those fifty sheets would last me several trips to Mexico.

Azimuth, depth, and distance. That's all that was required to be able to survey and map a cave passage. Oh, and patience. Lots of patience.

Some cave divers didn't bother to survey the passages they found. All they wanted was the glory of the find. They couldn't be bothered with doing the real work of documenting the find. They would let others that they thought less of do the menial task of survey.

I set the compass next to the line, making sure it was parallel, and rotated the bezel until the big N was lined up with the moving arrow.

I didn't think it was menial work. I liked creating the maps. During class we surveyed the cavern at Jackson Blue. Sure, there was already a map for it, but that map was old. Really old. Sheck Exley, the cave diver who was known as the father of cave diving training, created it decades ago.

That map was also small and not very detailed. I really enjoyed creating a larger, more detailed map of the cavern. It was fun gathering the data and plotting it on the computer. Then after printing out the basic map, I drew in details of the walls and the fallen boulders on the floor. There were computer programs that did that last part, but I enjoyed doing the creative part myself.

With N and the arrow lined up, I pulled the compass closer to my mask so I could read the tiny numbers on the bezel that lined up with the stationary arrow. Man, I wish those numbers were bigger!

I doubted I would get very detailed with the caves in Mexico. I had plenty of time to dive Jackson Blue and spend time in the cavern getting measurements and headings and details of what it looked like. I could hover in there for hours sketching the walls and the floors. I was only in Mexico for a week. I'd rather spend that week looking for virgin passage than drawing maps. But at least I could get some line maps and add that detail to the existing map.

Dammit! I think I moved the bezel. I placed the compass next to the line again to make sure the bezel was lined up properly.

The map of this cave was decades old and not very detailed. There were even passages in the cave that weren't on the original map. I had already discovered that. During the month leading up to this trip I studied the two maps I was able to find online. I studied them extensively. I had even memorized them. As we were swimming along the passages, I could see the maps in my mind and where we were on them. A few times we came across offshoots that weren't on either map. Just to be sure I looked at the maps after the dives and highlighted the route we had taken. Sure enough, there were tunnels we had passed that weren't on them.

I had moved the bezel. Only about an eighth of an inch, but that was enough to throw the entire survey off. I had to be more careful about that.

I penciled those tunnels onto the maps. I even did a quick survey in one of the shorter tunnels. Lindsey and Gary were a little annoyed at me over that. Granted, I was new to cave survey. The only time I had done any cave survey before this trip was in the class I took. I did some additional survey in the Jackson Blue cavern but that was a different type of survey than line survey. That was a much more detailed survey of the room.

I found I was being too much of a perfectionist. Yesterday it took me almost a minute at each survey station to get my data. Something that should have taken seconds. The hard part was the azimuth readings. The compass hashmarks were small and difficult to see in a dark underwater cave. And I kept leaving my fingers on the bezel and turning it as I pulled the compass from the line to read it.

I pulled the compass up to my mask again, this time being careful not to rotate the bezel accidentally. I squinted to read the tiny numbers.

By the end of the line in that tunnel, I remembered to let go of the bezel so it wouldn't move, and I got faster. It seemed like I was back at ground zero overnight and making the same mistakes. I managed to map the tunnel I found the day before, and I scaled it to the line map I had and overlaid it. I was looking forward to doing more, especially with the virgin tunnels I managed to find.

I read the number eighty-six on the compass. That correlated to the image of the map in my head. We had been heading south when I saw this passage to the left. So eastbound was correct. I wrote "86" under the azimuth heading and glanced at my dive computer. Forty-five feet deep. I jotted that number in the next column. I had cut the line about a foot short of the next knot and wrapped it around one of the cave fingers a few times, accounting for another foot. From where I was, I could see another knot about a foot in front of the next station where the line changed direction. So eight plus one gave me nine feet. I wrote that number in the distance column.

I set the wetnotes down in front of me again and focused my efforts on pushing back to the station behind me. That's when I saw a light behind me. And not the light from my backup light. A bright light. It was sweeping back and forth. That must be Lindsey or Gary.

6

Lindsey

Oh, thank goodness! Joey just moved. Was he trying to survey this tunnel? Still?? He'd been in it for almost half an hour! I shined my light beam at him and swept it back and forth slowly to get his attention. He wasn't turning around though. He was still too far away for me to touch his leg to get his attention. And I wasn't so sure I wanted to go any farther into this tunnel. It was already too small where I was.

I reached out and lightly touched a flat area on the floor with my fingertip. I held myself in place and waited for Joey to turn around. He didn't though. He was just lying there. It looked tight. I couldn't see any space above or below him. He was sandwiched in. Could he be stuck? Surely, he wouldn't be surveying if he was stuck.

Never mind. This was Joey we were talking about. Yes, he would.

I swept my light back and forth again. This time I watched as he moved his light back and pointed it toward me, aiming the beam right at my eyes and momentarily blinding me. I closed my eyes and shielded them to minimize the effect. That also meant I didn't see any light signal he may have sent me.

About thirty seconds later I slowly opened my eyes. Joey had his light back in front of him. I decided to wait for him rather than signal him and risk getting blinded again. Joey began to wiggle his body back and forth. He wasn't moving backwards toward me though. I watched as he moved forward a few inches and then pushed back again. He closed the distance between us by a few feet. It was difficult to tell exactly how much because he was at least sixty feet away from me. I saw him reach in front of him for something. It looked like his wetnotes.

So, the idiot child was stuck in a tight, low tunnel and had decided to pull out his wetnotes to get survey data! I was definitely going to have to talk to him about this tonight.

Joey wiggled again. This time he managed to move back another few feet. I could see him open his wetnotes and write in them. I considered going farther into the tunnel to grab his legs and pull him out. The small size of the restriction kept me from doing that. Just the thought of it made me feel that belt around my chest, gave me heart palpitations, and sent my respiratory rate up.

If Joey was in real trouble, like out of air trouble, I'd go in there without hesitation. Small restriction be damned. But he was obviously not in any distress if he was surveying. I decided to turn around and go look for Gary again. Hopefully, he wasn't acting a fool like Joey.

7

Joey

I swung my arm around behind me to signal whoever was back there that I was okay. No need to reveal I was stuck. I would eventually get out. Hopefully. With my hand along my side I rotated my light in a large circle. I moved the light back in front of me, partially shielding it, and waited for a response.

No signal came. Then, just as suddenly as the light had appeared behind me, it disappeared. Must have been Gary. Lindsey would never have left like that. I returned my attention to continuing to move backwards to the next survey station so I could get those numbers.

This time I moved much more easily. It seemed the tunnel was getting bigger. I did get stuck for a few seconds, but I was able to wiggle my hips around and get over the next bunch of fingers that kept trying to grab me. I pushed back more. I reached the next station where the line was secured around a large finger on the wall and went to grab my wetnotes.

Dammit!

I forgot to pick them up as I was backing out. I shined my light beam ahead to where I had set them down, and there they were, more than ten feet in front of me. I thought about leaving them there. They were so close though. I pulled myself forward, back toward the notes. For some reason, it was easier to move in this direction than it was to move backwards. When I got back to that last station I was going to have to try to turn around. Maybe it was more about moving forward than the direction I was moving in the tunnel.

Back at my wetnotes, I grabbed them and tucked them under my waist strap. No sense in putting them back in my pocket only to remove them again in a minute. I pushed back, this time remembering to wiggle my hips over the fingers coming out of the uneven floor that kept grabbing me. The return trip wasn't as slow going this time. I was getting better at it.

Back at the next station, number three starting from where I had cut the line and secured the end of it, I held the compass next to the line and rotated the bezel to line up the large red mark with north again. I squinted my eyes to read the tiny numbers.

108

I jotted the number in my notes beneath the *86*. I checked my dive computer for the depth. That was unchanged. I had passed one knot, giving me nine feet from the second station. From that knot to where I currently was looked to be about six feet. I estimated this by my height. I measured in right at six feet. In larger areas of the cave I could use my wingspan, fingertip to fingertip to measure the distance. That was something I had learned from my survey instructor. I didn't have that luxury in this small, low tunnel. And my instructor hadn't given us any helpful tips for situations like this. The distance from this station to the knot looked about right, though. It looked to be about my height. Close enough anyway.

I looked around the tunnel to see if I might be able to turn around. The walls had begun to get farther apart. The height was definitely a few inches more. I decided to try. I was closest to the right wall, so I swung my legs to the left. I got them angled about forty-five degrees off of the line when I felt my fin tips meet resistance. I swung my light around and looked at my feet. The tunnel was not quite six feet wide.

And with the fins adding another foot to my length, it meant I needed seven feet to rotate around.

I did have more room from floor to ceiling. I could bend my knees and bring them up toward my torso. I crawled my knees along the floor until I felt the ceiling against my back. I looked back at my feet. It looked like my fin tips could clear the wall in this position. I side crawled my knees to the left along the bottom, thankful that there was no silt or mud or anything else that could obliterate the visibility in this space. The rocky fingers in this area were also sturdy. I didn't feel anything breaking as my knees applied pressure. That would suck, but remaining stuck in here and dying would suck worse.

I got to where I was positioned at a ninety-degree angle to the tunnel. I had to bend my neck to the side to keep it from hitting the wall that was now in front of me. I had miscalculated the width of the tunnel. I should have continued moving backwards to the next station before attempting to turn around. Well, I was halfway through the turn. I might as well keep on going.

Except I couldn't. Something was keeping me from continuing my rotation. I pushed a little harder and gained maybe an inch before meeting resistance again. I swung my light alongside my body to try to see what was stopping me. Unfortunately, my head was bent to the right and the thing that was stopping me was to my left.

I felt around with my left hand. Maybe I could feel whatever it was that was preventing me from continuing to move. Sweeping my hand around, up and down, side to side, in circles, I felt nothing that would explain this cessation of movement.

I decided to rotate back to the right and continue backing up until the next station. Or the one after that. I'd have to do a better assessment of the area before attempting to turn around again. This time I'd use the old wingspan trick to make sure the walls were far enough apart.

I started a side crawl back to the right. I managed a couple of steps before the pressure on my head from the wall in front of me wouldn't allow me to move anymore. I had gotten into this position. I should be able to get out of it. I tried backing up away from the wall, but something was keeping me from moving in that direction. I wiggled my hips. This time that didn't work. I tried wiggling my legs, but my knees were now being jammed into the hard surface below me. I wiggled my feet. At least those could move. But that didn't really do me any good.

Suddenly I could no longer move my right foot. I tried wiggling it, but it felt like my fin was being held by something. I tried shining my light under my body toward my fin as I turned my head to look in that direction. Two fingers coming up from the floor were pinching my fin tip and holding it in place. The only way I was going to be able to get it out of their grip would be to move my fin to the left. But it wasn't moving.

Here I was, scrunched up in an almost fetal position, unable to move, in a small, no, very small, cave tunnel. I felt like one of those double-jointed contortionist street performers who squeezed themselves into glass boxes. Except, I wasn't in a box. I was more than two thousand feet inside a water-filled cave with a limited supply of air. FML!

8

Joey

I closed my eyes and focused on my breathing before the panic set in again. Although, breathing wasn't as easy in this scrunched up position. My diaphragm was compressing my lungs so I couldn't get a full breath. I continued to control my shallow breathing as best as I could while I assessed the situation I was in. I knew I'd done stupid things in the past, especially when it came to scuba diving, but this one took the grand prize.

After about half a minute the solution came to me, and none too soon as it was getting more difficult to control my breathing rate. It was increasing to the point where I was almost hyperventilating. I reached back to my right foot and felt around the heel. I found the fin strap that was holding the fin onto my foot and pushed it down and off my heel. I tried to pull my foot out of the fin pocket, but I couldn't move it far enough. My toes were still stuck inside the pocket.

I used my light to push the fin away from me as I bent my knee more, moving my foot up against my backside. I felt the edge of the fin against the bottom of my toes. *Almost.* I stretched a little more and pushed harder on the fin and wiggled my foot around violently. Well, as violently as the restricted space allowed. My toes cleared the bottom of the fin. My foot was finally free. I relaxed my arm and felt the fin rebound toward me, smacking the bottom of my foot.

With my right foot free, I pushed against the fin and stretched my leg back out to get it straight when it suddenly hit me. A charley horse! I forced my leg straight to try to relieve the pain I was feeling in my hamstring. I tried to reach back to massage it, but my scuba tank was in the way. I held my leg out as straight as possible and dug my toes against a cave finger trying to stretch the muscle. After a couple of minutes the charley horse finally subsided. I turned my focus back onto my breathing for the next minute to try to get that under control. I had gone where no one had gone before, but I was paying for it dearly.

Once my breathing slowed down, I turned my attention to my left foot. It wasn't stuck but maybe removing that fin would help me get the rest of my body unstuck. The fin tips extended more than a foot beyond my toes. Losing that length might just make the difference.

I reached for my left fin with my left hand and slipped the fin strap off the heel. I grabbed the fin and tugged on it. The left fin came off much more easily with the fin tip not wedged in between two fingers. I slowly straightened out my left leg, careful to not trigger a charley horse on that side.

With both legs somewhat stretched out, I worked out the cramps. I think I got the fins off just in time. Experiencing charley horses in both legs while scrunched up and trapped in a water-filled cave wouldn't have been any fun. It was bad enough to have it happen to one leg.

I thought about the predicament I had gotten myself into. This hunt for virgin passage suddenly seemed a little overrated.

Once my leg muscles calmed down, I turned my attention back to the situation at hand. I decided to see if I could continue to turn so I was facing the direction I was traveling. It might be easier without the fins on my feet. And it would definitely be easier to exit this tunnel being able to see where I was going. I wished I had paid more attention to the tunnel on the way in. But I was so excited about my find that all

I was looking at was where it went, not what it looked like. The twenty-four feet I had traveled backwards through didn't look so inviting backing out from it. Especially after getting stuck in it a few times.

I swung my legs to the left. This time, without the fins on, I was able to continue moving. Whatever it was that had stopped me earlier must have been grabbing the fins and not my legs. I continued moving my legs around to the left. My feet had finally cleared the wall enough that I could fully stretch both legs.

I was also able to back up a little allowing me to straighten my neck. *That was a relief!* I was starting to feel what Lindsey would call a crick in my neck. Those southern sayings. I always thought a crick was where you went fishing not something you had in your neck.

My body wasn't quite parallel with the tunnel but at least I could see the way out. I started to move forward but quickly stopped. My fins were still lying on the floor to my right. Well, the fin that came off my left foot was. The other fin was sticking up from the floor.

I grabbed the loose fin, passed it to my left hand, and brought it toward my foot. I slowly bent my knee to bring my foot closer. This wasn't going to be easy. It was difficult enough standing in a spring basin when I forgot to put them on before clipping my tanks on.

It went better than I expected. I managed to bend my knee enough to reach my foot and slip it into the fin pocket. I reached back and felt around for the fin strap, grabbed it, and pulled it over my heel.

One down, one to go. I was still feeling the aftereffects of the charley horse in my right leg. This was going to be interesting.

I grabbed the other fin and tried to bring it toward me, but it wouldn't budge. I tugged on it. The fin tip wouldn't move. Those fingers had a death grip on it. Okay, another not so great analogy. I pushed and pulled on it. I moved back so the fin was in front of me and grabbed it near the fingers. I used brute force on it. It wasn't coming out. I shook it violently back and forth. Nothing. I thought about just leaving it there. Maybe King Arthur would come along and pull it out. This was only the middle of our dive trip, though. I had two and a half more days of diving.

The dive shops we had walked into didn't sell dive equipment. They sold experiences. You could book boat diving with them. Some even offered shore diving. They all offered rental equipment, but you had to be diving with them to rent the equipment. Not only that, but I was almost half a mile from the cave opening. That would be a really long and slow swim wearing only one fin.

I shook the fin back and forth again even harder than before. The fingers finally let go. I held the fin in my hands. I was going to use my sharpie to write "Excalibur" on the fin later tonight. I inspected the fin tip and didn't see any damage. There were scrapes on it but no tears. At least it hadn't been turned into a split fin. I'd never live that down. I shoved the fin toward my foot and slowly bent my knee, trying to avoid another charley horse. I slipped my right foot into the fin pocket and pulled the strap over my heel. I felt a slight twinge in my hamstring and quickly straightened my leg. I waited a moment until the feeling passed.

Back to the survey and getting out of this tunnel. I noticed my wetnotes on the floor next to me. Strange. I had tucked them into my waist strap. They must have slipped out as I was trying to get myself turned around. I grabbed them as I moved back alongside the cave line I had just placed. I began to get another azimuth heading, placing the compass next to the line and setting the bezel. The red line was closest to me rather than the other side of the compass. That was strange. That wasn't the way it should be. Then it occurred to me. I had been getting headings while backing out of the tunnel. Now I was getting headings while moving forward in it. That was why I had to rotate it so much. That would also affect the data somehow. Maybe it wasn't such a good idea to turn around.

I closed my eyes and tried to think about it for a moment. When I converted the data in the evening, I always took the reciprocal of the heading to plot out the passage from the line I started on. But the first two headings I took were already the reciprocal. So should I convert them to match up with the data I was about to collect? Or should I write down the reciprocal of the numbers I was about to get.

My head started hurting just thinking about it. And in the meantime, time was ticking away. And the air pressure in my tanks was dropping.

9

Lindsey

I got back to the line intersection where our markers and Joey's stage tank were located. I thought about leaving a note on the line for Joey. I'd hate for him to get back before me and decide to head off somewhere else. I pulled my wetnotes out of my pocket, flipped them open to a blank page, and grabbed the pencil attached to the notebook with a bungee cord.

Looking for Gary. Stay put!!!

I tore the sheet out of the notebook, folded it in half with the writing to the outside, and set it on the line like a tent. I slid one end of the paper in between my marker and the line so it was secured in place and wouldn't accidently be knocked off. I turned back to where I had last seen Gary and started heading farther into the cave to look for him again.

Glancing at my dive computer, I saw eight minutes had passed since I got back to the line intersection. That meant I hadn't seen Gary in twenty-eight minutes. Surely, he was already heading back out of the cave from wherever he had gone. Thank goodness this cave was so shallow. We had plenty of air in our tanks. We could all easily stay underwater for three hours. Longer if we tapped into our reserve air. But that wasn't the plan.

The plan was for a two-hour dive. We were already at the point of exceeding that by several minutes. We were an hour and thirteen minutes into the dive. We should be starting our swim out in two minutes if we were going to make it out by two hours. Gary should be swimming back by now. I should see him at any moment.

I continued to swim farther into the cave, hopeful that each time I went around a corner I'd see Gary's dive light coming toward me. The cave ahead of me remained dark. Not just dark, but black. My dive light penetrated the darkness about fifty feet or so but beyond that all light was swallowed by the void.

I checked my pressure gauges. I still had 2400 psi in each of my sidemounted tanks. I had already breathed my stage tank down to 2100 psi. That meant I had a total of 300 psi to breathe from each sidemount tank before I tapped into my reserves. I started with 3100 psi in each tank. With 300 psi in each of the two tanks, I could search for about another twenty minutes.

We used one third of our air supply to penetrate the cave, one third to exit, and one third for emergencies. I liked to buffer that a bit. I usually only used 800 or 900 psi for penetration so I would have 1100 to 1200 psi for reserves in each tank. Better to have more air than not enough. Because we had all started with 3100 psi, I agreed to a 1000 psi penetration. That would still leave us with 1100 psi for reserves. I would have preferred only using 900 psi, but the boys begged.

"Com'on, Linds!" Joey pleaded. "It's only 100 psi. What's the big deal?"

"I could say the same for why we shouldn't use that extra 100 psi," I replied. "What's 100 psi more going to get us?"

"Using it still leaves us with 1100 psi for emergency use. And we have the stage

tanks. Besides, what could happen?" Joey ignored my retort.

"We've only been in this cave four times, Joey. And we're planning on going into a section of the cave we haven't been in before. We should have a bigger buffer."

"There are three of us, though." Gary interjected.

"What does that have anything to do with it?" I asked.

"What are the chances of more than one person having an issue? We have plenty of air reserves to deal with most issues."

"Unless we get separated from each other. Then what?"

"It's a shallow cave. We're not planning on heading into it all that far. And we'll still have a small buffer."

"Com'on, babe! Everything Gary said makes sense. And we will have a buffer."

While I didn't completely agree, I gave in. But I stuck to the two-hour dive time limit. I figured that would have us turn long before using 900 psi anyway. They hadn't thought of that. At least that meant we were all happy going into the dive.

The dive plan was to turn at an hour so we would be surfacing two hours after we began the dive. If we had breathed 1000 psi before that hour, we would turn then. No one turned at the one-hour mark and it didn't look like we were going to be heading out after having breathed 1000 psi, even if I found Gary in the next two minutes. If I was only 300 psi in each sidemount tank from reaching turn pressure, the air pressure we had agreed we would begin heading out of the cave, that meant the boys were only 100 psi or less from reaching that point because their breathing rates were higher than mine.

I looked back at my dive computer. We'd been on the dive for an hour and eighteen minutes. I was about five minutes from Joey's location, placing me fifty minutes from surfacing in the cenote. If we all started out now, we would be only eight minutes behind schedule. That wasn't going to happen though. I had already swum this passage looking for Gary about twenty-five minutes earlier. If he was back here, he should have been swimming out by this time. I should have encountered him already.

I'd go just a little farther.

Still nothing. No light. No line markers belonging to Gary. No line intersecting with the main guideline and going off into some small black hole. No stupid yellow fins. Where the hell was he??

1:22

That was the current dive time according to my dive computer. Only four minutes since I last looked at it, but it felt like twenty minutes. I checked my air pressure again. The needle was just above the 2100 psi mark. It was almost time to switch regulators and start breathing from the other tank. That also meant I only had another ten minutes to search before I started breathing my reserve air.

Time seemed to be going by quickly and standing still simultaneously. What a horrible feeling this was. I may not dive with these boys anymore, at least not on this trip. I didn't know if I could handle the stress.

1:23

I tapped on the display face of the dive computer. I could swear it had been more than a minute. I looked at the backup computer on my other arm. The times corresponded to each other. Either they were both running slow, or my perception of time was completely screwed. Should I continue swimming away from Joey to look for Gary? Or should I head back and get Joey so we could join forces?

What if Joey was still in that small hole too far in for my comfort level? He didn't even respond to my light signal earlier. What if he was out already and didn't see my note and took off somewhere? What if he thought we headed out and he started swimming toward the exit? Too many what ifs.

1:24

Still no sign of Gary. It had been more than ten minutes since I left Joey back in that hole. I recognized this part of the cave. This was where I turned around earlier to go back and check on Joey. Maybe I should continue for another five minutes. But then that would put me almost twenty minutes from Joey's location. And forty minutes separated from him. That was a lot of time. I didn't think Joey would wait around that long.

1:25

I knew I hadn't gone much farther than the last time, but I was too concerned about Joey taking off to Lord knows where. I was starting to feel anxious again. I could feel my heart beating in my chest. I turned around and started swimming back toward Joey. I hastened my pace while trying to control my breathing.

I checked my pressure gauge. I breathed through almost 100 psi since I last checked. I had also breathed one tank down to 2000 psi. That meant I could only use 200 psi from the other tank. I switched regulators. I was definitely going to be breathing from my reserve air. There was still lots of air, even with the reserves being used, but we were now looking at a two-and-a-half-hour dive time. That wasn't the plan we had agreed on.

1:26

I was heading back, quickly. The water flow wasn't helping. This tunnel was a siphon. The water was flowing into the cave rather than out of it. That meant we were swimming with the current on the way in and against the current on the way out. That meant the exit wouldn't take forty-five minutes. It would take longer.

So maybe closer to a three-hour dive time. This dive was spiraling out of control fast.

The water didn't siphon from the entrance of the cave. In the main tunnel, the one with the orange-colored line, the water flowed out of the cave. But we had gone off the main tunnel into this offshoot only about twelve minutes into the dive. About five minutes after turning into the offshoot tunnel, we realized the water was flowing the wrong way. I communicated this to the guys, but they blew it off. It wasn't a strong current, so I didn't push it. But I knew it would take a little longer to head out. Maybe only five minutes longer, but longer, nonetheless. The current felt stronger now, though. I didn't know if the current was increasing or if it was just my imagination.

I should have insisted we turned sooner. We should have turned instead of Joey and Gary going off to look for leads. But then they started poking around looking at what they thought might be unexplored tunnels and that slowed our penetration speed down so I thought it would be okay. I should have stuck to the plan.

1:29

This felt like it was taking forever. I shielded my light beam and glanced back.

Nothing but black.

Completely dark.

No Gary.

I continued swimming toward Joey. I should get to him in less than five minutes. I was swimming a little faster, even considering I was swimming against the water flow.

Another 50 psi breathed. I was only 50 psi from reaching my turn pressure. Even with the time limit out of the picture, we should be swimming out by now. I was about to start breathing my emergency reserves.

I still hadn't found Gary.

10

Lindsey

The needles on my pressure gauges had finally dropped to the turn pressure. The needle on the gauge connected to the tank I was breathing from kept dropping. I shouldn't have turned back to look for Joey. I knew where he was. I had left a note for him to stay put. I had no idea where Gary was. I was worried about Gary and what might have happened to him. What if Gary was stuck in some small tunnel and couldn't get out? What if he was hurt? What if he had a medical issue? What if he got a bad air fill?

* * *

A couple of years back, a cave diver by the name of Brendan had died in one of the caves on the island. The Mexican authorities were surprisingly efficient in doing an autopsy the day he died and immediately found the cause of death. The team of divers that was with Brendan was quick to get the word out – carbon monoxide.

Well, carbon monoxide didn't kill him. Carbon monoxide made him lose consciousness underwater. Drowning took his life. It was an avoidable fatality. Most cave diving fatalities were avoidable, for that matter. Carbon monoxide was known as the silent killer. It was an odorless, tasteless gas. It could be found in a variety of places where combustion was present – running a car or lawn mower, running a generator, using a stove or oven, burning wood in a fireplace. That's why it was recommended that anyone with a gas stove or furnace in the house or an attached garage should also have a carbon monoxide detector.

I was just a teenager when Hurricane Dennis hit the Florida panhandle, but I remember we were without power for a few days. My father set up a generator to plug our refrigerator into and provide us with some lights. He had placed the generator right outside of the kitchen door. Because it was hot outside, we kept the door open to allow a breeze to come in through the screen door. About an hour after he had started the generator, we all started to have headaches. We blew it off to the heat and the stress. Fortunately, we had a carbon monoxide detector in the house. It was in the kitchen near the stove. It sounded an alarm. My father ran to it to investigate. The display had the number forty-seven on it telling him the carbon monoxide level in the house was forty-seven parts per million.

The headaches were caused by the carbon monoxide in the exhaust of the generator. The breeze that was helping to cool us down a little was also bringing the exhaust fumes inside the house with it. We all rushed out of the house. My father shut off the generator and relocated it far from the door, as far as the extension cords would allow. It took about two hours for the carbon monoxide detector to stop alarming. Two hours before we could safely reenter the house. If it wasn't for the carbon monoxide detector, we would have lost consciousness and died that day. After that we always made sure the carbon monoxide detectors we kept in the house were up to date and functioning.

As a diver, I hadn't given it much thought. Carbon monoxide was mentioned in the training manuals. It had one line stating it could be an issue. Nothing about analyzing your tanks for its presence. Instructors glossed over it, stating it wasn't an issue and not to worry.

Then Brendan died because of it. Apparently, Brendan had about eight hundred ppm of carbon monoxide in his bloodstream. If you have more than ten ppm carbon monoxide in your scuba tank, you aren't supposed to breathe from that tank.

Eight hundred ppm.

* * *

What if Gary hadn't tested his tanks? After Brendan's death, I bought a carbon monoxide analyzer and analyzed every single scuba tank that anyone I was diving with, including my students, were about to use. Joey knew the story about Brendan. He didn't think the possibility of it happening again was that great, but he knew how passionate I was about analyzing our tanks for carbon monoxide, and he always checked.

Gary had been a little flippant about it. He checked the first couple of days, or at least he went through the motions. But I hadn't paid attention while we were setting up for this dive to make sure he was analyzing his tanks. I analyzed mine and Joey's and then left the analyzer on top of his equipment bag.

Had he analyzed his air? Or had he just tossed the analyzer into the car? What were the chances of Gary getting bad air but Joey and I having good air? I didn't think they were high, but the possibility was there. The tanks could have been filled at different times. The tanks Gary had could have been almost empty and our tanks only half empty. The tanks Gary had could have been emptied at some point and water gotten into them. There were so many possibilities.

What if Gary's air was contaminated and he had passed out and drowned somewhere in the cave? What if he had lost consciousness and dropped down into a crevice in the floor? Or he floated up into the ceiling disappearing into tannic water where we couldn't see him easily? I looked up and saw a tannic pond. I pictured Gary's lifeless body disappearing into it. I quickly blinked my eyes repeatedly to get that image out of my head.

I couldn't keep myself from thinking the worst thoughts. While it had never happened to me, I knew cave divers whose dive buddies died while they were diving together. Most felt horrible. I said most because there were a few that you'd think by their actions afterwards that they only felt an inconvenience at having to have been involved in the dive. But there were some that felt so bad they stopped diving after what happened.

I was more concerned about Joey than myself. How would he take it? Joey and Gary and Jim had become very close friends. Jim! How would I tell him about Gary? Jim and Gary had been together for a few years. They had been living with each other for the past couple of years. And recently they started talking about getting married. The only reason Jim wasn't on this trip was because he had work commitments that he couldn't get out of. How would I break the news to Jim? How would I tell him that his best friend and love of his life had died in a cave, and we hadn't found his body?

What about Gary's mom? I could picture her breaking down in tears as I told her the news. She was such a sweet woman. She had lost her husband, Gary's father, to cancer the year before. How would she take the news of losing Gary?

Stop it, Lindsey!!! Gary was not dead. He's poking around in some tunnel he found and just got caught up in the excitement. The same as Joey. They were two peas in a pod.

My tanks were already below turn pressure and both of those boys should have reached their turn pressures at least five minutes before me. Gary should be heading out and Joey should be waiting for me where I left him the note.

Hopefully, Joey saw the note.

Would Joey see the note? How could he not? It was plain as day.

But we were in a cave.

And it was Joey.

First things first. I needed to find Gary. Just as I saw Joey's stage tank sticking up in the tunnel from where it was clipped to the guideline, I turned around again and started swimming back toward where I had last seen Gary. Joey was behind me again, between me and the exit. Gary was not. Or at least I didn't think he was.

I had no idea where Gary could be. How could he disappear like this? Where could he have gone? And why didn't he tell us what he was planning on doing?? If I found him alive, I was going to kill him!

I shielded my light and covered my dive computer displays. I waited a few seconds for my eyes to adjust.

Pitch black.

No illumination whatsoever.

I pulled my hand away from the light and scanned the area around me. I felt a twinge of anxiety starting to build in my chest. Just a slight tightness this time, like I had tried on a bra that was a little too small for me. But the tightness was coming from the inside.

Such a strange feeling.

Maybe I should turn around and get Joey. Then we could both look for Gary together. Or maybe Gary would suddenly show up and we could all exit together. Then I'd be able to smack some sense into Gary once we were safely back on the surface.

The anxiety was getting worse. It was no longer just a tightness in the chest. The belt was back. I was also starting to feel like I had to throw up. And I was feeling a sense of hopelessness. What if I couldn't find Joey either? It would be one thing to lose one team member on a dive, but two. I couldn't bear that. And to make things worse, to lose them while diving in Mexico. What would I do? Who would I call? Would there even be anyone who spoke English?

After another fifteen minutes of swimming with no signs of Gary, I decided to turn around again. I had to find Joey first. I knew I'd feel better if I knew exactly where he was. I loved Gary like a brother, and I wanted to find him too. But Joey had to come first. If only because I knew where he last was. Then we could both look for Gary and hopefully find him alive and well.

11

Joey

I decided to write the numbers I was seeing and figure it all out later. I didn't have time to try to do math conversions on the dive. I drew a line across my survey notes under the last set of numbers I had recorded. That way I would know where the difference in recording started.

I held the compass next to the line and rotated almost one hundred and eighty degrees to line it up to the north. Wait! That's not right! I shouldn't have to adjust the bezel so much. I stopped myself. Dumbass! I had just worked this out and drawn a line in my notes. I was already getting confused. Maybe I should blow off the survey and come back to do it the next day.

No. It wasn't that much distance back to where I started. I glanced at my gauges. Plenty of air left before the gauges showed I was at the agreed upon pressure to turn and start heading out of the cave. I continued to survey the line in the tunnel as I made my way back to where I had started and back to my stage tank.

Then it hit me as I looked at my dive computer to record the depth. More than thirty minutes had passed since I started running line away from the permanent line and into this small lead. How had so much time passed? I hadn't let out much line. Was I stuck for that long? What had Lindsey and Gary been doing while I was in this tunnel? One of them was behind me at least once. Had they been patiently waiting for me to come back out?

It was doubtful that Lindsey was waiting so patiently. She barely tolerated our shenanigans when Gary and I were looking for leads. Gary had probably gone off to look for his own lead. That meant the three of us were all separated doing our own thing. But what was Lindsey doing? How upset was she going to be having to wait for me for so long?

I quickly abandoned the idea of trying to get any survey data and shoved the wetnotes into my thigh pocket. The survey would have to wait for another day. If Lindsey was upset with me for having to wait so long, she would come unglued if she saw me coming out surveying the line. With my notes safely tucked into my pocket I picked up my pace. I slid my hand gently along the line and counted knots as I moved back out of the tunnel toward my stage tank. At least I would have a rough idea of how much line I had put in here.

I rounded the next corner and saw the outline of my stage tank bottom end up resting on the floor where I had left it clipped to the guideline. I didn't see any sign of Lindsey or Gary. I didn't expect Gary to be waiting for me, but I did think Lindsey would still be there. Strange that she wasn't. I sped up even more. I was back at my stage tank within thirty seconds. I unclipped it from the line and clipped it to my harness, nestling it in the space between my left sidemount tank and my back. I looked around for any signs of Lindsey and Gary but didn't see anything. I shielded my light. Total darkness. I waited a few seconds for my eyes to adjust. Nothing but the dim glow from my dive computer displays. I was surrounded by a black void.

Where could they have gone?

Only two directions to go from here. Farther into the cave. Or back out toward the exit. Knowing Gary, he probably went farther into the cave. And Lindsey probably followed him. I checked my gauges. I had reached turn pressure sometime while I was swimming back out. I was about 100 psi beyond turn pressure. That meant I should be making my way out of the cave at this point.

Gary and I had similar breathing rates. We typically reached turn pressure within thirty seconds of each other. Lindsey had a better breathing rate. Not by much though. I'd been working on improving my breathing. If she hadn't already reached her turn pressure, she should be pretty close. I did have those couple of periods where my breathing rate increased. They didn't last long, though.

If Lindsey and Gary went farther into the cave, they should be heading out. Could they have passed by here already?

No. Lindsey wouldn't leave me in the cave. She would have been waiting for me with my stage tank.

Unless....

If something happened to Gary, she would have exited with him. I began to turn toward the exit to make my way out. I hesitated. But if they were still in the cave, the other way, and they got back here would they wait or continue to exit? I decided to turn back around and head farther into the cave.

Reserve air was meant to be used for emergencies. And team separation was sort of an emergency. Especially if something was wrong with either Lindsey or Gary.

I quickly calculated how much air I could use before I had to turn around and start heading out. One tank had 2100 psi and the other had 2000 psi. My stage tank still had 2100 psi in it. I had spent a bit of time in the tunnel I found so I only needed 1000 psi from my stage tank and about 700 psi from each sidemount tank to get back to the opening. That left me with about 1300 psi from each of the sidemount tanks and 1000 psi from the stage tank to look for Lindsey and Gary. I wanted to keep a little reserve just in case. I divided each by three. I would swim farther into the cave until the gauges read 1400 psi on the sidemount tanks, and then I would turn around. With or without Lindsey and Gary.

Too much math. My head was starting to hurt from all the math. Cave diving was supposed to be fun. It shouldn't involve so much math. Especially during the dive. I turned back and started heading farther into the cave hoping I would find them long before I got to my emergency turn pressures. Even though I had calculated the pressures of when I should turn back, I didn't know if I'd be able to turn and head out without Lindsey and Gary. I had to find them.

12

Joey

I glanced at my dive computer. Ten minutes had passed since I clipped on my stage tank and started making my way farther into the cave. Still no sign of either Lindsey or Gary. Where could they have gone? Maybe I should turn around and head out. Maybe they already started out of the cave. The plan had been to turn at 2100 psi of air pressure in the tanks or when one hour had passed since the time we began the dive. We had already passed both of those marks.

Just a few more minutes, then I would turn. I hadn't passed any line intersections in the guideline. They had to be close to the line I was following. Unless Gary went off without running a line and Lindsey followed him. But Lindsey wouldn't do that. She was too conscientious about safety. She was more than conscientious. She was strict about it.

Not that Gary and I weren't safe. We were just a little more relaxed about the rules and the dive plan. We were okay with swimming thirty or forty feet away from the permanent guideline without running a jump line. And so far, nothing had happened.

So far.

I quickened my pace. I shielded my light. My eyes adjusted to the blackness. No other lights. All I could see was the dim glow coming from the dive computer displays on my wrists. But the area farther from me was pure black. Completely devoid of all light and color. I couldn't think of anywhere else where it got this dark.

I moved my hand away from my light allowing the beam to escape and feeling an immediate sense of comfort in being able to see again. I glanced at my dive computers. Twelve minutes since I started farther into the cave. They couldn't have gone this far.

Could they?

I decided to give it three more minutes and then I would turn around. Where the hell had they gone? Why had I insisted on checking that lead and leaving them behind? Was it worth it? What was I going to do if I couldn't find them? It had been more than forty minutes since I had last seen them. Okay, maybe only twenty minutes. I did see that light behind me when I was stuck. And I don't think the second time it was my backup light.

The last time I knew I had laid eyes on Lindsey and Gary I was tying the line from my explorer reel to the existing line in the cave. I had seen a lead to the left that I wanted to check out. Before deploying the line, I had ventured in about twenty feet, going only far enough so I could still see the illumination from Gary and Lindsey's lights back in the tunnel where we had been swimming. I would have gone farther but I heard Lindsey's voice in my head reprimanding me for going off the guideline too far without running a line.

We hadn't found any new tunnels even though we checked every single area that looked like it might be one. And then I found the lead I disappeared into. As I looped the line around the line arrow I had placed on the existing line, I saw Gary continue to swim in the direction we had been going. I thought he was only going a few feet farther to see if there were any other leads in the area. I didn't think he would go very far.

Here I was, almost fifteen minutes of swimming, roughly seven hundred feet from where I had found that lead, and still no sign of either one of them. I wished Jim was also on this trip. Damn work! Jim had recently gotten a promotion at work, and he couldn't get away. Jim encouraged Gary to come down with us anyway. If Jim were here, he and Gary would be somewhere in the cave together and I wouldn't be worrying about where Gary had gone.

But here we were for a full week of cave diving in some of the most exotic caves in the world. Caves that hardly any other cave divers were given the honor of diving because the logistics didn't make it easy. And Jim had to miss out on it.

* * *

Lindsey and I had met a local diver the year before while we were on our first recreational dive trip together in Cozumel, Mexico, one of the diving meccas of the world. The diving around Cozumel was hard to beat. There were lots of divers that returned year after year, sometimes multiple times a year, to dive the reefs along the western shore of the island.

The dive master on the dive boat we were on happened to also be a cave diver. When he saw our unusual diving configuration, he began asking questions.

"What's up with the tanks on the side?"

"It's a configuration called sidemount diving," Lindsey answered, always the dive instructor.

"Yeah, but isn't that supposed to be two tanks? One on each side?"

"That's what you'll see most people doing. And we do that at home in Florida when we're diving in the caves. But since we're doing recreational dives from a boat, we decided to use one tank. It's called monkey diving."

"Yeah, it's a lot more comfortable than having a tank on your back. Keeps the valve and regulator where you can see them and keeps you in a lower profile," I chimed in.

"Doesn't it make you lopsided with the weight of the tank on one side and nothing on the other?"

"Not really," Lindsey answered. "There's only about a four-pound difference, and we get that much of a weight difference in the air we breathe from our steel sidemount tanks."

The divemaster thought about that for a moment.

"Oh, wait! Did you say you guys are cave divers?"

"Yeah, we live about an hour from some of the best cave diving in Florida."

"I wanted to go to Playa this week to dive those caves, but Lindsey insisted we do a recreational dive trip since I've never been on one before and have only been diving in salt water a handful of times."

"This is your first dive trip? Congratulations! You came to the best place to dive in the world! You know we also have caves here on Cozumel, don't you?" our guide asked us.

"You do???" We both yelled out at the same time.

That was how we came to meet Jose and learn about the caves of Cozumel. Jose was a cave diver and offered guided dives in the local caves. Unfortunately, we weren't equipped to do any cave dives during that trip. We had only brought our recreational scuba equipment with us. I did ask him about the possibility of renting dive equipment to go cave diving, but before he could tell us there wasn't any available, Lindsey interrupted.

"No sir! We won't be taking rental equipment into any caves! We would need time to familiarize ourselves with any equipment we would be taking into such an environment."

Always the safety czar.

After making the transition to sidemount diving in preparation for cave diving training three years earlier, I couldn't see myself diving with a tank on my back ever again. I didn't even own that old, used buoyancy compensator, BC for short, that I had purchased shortly after getting certified. I considered diving sidemount on this trip, but I wasn't sure if the dive center would be open to someone diving with two tanks on a recreational level dive. They'd be too concerned about me staying underwater longer than I should. I couldn't say that wouldn't be a valid concern. And trying to deal with gearing up with two tanks, dropping into the water with both tanks, and then getting back on the boat with them didn't seem like a fun time.

Maybe if we were heading out to sea caves and going to check those out, but we weren't. We were doing hour-long recreational reef dives. Totally relaxing and stress free. After some of the situations I had gotten myself into since first getting scuba certified, that trip was exactly what I needed.

When Lindsey suggested the trip, I wasn't too excited about it.

Where was Lindsey? Where was Gary? Why hadn't I found them yet? Why didn't they wait for me?

Lindsey wanted to do a recreational dive trip. I wasn't thrilled about it. I knew there were caves across the way on the mainland. Lots of caves. All the way from Tulum up to Playa del Carmen. How could I be on an island so close to one of the best places in the world to cave dive and not go cave diving? Lindsey wasn't having it though.

Ever since I got scuba certified, the only saltwater diving I'd done was at the St. Andrews Jetties in Panama City Beach, Florida. Well, technically, I did do a couple of dives in the middle of the Gulf of Mexico. Okay, I'm exaggerating a little. It wasn't exactly the middle. But it was still a good ten miles from the coast where we couldn't see land. At least I didn't think we could see land. These dives also happened in the middle of the night.

Anyway, the first dive at the jetties didn't go all that well. In fact, Lindsey and I almost got ourselves killed. No fault of our own. The tide charts were off. That tidal current was not a force anyone wanted to contend with.

So, Lindsey suggested a nice, easy relaxing trip to the Caribbean.

She had been to Cozumel on a trip with her dive shop the year before I met her and really enjoyed it. She wanted to share the experience with me. I tried to convince her to at least schedule a few days on the mainland to experience the caves there, but she was insistent this would be a reef and fish diving trip only. Oh, and some sea turtles and sea horses, if we got lucky. And sharks. She wouldn't even give me one day to dive the cenotes.

I thought about turning around. It was more than ten minutes since I started this way to look for Lindsey and Gary. I would just look around that next corner. Then I'd turn back.

I knew I wouldn't win the argument and eventually gave in. And, boy, was I glad I did! Otherwise, I would never have met Jose and would never have learned about the underwater caves on the island of Cozumel. The reef diving was also pretty good, for reef diving.

When we first started discussing the trip, the first thing I thought about was having to spend an entire week in single tank backmount configuration. I didn't relish that thought. I had also sold my old BC when it occurred to me that I hadn't used it for more than six months. It had served its purpose. I'd have to rent one in Cozumel. I'd also have to reconfigure my regulators to be able to use them on a backmounted setup. I wasn't even sure if I had a long enough high-pressure hose for the pressure gauge. None of that sounded too enticing. After selling the BC, I borrowed a BC and regulator set from the dive shop where Lindsey worked. She was teaching a class and doing checkout dives at the jetties, so I went along, a little concerned about the tide tables possibly being wrong again. I hated it. Not the diving. Diving was always good. I hated having a scuba tank on my back.

I made it to the next corner. I looked around it but didn't see anyone. The tunnel curved around to the right, though, so I couldn't see very far. I could go check that corner then turn back. Just one more corner.

Fortunately, the trips to the jetties didn't happen very often. Most times I would head to the Mill Pond in Marianna, Florida and dive with Gary and Jim. They had finally gotten themselves some diver propulsion vehicles, DPVs, more commonly referred to as scooters, so our options for diving had opened up quite a bit. On occasion, Lindsey still guilted me into going with her and getting some salt on my gear.

I did it. And I did kind of enjoy the environment that was so different from the caves I was used to. But I definitely didn't enjoy the tank on my back. So I did some research and found out about this thing called monkey diving. Diving with a single tank mounted on the side, just like sidemount diving but without the second tank. I experimented with it at Eddy Spring a few times while Lindsey was conducting the first day of open water scuba diver checkout dives with students. It felt amazing! It was almost like diving with no tank at all. It felt similar to what that monofin diver I'd seen several times at Eddy felt like. I couldn't believe I had never heard of monkey diving!

Nothing beyond that corner either. The tunnel curved back the other way about fifty feet ahead, though, so I couldn't see very far. One more corner, then I could turn back.

My usual sidemount BC was a little big and bulky for diving with a single aluminum eighty cubic foot tank mounted on the side, but it still got the job done. After some research I bought some two-inch webbing, a small buoyancy compensator bladder, and some stainless-steel hardware designed specifically for sidemount harnesses. I built my first monkey diving rig.

Monkey diving was even better in the minimalistic, low profile rig I had built. I managed to convince Lindsey to try it. She liked it so much I built her a low-profile rig. We used them on our first Cozumel dive trip. They attracted the attention of Jose and the other recreational divers on the dive boat.

After that first day on the boat when we had discovered we were all cave divers, we planned on heading out for dinner together one evening. While we were out to dinner at a local taqueria, Jose told us more about the cenotes on the island. Cenotes leading to miles and miles of underwater cave tunnels. Cave tunnels with speleothems, formations that were formed before the caves were flooded twelve thousand years earlier. There were also ancient Mayan artifacts in the caves.

Why had I never heard of these caves before??? We stayed at the taqueria late into the night with Jose describing everything he'd seen in the caves of Cozumel.

"You won't believe the things we see in these caves!" Jose told us excitedly. "They have sea life in them! Sea stars, eels, scallops, sponges, cowry. I even seen an octopus in one of the caves. Really freaked me out when I saw it because it was so far from any of the ocean entrances I know. Hell, it had to be about a kilometer in from the shoreline!"

"Get out of here! Really??"

"Yeah, and the formations are so pretty. I've never been diving in a cave outside of Mexico, but I've seen videos of the Florida caves. These are much prettier."

"Oh com'on, Jose! You have to experience the Florida caves in person before you can have an opinion about them. I realize they don't have the stalagmites and stalactites you see here in Mexico, but they have their own beauty from being carved out by the water flow that you don't see here." Lindsey argued.

The conversation went on like that for hours. Each arguing the beauty of our own local caves. Pulling up videos on YouTube to prove our point. No one gave in to the other side.

The next day on the dive boat we were exhausted. Even Jose was moving slower than usual. The late night of good beer and food had taken its toll on us. As we were drifting over the reefs looking for sea turtles, eels, and any other assortment of marine life, I couldn't help but think about the caves on the island. Especially the cave I had seen the entrance to without knowing there was a cave there. We had seen the water off the road as we were driving to the marina every morning and one afternoon decided to pull over and take a closer look. It looked like a small pond. I had no idea there was a cave with about four miles of tunnels below our feet.

That's the cave we were in at the moment. Jose had offered to guide us in the caves on Cozumel when we returned. He wanted to prove his argument in person that the caves here were better than the caves in Florida. So here we were six months later.

Nothing beyond that corner. I really should turn back. I've been heading this way long enough. They couldn't have gone this far.

13

Joey

We did a shakedown dive the day after we arrived in Cozumel. Jose took us to Aerolito, the most well-known cave on the island, and the easiest to access. When we had stopped to look at it during our previous trip, we only saw the first, larger part of the cenote where a cave entrance wasn't visible. The other end of the cenote was much smaller, maybe a tenth the size of the larger end. Had we gone all the way back to the other side, we would have seen the cave entrance. It's that obvious! It was on the very end of the cenote under a rocky shelf and was as wide as the cenote.

We did that first dive with Jose running the line from the opening to the beginning of the main line. We entered a smaller opening about halfway across the long end of the larger side. The dirt road to the smaller end was too rough to drive our rental car over so we parked near the paved road and set up our equipment there. Entering on the larger end gave us an opportunity to get situated in our gear and make sure everything was balanced correctly.

We descended below the surface and began to follow Jose over the lush green floor of the cenote. Jose quickly found the small opening on the right side under the dirt road. I would have never seen it if he hadn't shown it to me. It was hidden in the shadows. Jose anchored the line from his primary reel and started into the cave with us following closely behind. We followed him in. And in and in. He kept reeling out more and more line from his primary reel. I began to think Mexican caves didn't have line in them and we were going to have to run our own lines every dive. Gary and I both had explorer reels with more than a thousand feet of line on each, but we hadn't expected to have to use them just to dive the cave.

After about five minutes, we finally swam over a faded yellow stop sign. It was so faded we couldn't see any words on it. I descended to the floor in front of the sign to take a closer look. That's when I made out the very faint words that used to be red.

PLEASE STOP UNLESS CAVE TRAINED
We Care!

It was the same sign as the one in the cavern of Twin Cave back in Merritt's Mill Pond in Marianna, Florida. Except the letters on the sign in Twin Cave were not so faded. This was a milder version of the grim reaper sign that seemed to be more prominent in the cave entrances. The other sign had a drawing of a grim reaper with three skeletons in open water dive equipment at its feet and the words STOP! PREVENT YOUR DEATH! GO NO FARTHER on it. I don't know if it was more effective at keeping untrained divers out, but it was certainly more menacing.

I ascended back to the line from Jose's primary reel and saw it bend around a corner over a limestone bridge that was above the stop sign a couple of feet beyond it. I looked for the permanent guideline of the cave, but I still didn't see anything except Jose spooling out even more line as he went around another corner to the left this time.

As I swam around that corner, I finally saw the main guideline. It was about fifty or sixty feet beyond the faded stop sign, and close to three hundred and fifty feet from where we had entered the cave. Jose's reel was almost empty. That was the farthest back I'd seen the beginning of any permanent guideline in a cave. The lines in the Florida caves typically began anywhere from right at the entrance to maybe one hundred feet in. Definitely not three fifty! I'm not sure I could have found it without Jose there to follow. I wondered if it was just as far from the large opening.

The main line in Aerolito was orange rather than gold. And not as smooth. It also seemed much stiffer than the gold line seen in the Florida caves.

"Because Aerolito is tidally influenced and it has a saltwater layer that starts at about five meters deep, a sturdier line is needed. If we used the regular thin lines, they would have to be changed every few years because the saltwater breaks it down. As it is, we are already changing the thinner, white cave line we have in the side tunnels that we don't visit very often because it gets deteriorated within three years and breaks too easy. I've done a lot of time diving to fix and change broken line in those passages." Jose explained to us during the dive briefing.

Jose secured the line from his primary reel to the beginning of the main guideline, and we swam through a section that put us right in the middle of the halocline, an area where the saltwater and freshwater met. Undisturbed you could see the line of separation. Get in the middle of it, finning and moving, and the two waters started swirling around and mixing with each other. This obscured the visibility quite a bit. It wasn't like silt clouds. Silt removed the visibility. When it was bad enough you couldn't see anything, not even the light beam coming from a three-thousand-lumen dive light.

The halocline disturbance made it blurry. Really blurry! Like if you wear glasses or contacts and lost them blurry. Or like when you mix oil or gasoline in water. The saltwater and freshwater didn't want to mix. At times, the visibility was so blurry I could barely see Jose's light only ten feet in front of me. I definitely couldn't see the guideline below me, so I followed Jose with my thumb and forefinger making a circle around it. This was the universal scuba hand signal for okay, used as both a question and a response. It was also used to follow the line in reduced visibility to avoid putting tension on it.

About three minutes later, we finally broke through the halocline and descended below it into the saltwater layer. Man, did it feel warm! It kind of felt like I had peed in my wetsuit, only the pee was surrounding my entire body. It reminded me of that video Dr. Richard Pyle had made of a dive he and his teammate did off the coast of Christmas Island. They were ascending from four hundred feet deep and hit the thermocline where the water temperature went from fifty-five degrees Fahrenheit to eighty-six degrees Fahrenheit. The first words that came out of Pyle's mouth were "It feels like I'm swimming in piss!"

What made it even funnier was that Pyle was talking in that high pitched helium voice you get when you breathe from a helium-filled balloon because he had been breathing Trimix, a mixture of helium, oxygen, and nitrogen. He was breathing Trimix so he could decrease the effects of nitrogen narcosis. This was what Jacques Cousteau called the Martini Effect because each atmosphere of depth made you feel like you'd had the equivalent number of martinis. Four hundred feet deep would make you feel like you had thirteen martinis if you didn't have any helium in the air you were breathing!

The temperature contrast wasn't as significant for us as it had been for Dr. Pyle. It was only a couple degrees difference. It went from eighty degrees Fahrenheit in the freshwater to eighty-two degrees Fahrenheit in the saltwater. It felt like a much bigger difference, though, and the feeling must have been similar. I even talked through my regulator and said in a high-pitched voice, "It feels like we're swimming in piss!" I don't think anyone understood me, though.

The main tunnel of Aerolito wasn't very decorated. At least not what I could see of it. It was dark and wide, and my light didn't penetrate to the sides of the tunnel. I couldn't see the ceiling through the halocline. But the halocline was fun to play with. The tunnel was wide enough for Gary and me to swim side by side and we kept sticking our fingers up into the line the two waters formed and swirling the layers together, watching the waters mix and blur the visibility. It was really cool.

When we weren't messing with the halocline, I saw sea stars. More specifically, brittle sea stars. They were everywhere! And they were easy to find. As we passed by and I shined my light on them, they pulled in their tentacles and made themselves as small as they could. Some of them pulled themselves into small holes that they had dug right next to where they were hanging out.

"Aerolito is known as the cave with the most marine life that can be found inside a cave anywhere. There are species in Aerolito that are nowhere else in the world," Jose told us that night out at the taqueria. *"There is sixty-one hundred meters of line. I think that's about twenty thousand feet, in this cave. That's more than six kilometers! Can you believe?"*

"I believe it's that long. We have longer caves in Florida," I replied.

"Oh, Aerolito isn't the longest cave in Mexico, not even on Cozumel. The longest cave on Cozumel is la Cueva Quebrada, where the Chankanaab Nacionale Park is. That has almost nine kilometers of line in it. But Aerolito has more marine animals. There was a group of cave divers that were exploring it many years ago and they claim they added twelve kilometers of line, but they never share a map. I've been looking all over the cave and just come to dead-ends. I don't believe their claim."

"Twelve kilometers?? Wow!! That's..." I pulled out my phone to Google the conversion. *"That's almost seven and a half miles!"*

"Yes, if it was true, Aerolito would be the longest cave on Cozumel. But, like

I said, they never show proof, so it remains the second longest.”

“Four miles is still pretty long.”

“Yes, it is, but nothing compared to what there is in Playa. It is much more interesting though. I will show you everything that is living in there. Sea stars, sponges, clams, maybe we will even see some sea worms.”

About fourteen minutes after we had started the dive, the walls of the cave moved in closer to us until we were swimming through a corridor that was about six feet wide. Gary dropped back in line behind me. Lindsey was behind him. We were deep enough that we weren't disturbing the halocline anymore. That's when I first started to see some of the formations Jose had told us about. And some other marine life. That's right! The marine life wasn't just near the opening to the cave. We had to be at least six hundred feet in, and we were still seeing life in it. Big animals like red sea stars. In Florida, the only life we saw inside caves was barely visible to the naked eye.

Granted, Aerolito was connected to the ocean. In fact, on the other side of the cenote from where we entered was another tunnel called Shark Alley. Shark Alley connected from the cenote to the marina. It went beneath the jungle and a road. Jose showed us the area where it opened into the marina. We could see a boil on the surface from the water that was flowing out of it. The total distance was about eight hundred feet from the cenote. It was called Shark Alley because sharks were known to venture into that tunnel with the tide. I couldn't even imagine encountering a shark in a dark cave. I think I'd soil my wetsuit. And I don't mean by peeing in it! I'd have the old scuba Warhammer maneuver.

The marine life in the main tunnel, where we were diving, was mainly sea stars and sponges. We saw a couple of large sea stars, not the small brittle stars. The large orange/red colored sea stars like you find on the reef. And sponges hanging from the guideline. They had grown around the line. Some of them looked like softball size snowballs. I found myself hoping we didn't lose visibility. If we had to exit the cave using the line to guide us, it wouldn't be that easy with the sponges attached to it. I reached out and lightly touched one with the tip of my finger. It felt soft. I didn't want to have my hand run into one in the dark, though.

About twenty minutes into the dive, Jose stopped and deployed the line from one of his jump spools. We were moving from the main line to a tunnel on our right. This one had a gold line in it. Actually, it was bright yellow. Not quite as thick as the orange line in the main tunnel but still thicker than the cave line on our spools and reels. And very stiff. This was where things were supposed to get interesting. Jose was taking us to a place in Aerolito called Wonderland. That's all he told us.

"You'll see why it's called that when we get there. Patience. And make sure you keep an eye on the ceiling in the tunnel leading to Wonderland. You will be surprised by what's there."

Was I ever! There was a large rock sticking out of the ceiling. By large, I mean ten feet long. It was covered with scallops. They were every inch or so on the surface of this rock. What was even more interesting was that they were right above the halocline in moving water. I could see the water rushing by over the scallops, making them wave to us as we swam by. Below the halocline, in the saltwater, there was minimal current. While we waited for Jose to connect the guidelines of the main tunnel and the tunnel to Wonderland, I hovered motionless trying to discern any movement in the water. I thought the water was flowing out but couldn't be certain.

At the scallops, I could see the freshwater above the halocline moving by quickly. It was heading out toward the direction we had just come from. The movement of the water was significant enough that it disturbed the halocline and made visibility a little blurry. The scallops were in that disturbed layer of water that was about a foot and a half tall. They seemed to like the brackish water over the salt- or freshwater. I slowed down to make sure I could get some photos and video with my GoPro. Jose stopped and waited for me. I swear he had a huge grin on his face. I didn't know how he was able to seal his lips around his mouthpiece and breathe from his regulator with such a big smile.

After getting a bunch of photos and video, we continued farther into the cave. I saw several white lines going off into tunnels along the side of the tunnel we were in. I even saw another yellow line heading into a much smaller tunnel directly in front of us. It looked like a line intersection until we got right over it and I saw a gap about a foot long between the ninety degree turn in the line we were on and the line going straight into the restriction. We followed the continuous line toward the right and began to descend deeper.

We had only been about twenty-five feet deep to this point. We might have hit thirty feet a couple of times. This was a very shallow cave. Nothing like the typical Florida cave. I could spend hours in it with just two aluminum eighty cubic foot tanks and not have any decompression obligation.

Scuba diving causes your body to absorb nitrogen bubbles into the blood stream and into soft tissue organs. The deeper you were, the more nitrogen it absorbed. This made it necessary to ascend slowly to allow the nitrogen bubbles to escape your body slowly. If you didn't, you could get decompression illness, or the bends. At deeper depths, after a certain period of time, you needed to make decompression stops at shallower depths to allow your body to get rid of the nitrogen before you could ascend to the surface.

At twenty-five feet of depth you would never have to do a decompression stop. You could stay there forever if you had enough air to breathe. We weren't at twenty-five feet anymore. We had descended to sixty feet. That meant we might have a decompression obligation at the end of the dive. It also meant we would be breathing through the air in our tanks more than twice as fast as we had been in the shallower part of the cave.

14

Lindsey

About ten minutes after the last time I turned around, I thought I saw a light ahead. It was only a brief flash, like a lightning strike seen from miles away. It was there and then it was gone. I shielded my own light and was immediately enveloped by the darkness of the cave. Only the soft, dim blue glow from the numbers on my dive computer displays existed in this black void. I moved my arms toward my body to shield those as well. I wanted to be in total darkness. I wished I could hit a button to turn off the displays momentarily.

I waited.

I watched.

Nothing.

The flash of light must have been my mind playing tricks on me. I was so desperate to see Joey and Gary that my mind was creating illusions to make me think I was seeing signs of them. When you stared at something long enough you began to see things that weren't there. When you wanted something badly enough, your mind might make you think it was within reach. I unshielded my light and continued swimming toward where I had left Joey.

There it was again! Another flash of light!

I quickly covered my light and shoved my dive computers against my body to extinguish their glow and waited for my eyes to adjust. I was in a tunnel that ran fairly straight for hundreds of feet. Not many curves or corners. My dive light beam penetrated about eighty feet or so. I was sure it could be seen from much farther away, but only if someone was looking for it. I kept my light covered and waited. I waited a bit longer. I wanted to keep moving forward, but I couldn't maintain contact with the line that was keeping me on the path out while also shielding my light. So as much as it pained me to remain in place, I did. I held my position and waited for the flash of light again.

I had no idea if the light was coming from the tunnel I was in or if it was Joey or Gary coming out from an offshoot tunnel. I was still too far from where I had left Joey to see any light coming from his tunnel, but maybe he had made it back out and continued farther into the cave and found another lead. Even though he was certainly beyond his turn pressure, I wouldn't put it past Joey to get sidetracked with another lead while looking for me and Gary. He would even try to justify his actions.

"If we find anything before we hit our turn pressure, make sure to note the pressure in your tanks," Joey told Gary. "We can use that to recalculate our turn pressure and stay in the cave a little longer before starting to head out."

"What are you talking about, Joseph?"

"You know. Like we used to do at Hole in the Wall cave when I was only intro cave certified. We would swim the upstream section, turn around when we reached turn pressure, and swim back to the bottom of the chimney. Then we would recalculate sixths, move the line from our primary reel over, and swim the downstream section until we reached our recalculated turn pressure."

"It's one thing to recalculate your turn pressures when you're so close to the opening. That sounds a little dangerous to be doing so far inside the cave."

"Divers do it all the time when they're doing exploration. Otherwise, they would be turning back long before they had to and wasting a lot of time."

"I don't like it. It's too easy to get confused and breathe too much from your

tanks doing that. Let's just stick to one gas plan, one turn pressure. Sweet and simple."

"Com'on Linds! I've done it in Florida. And the caves are much deeper there. It's much safer to do here in the shallow caves in Mexico."

"You shouldn't be doing that in Florida. If I had known that we would have had this discussion a long time ago."

"Com'on Gary, help me out here!"

"Nope! I'm staying out of this one! I don't want her to threaten to call Jim again. Just let me know what to do when y'all decide."

Those boys were pushing all sorts of limits when I wasn't around. I began to worry about them cave diving on their own. They knew better than to do such things. They were complicating things that didn't need to be complicated. Now I didn't know what to expect from Joey. We decided to stick to a single turn pressure with no recalculations, but was he really doing that?

Hopefully, Joey saw the note I left him telling him to stay put. I didn't have a lot of faith that he would see it, or that if he saw it, he would wait for me. Once he started swimming farther into the cave, he wouldn't be able to help himself if he saw what he thought might be new, unlined cave passage.

Maybe it was Gary's light I was seeing. I didn't see any lines tied onto the permanent line and heading a different direction. Even though we had discussed not leaving the permanent guideline without running a line, I wasn't confident that either of them would remember that in the excitement of finding a potential lead. Maybe I passed Gary along the way and that was him coming back to this tunnel after investigating a potential lead.

A minute or two must have passed while I was contemplating the situation I was in. I hadn't seen any other flashes of light. Then, just as I was about to remove my hand from the light head, I saw another flash. This one was very distinct. Much more easily seen in the darkness I had allowed. It was definitely a light. No doubt about it. No mind tricks this time. It looked closer but still too far away to be constant. Whoever it was must be sweeping his light around the tunnel probably looking for another lead to explore.

I removed my hand from my light and began to quickly swim along the tunnel. I circled my thumb and forefinger around the guideline below me, keeping the light beam pointing down and slightly back. I wanted some light to keep me from swimming into a low hanging ceiling or narrow walls. But I wanted to preserve the darkness of the cave ahead of me as much as I could to help me see any more flashes of light.

I wanted it to be both Joey and Gary. Maybe they had found each other and were swimming back to look for me. Not likely, but I could be hopeful. I knew where Joey was, or at least where he had been. So I was hoping this was Gary. I had already had feelings of impending doom about Gary. Almost forty-five minutes had passed since I last saw his bright yellow fins quickly swimming off into the black void. I had followed the path I last saw him on twice. I saw no signs of him. It was like he had disappeared. Like he got sucked into the void never to return.

I guess this was similar to the way the family of that diver Joey found in Eddy Spring must have felt. Even though Joey and I knew what happened, no one else did. The family never learned of his demise. They never had closure. All they knew was that one day he was there, and the next day he was gone.

While I wasn't ready to give up on Gary, the thought of not being able to find him and not knowing what happened to him kept entering my mind. He had been gone far too long with no sign of where he went. What if he got stuck in a small tunnel? What if he had gotten bad air? If he had gone off to the side of the main tunnel and hadn't run a line, it would be almost impossible to find him in this cave.

The passages were too extensive. There were too many of them. That diver that died in Telford Spring in Florida years ago wasn't found until five years after he had gone missing. The diver that found him wasn't even looking for him. He was just doing a leisurely dive. I can't imagine how he must have felt when he found a dead body in the cave! Especially one that had been there for five years!

The line laid out in the cave was supposed to help guide us out to the opening. It also helped guide us in, although that wasn't its primary purpose. We had already found line that was deteriorating. We had to make a few line repairs the day before. It was so bad that I started testing the line after each tie off. I tugged on it to make sure it was still intact and would remain intact. A couple of times it gave way and fell to the floor in front of us. We had to run a short distance of new line to tie the broken ends together. If the boys weren't so excited about the caves here, I would have demanded we turn around and only dive in the tunnels with the thicker line.

What if Gary had followed an existing line and it had broken as he was going in and it was no longer connected to the main line in this tunnel? I hadn't thought to look on the floor of the cave for broken line. Even if I had, if the line broke because Gary's fin had caught on it and he pulled the line in behind him, I wouldn't see anything on the floor. So it wouldn't make a difference. And there was still line below me.

We could come back the next day to look for Gary's body.

Oh Lord!

Was he really dead? The thought of Gary's mom and Jim entered my head again. How was I going to break the news to his mother? How was I going to break the news to Jim? What if we couldn't find his body? Would Jim fly down here to try to find Gary himself? Would the two of them blame Joey and me for his death?

I didn't even know if I could come back here the next day to look for Gary's body. I didn't know if I could handle it. Could I keep control of my emotions? Could I stay focused enough to be in the cave without putting myself at risk? Probably not. As much as I would have liked to believe I could, I would only be fooling myself.

My mind kept going back to Brendan and the way he had died. His friends had posted an account of what happened on that dive. There were five of them on the dive. They were heading back to an area of the cave where they could surface into a large air-filled room. About fifteen minutes into the dive, Brendan suddenly began swimming very quickly, so fast that a couple of the divers on the team had fallen behind. According to the account of one of those divers, Brendan and two of the others swam around a bend in the tunnel and disappeared from sight for several seconds. As that diver went around the corner, he watched Brendan go vertical in the cave and ascend toward the ceiling. Then he saw a regulator drop down next to Brendan's feet.

All of the divers immediately rushed to Brendan's aid. One of them even stated he looked for air pockets in the ceiling, thinking that would be their only hope. There were no air pockets. The team surrounded Brendan, holding a regulator in his mouth, and tried to keep his airway open as they purged the regulator to try to get any amount of air they could into his lungs. They did this for almost ten minutes as they raced back to the opening of the cave, hoping to save Brendan. It was too late for him, though. Brendan had already breathed water into his lungs. They performed CPR on him once they got him to the surface, but it didn't help.

That was from only a fifteen-minute swim into the cave. We were forty-five minutes from the opening. Even if I found Gary as he was losing consciousness, it would be impossible to get him to the surface quickly enough. I glanced at the ceiling. There were no air pockets above me. Just a few small air bubbles from our exhalations. Nothing large enough to stick a head up into.

How was Joey going to handle it if Gary was dead? He would definitely want to come back into the cave to look for Gary's body. I didn't know if I could convince him not to. He would only be putting himself in danger, though. Joey definitely wouldn't be able to think straight. This wasn't something either of us should do. It wasn't something we could do.

I noticed my breathing rate was getting faster. There was almost a continuous escape of bubbles from my regulator. I slowed my swimming pace and focused on getting my breathing under control. I pushed the thoughts of Gary being dead out of my mind. We had plenty of air. He was probably off somewhere looking for virgin cave. We would find him.

Or maybe we wouldn't. All I knew at this point was I had to find Joey and we had to start making our way out of the cave. We still had almost an hour of swimming before we made it back to the cenote. Without Gary with us, that would be the longest hour of my life.

15

Joey

Fifteen minutes had passed. Fifteen minutes since clipping on my stage tank and swimming farther into the cave to look for Lindsey and Gary.

Fifteen minutes.

Still no sign of either one. They must not have gone this way. I turned around and began swimming back to the line intersection I had created. Maybe they were both there waiting for me. Lindsey would certainly be upset. I had just reached my turn pressure in my tanks, but we were way beyond our agreed upon turn time. Lindsey was a stickler to following the dive plan. And we had blown it. Boy, had we blown it!

Was that a light behind me? I turned ninety degrees and reached out for the permanent guideline while shielding my dive light. A few seconds later my eyes adjusted to the absence. I hovered a foot above the line in the dark and looked back in the direction I had just come, the direction I thought I saw a light flash come from.

Nothing. Just pure blackness. It was spooky how black it got in a cave.

I rotated my body so I was facing the way out again, keeping my light shielded a bit longer. I slowly swam along in the dark while maintaining contact with the line placed in this tunnel for that purpose. Guidelines were placed in underwater caves to guide us out should we lose visibility. Not so much for light failures. We carried two backup lights with us. The lines were there for when the silt got disturbed and made the visibility so bad we couldn't see through it to the cave walls around us.

The guidelines also helped us learn the cave tunnels. I was so familiar with the caves in Florida, where I went diving almost every weekend, that I didn't even reference the lines in them anymore. It was still nice to know the lines were there should the visibility be blown out like it had when the ceiling in Jackson Blue in Marianna, Florida collapsed. The lines were also there so the original explorers could survey the cave and stake claims to their passages. Not that everyone respected those claims. Most did, though.

After about thirty seconds of gliding above the guideline in the darkness, I removed my hand from the light head. The bright three thousand lumen light shot out like a light saber. I brought my hand up and flashed the light beam back and forth like I was Luke Skywalker in a duel with Darth Vader.

I thought back to the first time Gary, Jim, and I went cave diving together was in Jackson Blue. On the way back, when we reached the large room at the bottom of the chimney fissure, Gary stopped and turned toward me. He had fashioned a light cover made of yellow tinted plastic and slipped it over his light head. He began swinging his light beam around like a light saber.

Then Jim pulled out a red tinted plastic light cover, slipped it over his light head, and joined in a duel with Gary. After a minute, they turned toward me, and both started sweeping their tinted light beams at me.

I didn't have my own tinted cover, but I "fought" back anyway. We spent more than five minutes in a light saber duel with each other, each taking turns feigning a hit by the other's beam and dropping toward the bare limestone floor below. Before we hit the floor we would regroup, ascend, and rejoin the battle. The next dive together I had a blue-tinted cover for my light.

Gary and I had brought our light covers on the trip with us. The first day, right after we swam past the beginning of the main line, while Jose was pulling his primary reel, Gary and I whipped out our light saber adapters and began an underwater duel right there in front of Lindsey and Jose.

This was Lindsey's first time seeing this. Usually when the four of us went cave diving in Florida, we split up into two teams and didn't have the opportunity to duel with each other, so she had never witnessed it. I glanced at Lindsey during our duel and saw her with her hand over her mask and shaking her head. I looked back at Jose. He had just pulled the reel off the main line and started to spin the line back onto his reel as he was swimming out when he noticed what we were doing. He stopped and watched. I swore I heard him laughing.

Gary moved close to him and handed him Jim's red adapter. The three of us proceeded to reenact a scene from Star Wars while Lindsey watched, probably embarrassed for us.

I pulled my blue adapter out of my pocket and put it over my light head. I wanted to be ready for Gary when I saw him. The blue hue was comforting. Rather than having a stark, harsh white beam breaking the darkness apart, it produced a subdued light and allowed the darkness to take a stronger hold of my surroundings.

It certainly wasn't helpful for finding any new tunnels along the walls of the cave but at this point I was only interested in finding Lindsey and Gary. Reducing the light around me would hopefully help me see their lights. I continued swimming out while sweeping my light back and forth and occasionally covering it to see if I could see their lights.

Nothing but darkness.

I thought I saw another flash of light behind me. I quickly shielded my light and turned around to look. I waited as my eyes adjusted to the darkness. Because I had the blue cover over my light, decreasing its brightness, the adjustment went much more quickly this time. I still saw nothing there.

I turned and continued to swim out. I glanced at my dive computer. Twenty-five minutes since I left my new tunnel. I should be back there in five minutes. I slowed my pace a little. When I was about two minutes from there, I would shield my light and try to sneak up on Lindsey and Gary. I'd cut Gary in half with my light saber. He would never know what hit him.

Twenty-eight minutes.

I shielded my light as I reached for the line and formed a circle around it with my thumb and forefinger. I continued swimming into the darkness, looking for any evidence of light ahead of me.

Twenty-nine minutes.

I should have seen their lights by now. I couldn't be much more than fifty feet away and the tunnel was straight in this section. There were no corners to hide behind. My thumb hit a line arrow on the line. Then I felt a line intersecting the guideline I was touching. Immediately after the intersection, I felt another line marker, this one a cookie. I uncovered my light and confirmed I was back where I had started. Lindsey and Gary weren't there. I noticed a piece of paper on the line tucked against one of Lindsey's line markers. I slid it out and held it in front of my mask, lighting it with my dive light.

Looking for Gary. Stay put!!!

That was Lindsey's handwriting. Had this note been there earlier? I couldn't remember if it was or not. I was so focused on getting my stage tank clipped on I hadn't looked at the line. But that was thirty minutes ago. Maybe Lindsey had come back while I was gone and placed the note there. Probably not. It would make more sense that she placed it there while I was in my tunnel. That meant she left it there more than thirty minutes earlier.

Could she really be looking for Gary for that long? Why would she be looking for Gary? Gary should be here already. Were the three of us alone and separated from each other?

I was tempted to go look for Lindsey. I didn't know which way to go though. I didn't see her from where I had just come, but maybe I hadn't swum far enough. I did think I saw light flashes a couple of times. Could that have been her? I should swim back.

Or should I? What if Lindsey didn't go that way? What if she got back here while I was off looking for the flashing light. I couldn't just wait here. I could already start to feel the anxiety creeping in. I could feel my heartbeat getting faster. I had to do something. The problem was I had no idea what that something was!

16

Lindsey

It had been several minutes since I last saw a flash of light. Maybe I hadn't seen anything earlier. Maybe it was just my mind playing tricks on me. If someone had been swimming toward me, we should have encountered each other by now. What if the light flashes were from someone swimming out, though? If that was the case, then maybe it was Gary. It would only make sense that Gary had come out from wherever he had been and started swimming toward the exit. And I did leave Joey that note to stay put.

A sense of relief washed over me. Gary was okay. I must have missed him somehow when I was swimming back to look for him. All this worry for nothing. I should have just stayed at the line intersection and waited for Joey to make his way out. Now the two of them would be there waiting for me. At that thought I hastened my pace. I didn't want the boys to be waiting too long. There was no telling what kind of hijinks they would get themselves into without proper supervision. They might try to find more holes to explore.

I finned quickly while still trying to maintain a nice steady breathing rate. I had already breathed past my planned turn pressure. There was no point in using up the air I had left just to cut a minute or two off my swim back. I was going to hear it from Joey and Gary tonight. After all the nagging I did about sticking to the plan at dinner, I'll admit it was nagging, they weren't going to let me off easily.

Sure, it was their fault, Gary's specifically, that I was back here alone and not with them. I would be sure to point that out. Gary would be apologetic about it, but that wouldn't stop either of them from giving me crap about breathing through my turn pressure. Especially Joey. He wouldn't come right out and say anything at first. But he would figure out a way to slip it in. I could hear the conversation already.

"Should we go over the dive plan for tomorrow?" Joey would ask.

"Sure! We need to make sure we're all on the same page for the dive," Gary would remark.

"We gonna do another two-hour dive? Head in, turn at sixty minutes, and head back out?"

"Sounds easy enough. Shouldn't be hard to remember."

"Yeah, but just in case, I better write it down in my wetnotes. I wouldn't want to stay too long and keep everyone else waiting," Joey would say with a smirk and a touch of sarcasm. "I mean, it's one thing to get stuck in a tunnel and be a couple of minutes late, but to be swimming around sightseeing and thirty minutes late… That's something completely different."

I'd let them get in their jabs for a minute or two, but then I'd put a stop to it by pointing out that Gary was the one who had swum off and hadn't left any sign of where he had gone.

"But I was back at the intersection at the agreed upon turn time, Linds." Gary would probably point out. Even if it was a lie.

If the flashes of light I saw ahead were from Gary's light, then I knew he wasn't there when he was supposed to be. For me to see those flashes, he couldn't have been more than a three-minute swim ahead of me. Four tops. The thing was, I didn't have proof that those light flashes were him. I was too far away to see the fins and see if they were those loud, yellow fins Gary wore.

It didn't matter. They'd know they were in the wrong. They would get their ribbing in because boys will be boys, but deep down they'd know they didn't stick to the plan, and that caused all three of us to be separated from each other and put all of us at risk.

Another flash of light interrupted my thoughts. This time it looked closer. I must be catching up to him. I glanced at my dive computer. I was about five minutes from being back at the line intersection. Probably only four since picking up my swim pace. Gary would be arriving there in the next minute or so. Hopefully, Joey had seen my note and heeded it.

I checked my pressure gauges. I had breathed a lot more than I normally would have. I was now 200 psi in each tank into my reserve air pressure. That left me with 900 psi reserve in each tank. I prayed that both Joey and Gary would be at the intersection when I got there. I didn't have much reserve air to look for either one for long, and they probably both had even less air than I did.

A thought suddenly occurred to me. What if they weren't there? What if I got back to the intersection and no one was around? Could I leave the cave without them? Could I leave the cave even without one of them? Could I leave without Joey? What if Joey was there and he didn't want to exit without finding Gary? Did we endanger ourselves looking for someone who might already be dead? Or did we save ourselves and let more experienced cave divers look for his body?

Stop it, Lindsey!! Gary isn't dead! That had to be his light I was seeing. That had to be him.

17

Joey

I pulled out my wetnotes and dug out the pencil that was tethered to them. I flipped over the notepaper Lindsey had left for me and placed it against the hard surface of my wetnotes.

Went to log

As I was writing a note to Lindsey, I was interrupted by the appearance of a light coming from farther in the cave. I shoved the wetnotes into my pocket and started swimming toward it. I couldn't tell if it was Lindsey or Gary. Maybe it was both. I saw only one light, but it was still far enough away that there could be a second one coming behind it.

As we got closer to each other I saw it was just the one light. One diver. It looked like Lindsey, but I wasn't quite sure yet. She was still too far away to tell. I needed to know who it was. I swam faster. Thirty seconds later I was close enough to see black fins. It was Lindsey!

Another minute and we were facing each other, only a couple of feet apart. I looked into Lindsey's eyes through her mask lens. Even in the dark cave I could tell she was worried about something. Given that she was alone, and she had left a note saying she was going to look for Gary, I guessed she hadn't found him. I looked at my dive computer. One hour and forty-five minutes since we had started the dive. We should be surfacing in fifteen minutes. But where was Gary? I couldn't leave without Gary.

I looked at my pressure gauges. *Holy crap!!!* I had breathed 400 psi past my turn pressure. Did I even have enough air left to look for Gary? What about Lindsey? She probably had more air than I did, but would she want to stay and wait for him? Would she want to go look for him again?

I stopped myself. Gary had to be okay. There was no way he wasn't. Maybe Lindsey had found him, and he was on his way to us. It would make sense that Lindsey would have swum faster to get to me to make sure I didn't head off anywhere like I had been planning. Gary would be along shortly.

I made the buddy signal to Lindsey by bringing both index fingers together and apart a couple of times. That was our hand signal for where's your buddy. Lindsey responded by bringing her index fingers together followed by a question mark and shaking her head back and forth. My shoulders slumped. She hadn't found Gary.

She brought her index fingers back together and apart and then threw her hands up while she shrugged her shoulders. She had no idea where he was. Lindsey had been gone for forty-five minutes, though! How could she not have found Gary? Where could he have gone? Our plan had gone bad. Very bad.

The evening before, after we had gotten back to the house we had rented for the trip, Gary and I sat outside for a while enjoying the evening while Lindsey went inside to read. We discussed our own private dive plan to supplement the plan we had all agreed to at dinner. It wasn't that we were going to blow off the dive plan we made with Lindsey. We were planning on still sticking to turn pressures and turn times. We were going to do something extra though. Something that Lindsey probably wouldn't have approved of. I regretted that decision.

"Let's talk about tomorrow's dive," Gary started.

"What's up?"

"What we've been doing isn't working. We're not finding any new leads in there. Don't get me wrong. The cave diving here is amazing, but I'd really like to find some virgin cave passage to lay line in. Even if it's only a few hundred feet of it."

"What do you propose? I don't see what we can do any differently that will help us find tunnels no one has found before."

"Well, first off, we're wasting a lot of time sticking together. Earlier today, when you were off surveying that one tunnel you found that's not on the map, Lindsey and I were just hanging out in the main tunnel waiting. It took you a long time to get that survey done."

"Oh com'on! To be fair, I haven't been doing survey for very long. We only took the class a few weeks ago!"

"I know. I know. Cool your britches! I'm not criticizing you. I don't know that I would be any faster at it. But it didn't do me any good to just hang out waiting for you. I could've been looking around for my own tunnel or lead to check out."

"What do you want to do then?"

"Let's split up if one of us finds something. Most of the stuff we're finding is on the small side and two divers in there wouldn't be much fun for the second guy. And even if the tunnel is big enough for all three of us, I'd rather be off looking for another lead."

"Lindsey will never go for splitting up the team."

"We don't have to tell her. Next time you head off to check out a lead I'm just going to keep going to look for my own lead. Lindsey will likely stay and wait for you."

"You know she'll be pissed about that, dude. You'll never hear the end of it. She might even go out and buy a leash to keep you on."

"That's alright. I'll deal with her. I'm not the one sleeping in the same bed as her. She can be pissed at me."

"She's going to take it out on me, too."

"She'll be more pissed at me. You do what you want to do. If you want to wait around while I'm checking out a lead, that's fine. But I'm going to keep going. Just don't mention any of this to her before the dive otherwise she'll be watching me so closely I'll never be able to get away."

And that was how it went. Gary was so focused on finding his own virgin cave tunnel that he was going to do what he was going to do. In hindsight, I should have said something to Lindsey once we were alone in our room. I should have told her Gary's plan. Instead, here we were, forty-five minutes since either of us last saw Gary. Lindsey had gone to look for him. I had even gone to look. Gary should have been back by now. When he mentioned heading off to look for his own lead, I had no idea he meant he would be gone for so long. I thought he would be gone for ten minutes, maybe fifteen.

Here we were, long beyond our agreed turn time and pressure. No sign of Gary anywhere. We had almost an hour of swimming to get back out to the cenote where we had entered the cave. That was going to be the longest swim of my life.

18

Lindsey

The light flashes turned out to be Joey. Not that I was upset over that. I was glad Joey hadn't gone off after he came out from his new tunnel. But that meant the last contact we had with Gary was more than forty-five minutes earlier. Joey asked me where Gary was. I shook my head and threw my hands up. I had no clue. Joey appeared to flinch. He could probably tell I wasn't happy with the situation.

We were almost an hour beyond the time we should have turned, and I had breathed more than 300 psi into my reserve air trying to find Gary. That meant Joey had even less air left in his tanks. I reached out and grabbed the gauge on Joey's left tank – 1600 psi. He was 500 psi into reserves on that side. I checked his right tank and it read 1700 psi. I had about 100 psi more in each tank than he did.

We could look until Joey had 1500 psi in each tank. That would allow him to have 1000 psi for the exit plus an additional 500 psi in case anything else happened over that hour long swim. But that also gave us less than ten minutes to look. Would Joey stick to that plan or would he want to keep looking for Gary? Maybe it was best for us to just exit. What good would another eight minutes of searching do? Actually only four minutes because we'd have to be back at this location in eight minutes.

Gary got himself into this mess by swimming off. He had to know

I would stay with Joey. But why would he do that? Why would he go off on his own after he saw Joey head into that tunnel? It didn't make sense. He hadn't done anything like that before. We had discussed it several times. If one of us, meaning one of them, was poking around looking at a potential lead, the other two would hang back and wait. That way we all stayed together. If a tunnel was big enough for all three of us, we'd follow. But the only separation would be one of us checking a lead and making sure to be back within ten minutes.

It hadn't been ten minutes when Gary took off. In fact, it hadn't even been one minute. As soon as Joey had pulled his explorer reel off the D ring where it was stored, Gary was swimming away. I was foolish to think he would be back after a few minutes. I should have known that if he was going to break the rule we had set for ourselves to stay together, he would break the other rules, too.

I pulled out my wetnotes and jotted a quick note on them for Joey.

We look 4 Gary til 1500psi. No more! Then head out.

I turned the page toward Joey. He took a second to read it and then looked at his gauges. After a few seconds of thought, Joey looked at me and nodded his head.

I knew it would be tough for Joey to turn and begin to exit without finding Gary. It was going to be tough for me, too. But we couldn't put our own lives at risk. One fatality was better than three.

Stop that, Linds! Gary isn't dead!

Chances are we wouldn't even find Gary at this point. This cave was too big and too extensive. It was literally a maze. Gary could have gone anywhere. Without seeing a line marker on the line or another line heading off into some dark hole, we would never find him without pure luck.

I considered swimming out of the cave to look for Gary. What if he had somehow gotten around us and started making his way out already? What if he was just about to surface and was wondering where we disappeared to? I had already headed farther into the cave twice without seeing any signs of Gary. Maybe he had found a tunnel that looped back to the tunnel we were in, and it brought him out somewhere between our location and the cave opening. I didn't see any point in heading back the way I had just come for a third time. The first two times didn't reveal anything. I pointed behind Joey and told him to start swimming.

Joey immediately held his hands up and shook his head. I knew he thought I had decided to just exit and not look for Gary. I had to communicate to him that I wanted to look for Gary that way instead. I didn't want to waste time writing it all out on my wetnotes. I pointed behind Joey again and put my hands up to my mask like I was holding binoculars. I pointed around the cave behind Joey, trying to tell him I wanted to look there.

Joey pointed behind me and pumped his hand a couple of times to tell me he wanted to go that way.

I formed the hand binoculars as I swept my head back and forth, then pointed behind me, and shook my head side to side. *I had already looked back there, and he wasn't there.*

Joey pointed and pumped his hand again. He wasn't going to give in so easily.

I pulled out my wetnotes and quickly jotted another note on it to show Joey.

Looked. 20 min swim, 2x, not there. Look that way. Maybe got around us

I turned the page toward Joey. He read it. He seemed to be thinking about it. I thought he was going to refuse. I thought he was going to want to look for himself. But Joey surprised me. He handed my wetnotes back to me, turned around, and started swimming while sweeping his light back and forth, up and down, looking in every single crevice he could find.

This exit would take a lot longer than an hour. But at least we were heading in the right direction. I hoped that Gary had somehow gotten around us and was at the surface wondering where we were. Sadly, I didn't think that was the way it would turn out.

19

Joey

Fifteen hundred psi. That only gave me 300 psi total to look for Gary. Then we would have to head out of the cave. We would have to leave Gary behind. Was this how Mike felt when he left me in Jackson Blue last year? I knew he struggled with the decision, but I had no idea it could feel the way I felt at the moment. It was a horrible feeling. I didn't know how he was able to do it. I didn't know how I was going to do it.

We were still shallow enough that if I kept my breathing in check, I could stretch that 300 psi out to at least ten minutes, maybe twelve. But that only gave me five to six minutes of searching before having to turn around. Then what? At least Mike knew where I was when he started out of the cave. He watched me go into that restriction and saw the silt billowing out of it. I had no idea where Gary was. I didn't see where he last went. There was hardly any silt in the tunnel where we were located. I had no idea what had happened to Gary.

Another hour swimming out wondering what happened to Gary. An hour of pure hell. Actually, more like purgatory. The hell would begin on the surface once we had to start making calls. A call to Jose. A call to local authorities. Dealing with the Mexican police. What if they thought we broke the law somehow?? What if we had broken some obscure Mexican law! Would they throw us in jail? I heard lots of horror stories about Mexican prisons. I wondered if there was any truth to them.

That didn't matter. Mexican prison would be welcome over having to call Jim and tell him Gary didn't surface from a cave dive. As cave divers, it was something we had considered. Gary, Jim, and I even discussed it. We never thought it could happen to any of us.

And then having to call Gary's mom to tell her. Would she understand? Had she ever even considered the possibility of losing Gary in such a tragic manner? I had no idea how I would even begin those conversations.

Even worse would be telling Gary's mom and Jim that we had no idea what happened to Gary. He had swum off somewhere and we weren't able to find him. We didn't know where his body was. We didn't know what happened to him. We didn't know why he died. At least if we had found him, even if he was dead, there could be some closure. We might not know the cause of the death, but we'd be able to get Gary back home. Without a body, the disappearance would forever haunt them. It was going to haunt me.

Memories from three and a half years earlier came rushing back in. With those memories came an overwhelming sense of guilt. The family of that diver I found dead in Eddy Spring never got complete closure. The body was never found. They didn't know what happened. As far as they knew, the body vanished into thin air. Or would that be thin water?

I often thought about contacting them and telling them what happened to their son. At least they could be at peace with knowing he had died in the cave and his body was removed. Even if the rest of the story wasn't so peaceful. But I was afraid of what would happen to me. I was being selfish in a way. I was forced to do the things I had done, though. There was no way out of it. At least I couldn't think of a way to get out of it at the time. In hindsight, I should have just called the police and told them everything. But I was more afraid of Earl and what he might have done to me.

Could this be karma? Could this be my punishment for doing what I did to that family? Now I had my own missing friend and had no clue what happened to him. Gary was more than a friend. He was like a brother to me. As big as this cave was, no one may ever find his body. Wherever he was might be his final resting place.

Stop it! Gary couldn't be dead. He was a better diver than that. He was just off looking for virgin cave passages. By now, he had to be on his way out toward the cenote and we should see him any minute.

I wanted to head back into the cave to look for Gary. Lindsey stopped me though. She signaled me but I didn't understand what she was trying to say. She just told me 1500 psi. She was telling me to start swimming out. I pointed behind her and pumped my fist to indicate I wanted to go that way. She signaled me again, but I still didn't quite get what she wanted. It looked like she wanted to look behind me, but why would she want to do that. I saw which way Gary headed. And Lindsey had just come from that direction. No way Gary could have gotten around us and started heading out already.

I pumped my fist again while pointing behind Lindsey. I wanted to go look that way. I watched as Lindsey pulled her wetnotes out again. I waited impatiently as she jotted a few words. This was a waste of time. We were breathing the air in our tanks while we should have been looking for Gary. Lindsey turned the page toward me. I read the words she wrote. I read them a second time. Lindsey had already been that way twice. One time she swam twenty minutes. That equaled about one thousand feet. There was no way we could get that far before my air supply dropped to 1500 psi.

I thought about suggesting that we should split up and look for Gary in different places. I thought better of that. I didn't want to be alone in the cave anymore. I wanted to find Gary, but I needed the comfort of knowing Lindsey was right there and not having to worry about her as well. What if we did split up, she found Gary, and he was low on air, but she didn't have enough to get them both out? Then what? Would Lindsey ditch Gary and leave him behind, or would they both drown once the air in her tanks was depleted? I couldn't bear the thought of losing both of them.

I gave in. I turned and started swimming back toward the exit. I swam slowly. I swept my light back and forth and up and down. I checked every dark shadow in hopes of finding a tunnel and seeing a light coming toward me from within. I tried to keep the hope alive that Gary was in some new tunnel laying line and surveying it and we would run into him soon.

Despite all the positive thinking I was trying to force on myself, I couldn't help but feel a deep sense of foreboding. I couldn't help but think I was only fooling myself. I couldn't help but think about the people I was going to have to call once I surfaced from this dive.

20

Lindsey

As I followed behind Joey, searching the walls and the ceiling, looking for any signs that Gary might have recently been where we were, my mind started to wander. I couldn't help but think the worst. We weren't going to find Gary because Gary was dead. Something had happened to him, and he had drowned in some small offshoot tunnel, probably pinned in between a low ceiling and floor. Did he breathe all of his air, or did he panic and spit out his regulator and die with air still in his tanks?

Gary was a level-headed guy. I had never seen him panic or even so much as stressed out. Between Gary, Jim, and Joey, Gary was the calmest and most responsible of the group. But when a person finds himself in a hopeless situation, a situation that he never expected to happen because he had this perception that he was invincible, there was no telling how he would react.

I didn't know which would be worse. To be stuck in a tight space in a cave, all your efforts to get loose failing. A sense of futility falling over you. Panic rising and taking over. Pure terror because you knew you were about to die in this small space. Becoming so panicked that you started to thrash about and lost the regulator from your mouth. The next breath that came contained nothing but water. No air whatsoever. The sharp searing pain of the water as it traveled past your vocal cords and entered your lungs.

Would it go quickly? Would it be over before you even realized what was happening? Or would unconsciousness take a while to happen? Would you suffer, trying to scream in pain but no sound coming out because your lungs were full of water and not air?

Or would it be worse to slowly breathe away the limited air left in your tanks. Watching the needles on your gauges slowly dropping toward zero. Knowing that the end was coming. The time dragging by slowly, prolonging the agony of knowing you were about to die and there was nothing you could do about it. Watching the minutes pass on your dive computer. Wondering what that first breath of water would feel like. Anticipation building. Fear taking over.

I decided it would be better to go fast. To be panicked and have it happen all at once. The suffering would be minimal that way. You wouldn't have time to think about your circumstances. There wouldn't be any anticipation. The anticipation would be worse than the act of dying.

I heard of cave divers that knew they were near the end. Knew they were about to die in the cave. They took actions to make sure it would be easier for the recovery divers to find their bodies. One example was Steve Berman. He was working on his map to the Devil's Cave System at Ginnie Springs in High Springs, Florida. His body was found clipped to the line, only one hundred feet from his stage tank.

One hundred feet.

Two minutes of swimming at the average swim pace for cave divers. It could probably be done in one minute swimming fast. Especially with the water flow in the cave behind you.

One hundred feet.

Some people might wonder why Berman didn't swim that last hundred feet to his stage tank, why he just gave up and clipped himself to the line. He was so close. He could have made it. What they fail to consider was that Berman probably ran out of air one hundred feet back from where his body was found clipped to the line. He probably knew his stage tank wasn't far, but he could no longer hold his breath. He must have been trying his hardest to get to the tank, knowing death was imminent if he didn't reach it. And then he couldn't hold his breath any longer.

I couldn't even imagine what it must have felt like to know that was all you had, that was all you could do. You had tried your hardest. You had done everything you could, but you couldn't hold your breath any longer. You knew your next breath was going to bring water into your lungs. You were going to die in a cave, several thousand feet back from the opening.

Otherwise, why not keep swimming that last hundred feet? Why give up? I didn't believe Berman gave up. I believed he ran out of air long before he stopped. And he knew he could no longer hold his breath. His last conscious act was to clip himself to the line. He didn't want his body to be pushed off somewhere by the current where it would be more difficult to find. He wanted the recovery divers to have to make the least amount of effort in recovering his body. Even in those last moments, he was being selfless.

The recovery divers had been able to find Berman's body very easily. It was clipped to the main guideline only one hundred feet beyond his stage tank. The current in the cave was significant enough that his body was probably hanging like a sail in the wind. That had to be a rough exit, towing Berman's body out from the cave knowing he had been so close to surviving. So close to making it out on his own. Knowing it was his time and he had clipped himself to the line as his last selfless act.

No one knew exactly what happened to Berman. He had been working on a map of the Devil's cave system at Ginnie Springs. It would be the most comprehensive, most detailed map of that cave at the time. He was in the cave surveying tunnels a few thousand feet back. Based on his survey notes, it appeared he was surveying an offshoot tunnel that was supposed to loop back into the main tunnel. The problem was it didn't. The end of the line in that loop didn't come anywhere near the main guideline. Some people assumed Steve had gambled his life on the belief that it would and pushed on beyond his safe turn pressure. If that was the case, he lost that bet. If it wasn't, then maybe he had issues on the way back that delayed his exit. We would never find out. All we knew was that he wasn't able to make it back to that stage tank.

This wasn't going to be the case for Gary. First, I never saw Gary's stage tank when I went looking for him. Either he still had it on him, or he had taken it off somewhere away from the guideline.

The stage tank! I didn't account for the air in our stage tanks. We still had at least 2000 psi in those tanks. We could spend a little more time looking for Gary. I signaled Joey so I could check his stage tank pressure and we could recalculate our air and time in the cave. I swept my light to the right. Then a thought occurred to me. What if Gary had somehow gotten around me? What if he had started heading out when I was off the main guideline watching Joey?

He should have seen Joey's stage tank on the line. But what if he wanted to check out some leads between where we were and the exit. What if he decided to end the dive and exit the cave because he had reached his turn pressure? Gary should have come back to see if Joey's stage tank was where he had last seen it. But maybe he didn't. Maybe he had forgotten about it.

I decided it was best to continue to make our way out of the cave. We would look for Gary and hope for the best. Hope that he had decided to head out and was waiting for us on the surface. Maybe he was even upset at us for not sticking to the dive plan and taking so long to get out. Maybe he was on the surface thinking we both died in the cave and having the same thoughts about us that I was having about him.

I thought about the feelings I had thinking Gary might be dead. It would be so much worse if I thought both Gary and Joey were dead. Then to be all alone in a foreign country, unable to speak the language, and having to deal with the aftermath. The phone calls back home. Being unable to explain to their families that I didn't know what happened. I didn't even know where their bodies were. Would Gary have already started making phone calls? Would he be waiting for us hoping we would be surfacing any minute? Or would he be despondent, not knowing what to do?

I checked the time on my dive computer. We were still thirty minutes from the exit. We were moving slower than when we had entered. We were also swimming against the water flow. I decided I wanted to speed things up. We could look for signs of Gary on the way out while moving faster. I grabbed my wetnotes from my pocket and jotted a quick note to Joey as we continued to slowly make our way out of the cave.

Faster Gary may be out

I hastened my pace and quickly caught up to Joey. I shoved the page in front of his face as I illuminated it with my light. Joey read the note and signaled me the okay sign with his thumb and forefinger. He then hastened his pace. I could barely keep up with him. This time I wasn't going to try to slow him down. I followed closely, occasionally grabbing onto a solid formation next to me to pull myself along even faster. Gary had to be on the surface waiting for us.

21

Joey

We hadn't seen any signs of Gary as we slowly made our way out. I didn't think we would. Gary and I had checked the cave passage extensively on the way in. Neither of us had seen any leads that looked promising. But I also knew that things looked different going out than they did heading in. I might see something from this vantage point that I missed from the view I had heading in. I wasn't finding anything new, though.

Then Lindsey appeared next to me and shoved her wetnotes in front of my mask. For some reason, she thought Gary was already out of the cave. I couldn't figure out why she thought that, but I had spent more than half an hour in my new tunnel, laying line, getting unstuck, and surveying part of it while she was looking for him. Maybe she saw something that made her come to that conclusion. Or maybe she remembered something.

I swam faster. If Gary was already on the surface, I didn't want to prolong the exit any longer. I glanced at my dive computer display. We had already been on this dive for two hours and ten minutes. Ten minutes past due from when we were supposed to surface. We still had another thirty-five minutes to go before we would be back in the cenote and breaking the surface.

With a quickened pace I was confident I could cut that down to twenty-five minutes. As I kicked my fins harder and faster, I also focused on my breathing. I had plenty of air left, but if my breathing rate increased too much I might not. I even started to skip breathe – holding my inhalation a few seconds longer before releasing it.

I knew I shouldn't be skip breathing. It deprived my body of much needed oxygen. It allowed carbon dioxide to build up in my lungs and bloodstream. It could cause a headache and nausea. It was highly frowned upon, but I needed to conserve my air. Better to have a headache and a little nausea than to be dead in the cave with empty tanks.

As I swam along the tunnel, I occasionally covered my light to make sure Lindsey was behind me. She was keeping up somehow. She was used to me swimming much faster than her. She had even come up with a light signal to let me know I was swimming too fast and needed to slow down. Instead of the usual horizontal right to left to right light signal used to get my attention, she would sweep her light vertically up and down. That meant slow down. Similar to taking your hand, palm down, and bringing it up and down to tell someone to slow down. The light beam was just an extension of the hand. But Lindsey wasn't doing that. She was keeping up. I wasn't sure how. I didn't want to slow down to look and find out. As long as I could see the illumination of her light behind me, I knew she was not far.

I needed to get to Gary.

Ahead, I saw the line transition from the white cave line we had been swimming along to the bright yellow line that had been placed in several of the tunnels in this cave. The yellow line was much more durable and lasted longer than our standard cave line in this harsh environment. Jose had told us it had been there for years with no signs of breaking down. What it really meant to me was that we were only about a twenty-five-minute swim from the cenote. That is if we were swimming at a normal pace. We weren't. It might take us twenty minutes, maybe less. Definitely less. I wasn't planning on removing the jump spool or primary reel. That would only prolong our exit. And if Gary was still inside the cave, he would need those lines to continue out of the cave.

He couldn't still be inside.

I glanced at my dive computer again.

Dive time was 2:27.

Twenty-seven minutes overdue.

He had to be outside. What could be going through his head? We were almost half an hour late and by the time we surfaced it would be closer to forty-five minutes. Would he still be there waiting for us? Or would he take off to get help? Would he try to find Jose? Would he think we had died in the cave?

I followed the guideline to the right as the cave transformed into a narrow fissure. The walls on either side were close enough for me to reach out with both hands and touch them at the same time. The cave also got shallower at this point. It put me right in the middle of the halocline. Lindsey wouldn't be able to see much behind me, if she could see anything. I tried to get below the halocline to minimize the disturbance of the two waters so Lindsey wouldn't have to contend with blurry vision. There wasn't enough room below the halocline, though. The halocline was only a couple feet above the silty floor. I would only end up disturbing the silt and making the visibility worse. Better to have blurry visibility from the fresh and saltwater mixing than to have no visibility from silt.

I moved up into the freshwater layer. Not only was it much colder up there, but the visibility wasn't that great. There were tannins seeping in from the jungle floor above giving the water a yellowish-brown tint and limiting visibility to maybe ten feet. And I couldn't see the guideline in the saltwater layer below me. I decided to stay just below the halocline, where it was warmer, and as far to the left side of the tunnel as I could. This would allow Lindsey to stay to the right side, near the line, and maybe preserve some visibility for her. If not, she could always make contact with the line to stay behind me.

Another issue with this part of the tunnel was the water flow. Because the cave got smaller and narrower, it acted like a bottle neck. All of that water current moving through the tunnel from the much larger main tunnel at the other end came through much faster. We had to swim against it. The water current didn't seem that consequential when we were moving with it on the way in. It was definitely noticeable going out. It was also aggravating. And it didn't make sense. The cenote wasn't this way. Where was the water going?

When I wanted to be moving faster, I couldn't. I finned as fast and hard as I could, but it didn't seem to help. I started looking for handholds on the wall to my left to help pull myself along more quickly. There weren't many available. On the few occasions I saw a handhold I grabbed it and pulled myself forward as forcefully as I could.

I continued to shield my light to make sure Lindsey was still behind me. I had to drop my head and look back. The halocline mixing made it so her light beam didn't penetrate as far and wasn't as easy to see. I brought my head back up to look forward and I swam right into a large formation that was sticking up out of the cave floor. Head first. I saw stars momentarily. I began to feel some slight dizziness. It felt like it was getting worse. I reached for the line to my right hoping I wouldn't pass out. I remained in that position for a few seconds trying to clear my head.

I shook my head and rubbed it. The dizziness increased even more. The stars I saw began to dissipate, though. I felt a tinge of nausea and concentrated on not throwing up. I didn't want to throw up through my regulator. The dizziness subsided a little and I shook my head again, more slowly this time. The dizziness was still there, and I felt a slight headache where I had smacked my head into the hard formation. Not only had I been swimming faster than usual, but I was also moving my head up toward the formation, creating more momentum and hitting it harder.

Dammit! I remembered that column from our swim in. It made it necessary for us to swim around to the left and squeeze through between it and the wall across from it. I looked back and saw Lindsey getting closer. She must have fallen behind more than I realized. I rubbed my head lightly and could feel a goose egg already starting to form on my forehead. If I wasn't wearing a thick neoprene hood, I probably would have been knocked out. The neoprene absorbed some of the energy of the hit.

A moment later, feeling a little better, the nausea subsiding, I felt good enough to start swimming again. I grabbed the formation that I had swum into and pulled myself forward and around it, pushing myself off of it once I was on the other side. I could now see Lindsey's light beam without looking back. That would have to suffice the rest of this exit. At least while we were in this narrow tunnel. I didn't want to hit my head again.

I tried to remember how far that formation had been from the main tunnel where we had come from. It couldn't have been more than five or six minutes of swimming. But that was with the current. If I kept up my pace swimming against this water flow, I might be able to make it back to my jump spool in eight or nine minutes.

The tunnel got smaller and narrower. The water current got faster. It got harder to swim against. Fortunately, I was able to find a lot more handholds and pulled myself along faster. Normally, I didn't like to touch the cave, small tunnels being the exception. I mean really small tunnels like the one I was in half an hour earlier. Even in those I didn't like touching the cave, but it was necessary because otherwise I wouldn't be able to get into them. This was another exception. We were already deep into our reserve air, and I had to get to Gary. I just knew he was out of the cave waiting for us at the surface of the cenote. He had to be there.

I swam and pulled and moved as quickly as I could. The visibility got worse. Now it was blurry for me as well. I shook my head. Was it blurry or was it that smack on the head? I dropped my head lower beneath the halocline and my vision cleared. The tunnel had gotten small enough that not only was I causing the different waters to mix, but I was pushing the mixture ahead of me. I could only see about five feet in front of me. And it was five blurry feet.

I still saw flashes of Lindsey's light behind me. Somehow, she was keeping up. Was I swimming slower because of the knock on the head? Maybe it was the water flow. I was bigger than Lindsey and created more drag. It would make sense that it would slow me more than it would her.

The line crossed from the right wall to the left wall. It didn't matter. There wasn't enough distance between the two walls to make a difference in how my movement through it would affect the visibility for Lindsey. I could now touch both elbows to both walls at the same time. About a minute later the tunnel got wider. The ceiling began to rise up and away from me. I waited for my jump spool to come into view any moment.

The visibility got even worse, so I decided to make contact with the guideline to make sure I didn't lose it. This was exactly why these lines were in the cave. I felt the line dropping closer to the floor. I thought I saw my jump spool ahead through the blurriness. I couldn't be certain. It could be a sponge on the line. A couple of seconds later I was at the end of the permanent guideline and directly above the jump spool I had looped around it.

I looked at the line markers we had placed on the jump spool line indicating we had come this way and into this tunnel. There was my line marker, Lindsey's line marker, and Gary's. Gary hadn't exited the cave.

22

Lindsey

I followed Joey as closely as I could. I hated when he swam fast. Joey was usually so excited about being in a cave he didn't pay much attention to his swim pace and would get so far ahead. His legs were much stronger than mine and there was no way I could keep up with him. This time I was glad he was swimming fast and I tried to keep up with him as best as I could. I pulled myself along wherever I could find a handhold in the tunnel. I hated touching the cave, but this was an exception. My fingers were going to be torn up. The walls felt like sandpaper.

I started to fall behind, but I could still see Joey, so I let him go. Even if I lost sight of him, it would be okay. One of us needed to get to the surface to see if Gary was there. We had to let Gary know we were okay.

We arrived at the Y shaped intersection. I saw my line marker on our exit guideline. The boys had neglected to mark the line on the way in. The guidelines were different enough, but they still should have marked them. I grabbed my line marker off the line. We were more than halfway back. It should only be another twenty-five minutes before we made it out, twenty if we could keep up this pace. Then the walls started to get closer to each other, almost like they were swallowing us in. One minute I saw Joey ahead of me with plenty of room around him. The next minute he was being squeezed in by the walls. I felt a little bit of panic start to rise from deep within me. I could feel my claustrophobia rising to the surface.

I shook it off. I didn't like small passages. Definitely nothing as small as what Joey had been in thirty minutes earlier. But this tunnel wasn't that small. I had already been through it coming into the cave. It was just the stress of losing Gary along with the visual optics of seeing the cave walls closing in on Joey.

Panic.

Push that thought away! Stop thinking about walls closing in!

I stopped watching Joey and instead focused on looking for handholds to keep pulling myself along behind him. Then the visibility got blurry. We were in the halocline. There was nowhere I could go to avoid it. I watched as Joey tried dropping below it and then rising above it. He then settled right back to where he had started. The tunnel had gotten small enough that we couldn't help but swim in the halocline. Joey moved to the left, away from the line, probably to give me some clear water to the right, near the line. The thought was a good one, but the tunnel was so narrow it didn't make a difference.

I kept swimming and pulling myself along. I could no longer see Joey's light continuously. I would see sparks of light every now and then when the blurriness from the halocline allowed. Mostly I saw distortion. This must be what it's like to have to wear eyeglasses. I couldn't imagine waking up to this every day. At least those people could grab their eyeglasses and clear the blurriness away. There was nothing we could do to clear this blurriness.

I focused on getting through the tunnel. I knew the other end was only about four hundred feet away and then we would be in a much bigger tunnel, away from the halocline and with exceptional visibility. I was no longer seeing the sparks of light coming from ahead. Joey must have gained enough distance or gone around a corner. I kept moving. Looking for handholds and focusing on keeping my breathing under control.

I went around a slight bend to the left and saw light ahead. It wasn't moving, but it was too blurry to see what was going on. Had Joey found Gary? I strained to try to make out two lights, but the blurriness wouldn't allow me to distinguish that. It might be two lights, or it was just one being distorted. I tried to speed up, but I was already giving it all I had. I kept doing what I was doing.

About thirty seconds later, the light started moving. Then it disappeared again. I made it to where the light had been and saw a column on the left side of the tunnel. I remembered it from our entry a couple of hours earlier. The water in this area was even more blurry. I wondered why Joey had stopped as I grabbed the formation and pulled myself past it. Maybe he found Gary and they had to share air and hurry out. That would explain why he didn't wait for me.

As I got around the column, I saw Joey's light again. I had gained some distance on him. There was only one light. I knew it was Joey and not Gary because I could see the blue of his fins. Gary was on the surface anyway. He had to be by this time.

I followed the light. I felt the force of the water flow increasing. I positioned myself directly behind Joey. I was close enough that his body was deflecting the water flow around him and away from me. I was able to keep up with him this time. We moved along the tunnel. The visibility was getting worse. Even though I was right behind Joey, I could barely see him. His bright dive light was just a dim glow throwing off occasional sparks of light as the halocline allowed.

The only good thing about the bad visibility was that I couldn't see the walls or the ceiling. There was nothing to make me feel claustrophobic. I thought back to when we first approached the tunnel earlier and how small it looked. I almost stopped and turned around. I've been in smaller tunnels, like when I had to retrieve Joey's stage tank from that tunnel in Jackson Blue where he got stuck. That was different. I had good visibility, and I was on a mission. That kept my focus occupied. Later that day, back home, I thought about the dive and got a little freaked out. I almost started hyperventilating.

This tunnel was bigger, but the lack of visibility made a difference. I thought not seeing the walls would make things better, but it was actually making it worse. I was feeling more claustrophobic. I made contact with the line with my right hand and brought my left hand up in front of my head to protect it. I closed my eyes. I would follow behind Joey along the line like this. If I couldn't see what I was in, it wouldn't bother me as much. It helped a little. I still knew what the tunnel around me looked like, though.

I felt the line crossing from the right to the left below me and swapped hands so that I was maintaining contact with my left hand while my right hand protected my head. I chanced a peek. The visibility was still horrible. I could no longer see Joey's dive light. I also couldn't see the walls. I felt the vibration of Joey's hand moving along the line ahead. The visibility must have been bad for him, too. That meant the tunnel was even smaller. Bad thought!

Even with my eyes closed I could feel the walls closing in on me. I hadn't noticed the size of the tunnel on the way in because I took the rear in our team of three. With Joey and Gary swimming through the halocline, I had no visibility, so I made contact with the guideline and closed my eyes. The claustrophobia didn't affect me then. Probably because I hadn't been able to see just how small the tunnel was. Coming from the opposite direction this time, only behind one other diver, I did get some glimpses of its size. And I wasn't impressed.

I took another peek. Joey's light visible again. We were getting closer to the jump spool. Closer to being out of this coffin and into the main cave tunnel. Closer to seeing Gary again.

I closed my eyes and continued to swim. About a minute later I swam into Joey's fins. Why had he stopped?

I opened my eyes. It was still blurry but not nearly as bad as it had been. I could clearly see Joey and his light. I could also see that the cave had gotten considerably larger. I looked down at the guideline and saw Joey's jump spool secured to the yellow line. Then I saw what was probably the reason Joey had stopped.

Three line markers on the line. Mine, Joey's, and Gary's.

23

Lindsey

If Gary had come out this way, he should have retrieved his line marker. Had Gary forgotten to retrieve it or was he still in the cave behind us? I looked at my pressure gauges. About 1100 psi in each tank. I hadn't used my stage tank on the way out so it should still have 2200 psi. We could head back into the cave to look for Gary. But should we? How far would we get? Would it be worth the effort?

What if Gary had issues that caused him to exit the cave? What if he swam right past his line marker without bothering to stop to retrieve it. The line markers were there to communicate to each other if we were still in the cave or not. This was something we had discussed before the trip.

"Alright guys, I know this is what we were trained to do, and it should be something that happens without thought, but let's go over it anyway. Mainly because y'all dive together more than I dive with y'all."

Joey and Gary put their phones down and nodded in agreement and maintained eye contact. They knew my instructor voice when I used it, and they knew it was best to give me their undivided attention.

"Mexico is known for its extensive caves and the complex navigation in them. Unlike Florida where most of the caves have one main artery with shorter tunnels that go off for a few hundred feet or maybe loop back a few hundred feet later,

Mexican caves are different. They're kind of like the area back in the Middle Grounds of Jackson Blue, only more mazelike. Once we're off the main guideline, which isn't necessarily the main artery of the cave, we could find ourselves in a maze of tunnels. We'll need lots of non-directional line markers because there's a good chance we'll be running into lots of line intersections and putting in jump spools from one line to another." I paused for some dramatic effect. "We have to mark every single navigational decision we make. We EACH have to mark them."

The boys sat there and nodded. No dissent yet.

"We'll start with leaving a line marker at the beginning of the line next to the primary reel. That way if we get separated in the cave for any reason, when we get back to the primary reel, we'll know who is still in the cave and who isn't."

"Wait. So we each have to put a marker on the line? Not just a team marker?" Gary asked.

"That's what I just said. No team markers. That won't help us keep track of each other if we get separated..."

"But why would we get separated from each other?" Joey interrupted. "Are we planning on splitting up?"

"No, we're planning on staying together. But we have to plan for the worse scenario, too."

"Okay, so we each place a marker on the line by the primary reel?" Gary clarified.

"Yes, then we do the same at every line intersection and at every jump spool we deploy." My L

ord! This isn't rocket science!

"That's gonna be a lot of cookies!" Joey remarked, referring to the non-directional line markers by their common name — they were round like cookies. Cave divers had a saying to try to entice non-cave divers to become cave divers - 'Come to the dark side. We have cookies.'

"It might be. That will depend on where we end up finding ourselves. I don't want to complicate the dive so much that we have to each leave a dozen cookies on the line. We should start off slowly. By the end of the week, we might be doing dives

that extensive, but I doubt it."

"I'll have to remind myself to do that." Gary said. "Jim and I usually just leave one marker for the two of us. And Jim usually handles that part."

"We'll start off the first couple of days with you being in the middle between me and Joey. We've always deployed individual markers rather than team markers, so it's already ingrained in us to do that. When you see me or Joey leaving or picking up a marker, that should remind you to do the same. And when you see one of us removing a marker from the line, that should remind you as well." I paused again to let that sink in. "If you do get separated from us for any reason, just remember to grab your markers on the way out. That way when we exit, we'll see your marker missing and know you already went past that intersection or jump."

That was how the discussion had gone the week before we left for our trip. And the first two days, Gary did well. He remembered to put a line marker on the line on the way in and to remove it on the way out. Every time except once. That happened the day before. We were exiting the cave. We arrived at a line intersection and there happened to be another line about ten feet away from the line leading into some other tunnel. Because of the angle of that guideline in relation to the tunnel we were in, we hadn't seen the line on the way in. It was very evident on the way out though.

Joey and Gary both headed off the line to check out the "new" guideline they had just discovered. After looking down the tunnel and Joey pulling out his wetnotes to jot down its location because it apparently wasn't on either of the maps he had memorized, the boys headed back to the guideline we were on. Joey dutifully retrieved his line marker. Gary started to head out behind me. Joey had to signal Gary to return to get his line marker. The excitement of finding that tunnel had made Gary forget about our protocol. We had a discussion about that as soon as we surfaced while we were floating in the water recounting the events of the dive. I didn't chastise Gary for forgetting to pull his marker, but I did reinforce the need to remember the markers.

It was feasible that Gary could have forgotten to retrieve his line marker, especially if he was having an issue that caused him to have to exit. But even if he wasn't having an issue, he was exiting alone, without me or Joey. And he didn't know where we were. That might have been enough to stress him out and cause him to forget to retrieve it. In addition to that, the visibility wasn't great because of the halocline.

I signaled Joey to keep heading out. Joey shook his head no and pointed at Gary's line marker, then pointed behind me toward where we had come from. I pointed at Gary's line marker, then pointed at my head, followed by the international signal for broken, motioning my hands as if I were snapping a pencil in half. I wasn't sure if Joey would understand what I was trying to tell him. I was trying to communicate that Gary had forgotten to remove his marker. I signaled Joey with my thumb up while pointing toward the exit with the same hand, telling him to continue to exit.

Thankfully, Joey understood. Or at least, he didn't argue. It could have been either one. We had been trained that if we couldn't communicate with a few simple hand signals, it was best to end the dive and exit so we could discuss it rather than try to have a written conversation using wetnotes. We had also been trained that when one diver signals to end the dive, there were no questions asked. We ended the dive and exited the cave. Those rules were during somewhat normal circumstances. This was anything but normal.

Hopefully, Joey understood and didn't think I was giving up on Gary. I was hoping Gary had forgotten to grab his line marker as he exited and was waiting for us on the surface. We still had markers at the beginning of the main line near our primary reel. Maybe Gary had remembered to grab that one.

24

Joey

Gary was still in the cave. He hadn't exited like we thought. Like we hoped. I turned to head back in to look for him and saw Lindsey checking her gauges. I should have checked mine as well. I glanced at them – 1100 psi in the right tank and 900 psi in the left tank. *Dammit!* That wasn't enough to go very far. I could use 300 psi at most from each tank. We might get to the area where we leave the halocline and the tunnel widens, especially with the help of the current pushing us. Would that leave me with enough air to swim out against the current, though? Probably not.

Then I remembered the stage tank I had mounted above my left sidemount tank. I hadn't touched it since clipping it onto my harness where I had begun lining the tunnel I found. Last I checked it had 2100 psi in it. That added another 700 psi to what I could use to look for Gary.

Lindsey had other ideas. She pointed behind me, telling me to keep exiting. I wanted to scream at Lindsey – *GARY'S STILL IN THE CAVE!* Lindsey pointed at Gary's line marker, then her head, and motioned like she was breaking a stick in half. Gary had forgotten his line marker the day before when we found that tunnel that wasn't on the maps. If it wasn't for me, his cookie would still be at that line intersection. What if he forgot this one today? What if he surfaced and was waiting for us, worried out of his mind. Like we were worried about him.

I grabbed my marker off the line, turned around and began swimming along the jump spool line toward the main guideline. Thankfully, the cave got a couple of feet deeper at this point and allowed us to get below the halocline. The visibility was no longer blurry. I saw where I had tied the jump spool to the permanent line twenty feet ahead. No personal markers on the guideline. But none of us had placed any there.

"Where do we place our cookies at the jumps?" Gary asked.

"Joey and I only place them next to the jump spool on the far end of the jump, the end we encounter first when we're exiting. This is to let other team members know whether a jump spool can be retrieved or not. If there's a line marker on it, then the jump spool stays in place. If there aren't any line markers, then we can pull the jump spool feeling confident no one is being left behind in the cave without a continuous guideline out."

"Okay, makes sense. Jim and I have always left our cookies on the exit side of the line that we loop our jump spool line onto. That way there's no confusion as to which way leads out of the cave. I like the way you do it though."

"I don't see a need for that. We'll never jump off a line without having a directional arrow in place, either the permanent ones already on the permanent guideline in the cave, or one of our personalized arrows that we place before setting the jump spool line."

"That makes perfect sense." Gary replied.

I wished we had implemented both. I understood Gary leaving the last cookie in place. The jump spool was tied to the guideline right in the middle of the halocline. The visibility was blurry and made it difficult to see the small spool. The two lines were also lined up straight with each other. That could be easy to swim right past without seeing the spool and cookies there. But this end of the jump spool line was tied onto the main guideline creating an actual T. It was looped in around the guideline between two permanent line arrows that marked the location of the tunnel we had just come from. As I approached it, I could easily see the line arrows and would have been able to easily see cookies as well.

Except we hadn't placed any cookies there. Maybe from now on we would place cookies on both ends of the jump line. Maybe that would help Gary to remember to grab his cookies on the way out. Unless he was still in the cave behind us.

I quickened my pace and turned to the left, cutting the corner made by the two lines. We weren't that far from the exit. We were only about five minutes from the beginning of the guideline where our primary reel was looped around it. And where the next set of cookies would be. Those would be easier to see because the primary reel was much bigger than the jump spool and the lines were perpendicular to each other. Gary should have had no problem seeing his cookie and remembering to grab it.

Three minutes later I was swimming over a mound that was less than one hundred feet from the beginning of the guideline. I was desperately hoping to see only two cookies on the line. As I ascended above the mound the visibility got blurry again. I was back in the halocline. Then I remembered. The beginning of the main line was less than a foot below the halocline. That meant Gary might not have seen his cookie when he exited so there might still be three cookies on the line. My heart sank. I still wouldn't have any clue as to whether Gary had surfaced or was still somewhere inside the cave.

I saw the familiar surroundings of the cave that I had become so acquainted with over the past couple of days. About ten feet ahead I would pass around a bend and see our primary reel attached to the main guideline. I swam around the bend and saw the reel. The visibility was too blurry to make out the cookies on the line to the left of the reel. I gave a few hard kicks to get me there faster. When I got within a couple feet of it, I saw the cookies we had left more than two and a half hours earlier.

There were three of them on the line. Mine, Lindsey's, and Gary's.

I quickly rotated toward the way I had just come from, back toward Lindsey just as she was swimming around the bend. I swept my light beam back and forth, trying to tell her that Gary hadn't pulled his marker. I considered turning back, certain that Gary was still in the cave. But we were so close to the exit. Less than four minutes if we swam fast. I grabbed my line marker off the line, turned back toward the exit, and started swimming as quickly as I could. Gary had to be on the surface.

25

Lindsey

I grabbed my marker off the line, leaving Gary's there alone, a solitary reminder of what we had just done. We had left Gary behind in the cave. I followed Joey toward the main guideline forty feet away. We both cut the corner to the line intersection formed by our jump spool line and the permanent guideline. I had trouble keeping up with Joey. When he wanted to, which was most of the time, he could swim much faster than I could.

I followed as closely as I could. I gained a little bit of distance shortly after we were back on the main guideline. There was a dip in the ceiling directly over the line and Joey took a wide path around it. The dip came close enough to the floor that I barely got through. If I wasn't trying to keep up with Joey I would have looked back and I'm sure I would have seen a cloud of silt hanging in the water. There was no way I could move through there so fast without stirring up the silt.

We made it to the beginning of the guideline and our primary reel in record time. I didn't have much faith in learning anything new at that point. If Gary had forgotten to retrieve his line marker from the jump spool line, he wouldn't have been likely to remember to pull the marker at the primary reel either. Unfortunately, both transitions were situated right in the middle of the halocline. That complicated things. There wasn't much we could do about the transition where the jump spool was. The line for that tunnel was only six inches above the cave floor. Repositioning it higher would only put it in the freshwater layer where the visibility was reduced due to the tannins seeping down from the jungle floor above our heads. The beginning of the main guideline could have been repositioned. It was at least eight feet off the floor. I would have tied it off somewhere lower and farther away from the halocline layer.

To be fair, this close to the entrance, the halocline layer changed its depth regularly. The cave wasn't far from the sea. Its opening began in the marina, so it was affected by the tide. The farther into the cave we got, the less the halocline depth was affected. But at this point it probably moved a couple of feet up and down. The tie-off should still have been placed closer to the floor.

As we arrived at the primary reel, I saw Joey hesitate. There must have been three line markers on the line and he was considering turning around again. We were too close to the cenote to not at least pop our heads up and check to see if Gary was there. Fortunately, we didn't have to have another discussion about it. Joey swam off quickly, the fastest I've ever seen him swim.

As I rounded the corner at the beginning of the line, I tried to get a glimpse of the wall below it. I wanted to see if there was anywhere else to tie the line to. The visibility was too blurry, though, and I couldn't see anything. I didn't have time to look, either. I would look the next day.

That is if Gary wasn't dead, and we would be diving again the next day.

I grabbed my marker off the line as I followed Joey as quickly as I could. Joey was swimming so fast he was increasing the distance between us again. There was no way I could keep up with him. By the time he got to the surface and looked around, I might be coming up below him. I would have to be fast because if Gary wasn't on the surface, Joey would want to head back in. I wanted a chance to talk to him. We had to have a plan and not just swim around aimlessly.

About a minute after swimming past the primary reel, I started to see thin rays of daylight poking through the small openings in the limestone to the right. Those would lead to the main entrance of the cave. We hadn't entered that way, though. The dirt road from the paved road back to this end of the cenote was too rough to drive a car over. There were lots of deep potholes. We tried to follow Jose back there on the first day, but the car bottomed out ten feet in. Jose stopped and decided we should enter through a different opening. We backed up the car before we destroyed something beneath it.

We parked on the other end of the cenote, near the paved road and the sign telling tourists about the cave and to watch for cocodrilos - crocodiles. We hadn't seen any yet, and at the moment crocodiles were the least of our worries. What that meant was we had another minute of swimming to follow the line from our primary reel out to open water where we could surface, and hopefully where Gary was waiting for us. Probably less than a minute for Joey because of how fast he was swimming.

I watched as Joey turned to the right and ascended into a beam of sunlight that was penetrating the cave from the surface through one of the openings above. The rays surrounded him, bathing him in a blue hued light, making him nothing more than a black silhouette against the rays. He almost looked like an angel ascending to the heavens above. And then his outline disappeared. I blinked rapidly several times. What just happened? How could Joey have vanished?

Then, just as suddenly as he had disappeared, Joey reappeared in the sun's rays that were coming from the other opening. Joey had been framed from the rays of one opening and then disappeared into the darkness of the wall and ceiling between the two openings before reappearing in the rays of the other opening. If I wasn't so stressed about Gary, I would have appreciated the optical illusion that just occurred. I really hoped Gary was already out of the cave and alive and well on the surface. Not dead somewhere far inside the cave. I wouldn't even be mad at him. Not that mad, anyway.

Thirty seconds later I was under the opening Joey had exited through. I turned and ascended over the rocks and back over the lush green carpeting of the cenote. The green plant life that covered the floor of the cenote danced back and forth beneath me as my movement over it caused the water to move it around. I saw Joey's blue fins directly in front of me, hanging below his body. His head was already above the surface, making him appear to be headless. Joey kicked his fins and spun around. He was looking for Gary around the edge of the cenote.

I began my final ascent through the last ten feet of water to the surface only five feet from Joey. When my head was about three feet below the surface, I saw Joey begin to descend back under water. I reached out and grabbed him. I could feel him stiffen and flinch. He must not have realized I was right next to him. He arrested his descent, grabbed me, and we both broke the surface again.

"He's not out here! I looked all around. I yelled out his name. He's not out here! We have to go back!"

"Hold on a minute, Joe! Take a breath. We need a minute or two to figure out what we're gonna do. We need to have a plan. We can't just go back in."

As I said this, I scanned the perimeter of the cenote. I didn't see anyone. Not even the usual cruise ship tourists we had seen that were brought here by various island tour guides so they could see their first, and probably only, cenote ever, and maybe catch a glimpse of a crocodile.

I stretched my neck to see if I could see any scuba tanks laid out on the rocky shore surrounding us. The rental car was parked under some trees near the entrance just off the paved road. I couldn't see anyone or anything around it. There weren't any signs of Gary anywhere else. If Gary had surfaced a while ago, he would have had plenty of time to get his dive equipment off and stored in the car. We had hidden the key a few feet off the dirt road under a rock and he knew where it was.

But we would either see Gary or the car wouldn't be parked where we had left it. I couldn't think of any reason for him to take off on foot except maybe to go relieve himself next to a tree. He and Joey had done that each time before our dives, hoping to minimize the amount of urine that would go into their wetsuits. They hadn't gone very far past the tree line. I could see their backs every time. I looked toward the area they had been ducking into but saw no sign of him.

Gary must still be in the cave.

26

Joey

When I got to the cenote I quickly popped up to the surface. Probably much too fast. I pictured the tiny bubbles of nitrogen in my bloodstream quickly expanding as I darted up, much like the bubbles in a bottle of soda when you first unscrew the cap. I hoped I wouldn't end up with the bends. Despite those thoughts I couldn't slow myself down. I couldn't control my ascent. I had to know if Gary had gotten out of the cave.

Once on the surface, I spun around looking for him. Looking for someone to ask if they had seen Gary. Looking for any sign that he had surfaced. There was no one around. I could hear scuba tanks clanging in the distance. The distinct bell-like sounds penetrating through the thick jungle between us. We had heard the clanging on the previous two days. Jose told us it was coming from the marina located nearby.

I looked along the shoreline for Gary's tanks, hoping to see them prone on the ground near the car. If he had exited a while ago, his tanks and dive equipment would likely already be in the trunk of the car. But why would Gary surface, pack up his equipment, and then walk off. The rental car was still parked exactly where we had left it.

Gary had to be inside the cave. I let the air out of my BC and started to drop back underwater. As I was descending, I felt something grab me. We hadn't seen the crocodile that the sign warned about…yet. I kicked my legs out to move myself back away from its grasp before its numerous, sharp teeth sank into my calf. This was all I needed. A crocodile attacking me in the middle of the cenote.

There were stories about a crocodile that had lived in this cenote. Jose had even told us about tour guides that would come out to feed the crocodile in the evenings. They trained it to come when they wanted so when they brought out the cruise ship tourists, they could get a close up look at a real live crocodile in the wild. It appeared I was about to have my first encounter with one in the wild myself.

"So, there's a tour guide, maybe more, that comes in the evening and slaps the water. He tosses few pieces raw chicken in the water and waits. The cocodrilo smells the chicken and comes to get her snack," Jose told us. "He done this enough times now and when the cocodrilo hears water being slapped, it comes to the sound to get chicken dinner."

"Winner, winner! That's a pretty smart tour guide!" I responded.

"Yeah, except a few months ago, some guy was here in the middle of night. I think it was after midnight. Probably drinking, getting drunk. That's what some people do here."

"They do that everywhere, Jose," Lindsey interrupted with a laugh.

"Yeah, I guess they prolly do. Anyway, it was in the middle of summer and very hot. Even at night. So the guy decides he wants to swim in the water. He jumps in. The cocodrilo hear the splash and come for her chicken. But there was no chicken. Just a marinated loco taking midnight swim."

"Holy crap! Did he die?" Gary asked.

"No, fortunately, he no die. He just have his hand and arm bit. I guess he don't taste like chicken." Jose laughed at his joke. "He's okay, though. They come and remove the cocodrilo from the water and put it somewhere else."

"Do you think there's a chance of another crocodile coming to live here?" I asked.

"There's always a chance. But I no see one here in a while."

Supposedly there was no longer a crocodile in the cenote. That didn't keep me from being spooked about one having been here before. I began thrashing my legs, trying to scare the crocodile away. Then I saw blond wisps of hair sticking out of Lindsey's neoprene hood as she reached out for me. She was next to me ascending to the surface. I pulled her into my arms, trying to protect her from the crocodile and returned to the surface. That's when I realized what I felt was Lindsey touching me, not a crocodile. I screamed at her in a panic.

"He's not out here! I looked all around. I yelled out his name. He's not out here! We have to go back!"

"Hold on a minute, Joe! Take a breath. We need a minute or two to figure out what we're gonna do. We need to have a plan. We can't just go back in."

I knew I should take a breath like Lindsey had suggested and calm myself down. I wanted to go back in the cave to look for Gary, but she was right, I wasn't in the right state of mind to do that safely. I stopped myself and took a deep breath. I held it in for a few seconds letting the oxygen work its way into my body. I blew it out through my nose. I repeated the actions. I felt a calm settling over me. I could do this. I had to do this if I was going to be any help to Gary. *Gary!!!*

The thought of Gary lost inside the cave, possibly hurt, or worse – dead – got my heart racing again. I took another deep breath and held it. I repeated to myself over and over, *He's okay, he's okay, he's okay.* Gary had to be okay. Lindsey and I still had enough air to continue to look for him. He must still have air in his tanks as well.

I looked at my pressure gauges. I had only used 300 psi from one tank since I had last checked them. So I still had 2000 psi in my stage tank, 900 psi in one of my sidemount tanks, and 800 psi in the other.

I wished I had at least one full tank with me. I could use 1000 psi from my stage tank to swim in and look for Gary again and the other 1000 psi to exit. That would have left me with the air in my sidemount tanks for emergencies. This was an emergency! Maybe I should use more to look for Gary. But what if he breathed through all of his air and needed to breathe from one of my tanks? An average of 850 psi between the two sidemount tanks should be plenty if I needed to donate one of my regulators to Gary. Almost double what I would be using to penetrate into the cave. I had to reserve the air in my tanks for Gary.

"I have plenty of air left. I haven't even touched the air in my stage tank since we made our way in earlier. I can use that to look for Gary and use the air in my sidemount tanks for emergencies," I quickly explained to Lindsey.

I watched as she looked at her own gauges and did the calculations in her head. I was more math inclined than Lindsey. I could quickly run the numbers in my head, but it took her a little longer. I waited, impatiently, hoping she would be able to figure it out without having to pull her wetnotes out and write it all out. My patience was already being put to the limits. I could barely stand waiting for her as she was doing the calculations in her head! I looked around the cenote one more time while Lindsey was figuring out her air and air reserves hopeful that maybe I had missed evidence that Gary had gotten out of the cave. Maybe I had missed his tanks lying on their sides near the car.

Unfortunately, I still didn't see anything. Gary had not exited the cave. He had to be in there. Hopefully alive.

"Okay, I have 2200 psi in my stage tank. And I have 900 psi in each sidemount tank. We'll go with your plan, Joe. We'll use the stage tanks to look for Gary. Breathe half going in and the other half coming out. We do not breathe from our sidemount tanks unless our stage tank empties or there's an unexpected event. The air in the sidemount tanks is for emergencies only! It's not to look for Gary."

"Yeah, yeah, that's fine. Let's go!

"Hold on, sweetie. We need to formulate a plan. We can't just go back in there and haphazardly look for him. That won't do us any good."

"Aren't we going to head back to where we came from and just look for him? What else can we do?"

"Yes, we'll head in toward the area where we last saw him. I doubt we'll get as far as we were with the air we have left in our stage tanks. Hopefully we'll run into Gary as he's swimming out. My biggest concern right now is that he may be low on air and need to breathe from our tanks." Lindsey paused with a thoughtful look on her face. "Actually, let's breathe from our sidemount tanks going in and coming out. What are your pressures?"

"I have 800, 900, and 2000 psi," I rattled off impatiently.

"Okay, breathe from your 800 psi tank first. When it starts getting hard to breathe, we'll turn around and head out while you're breathing from your other sidemount tank. Let's reserve the stage tanks for Gary in case he needs one of our tanks. In fact, I have more air than you so if we don't find Gary, I'll leave my stage tank clipped to the line. That way if he is swimming out and comes across it, he'll at least have a fighting chance."

I didn't like it. I didn't like the plan at all. I did like leaving a tank behind for Gary if we didn't find him. And I did like reserving our stage tanks for him. What I didn't like was using only 800 psi, less really, to look for Gary. That was 200 psi less than I had planned on using. But Lindsey was right. It was better to be able to hand off a stage tank to Gary than to be tethered to him by a hose if we had to share air with him. And 200 psi wouldn't get us all that much farther into the cave. Besides, we had to find Gary on the way in. He had to be coming out by now.

"Okay, sounds good!" I said after taking a couple of seconds to contemplate the plan. "Can we go now? We're not going to find him floating here on the surface talking about searching for him."

Lindsey's face transformed into a scowl. I deserved it. I was being an ass. But I was stressed and wanted to get back into the cave and look for Gary. Lindsey decided not to say anything about my comment. She placed her regulator into her mouth, and I watched her hooded head disappear below the surface. I quickly followed her down to the mossy green floor of the cenote and swam past her into the cave.

27

Lindsey

Joey was being an ass. I overlooked it. I knew he was stressed about the possibility of losing one of his best friends in a cave diving fatality. I was also stressed about it. It was always a distant thought in our minds. While cave diving was a very safe endeavor if all the training rules were followed, it was not uncommon to hear about fatalities happening in caves. There had just been a cave diving fatality in Florida a few months earlier. Joey and I didn't know the diver personally, but we had interacted with him online. Joey had taken it pretty badly. Unfortunately, we didn't know what had caused that fatality and it wasn't likely we would ever find out. Those things weren't discussed any longer.

Years ago, cave diving fatalities were analyzed and discussed so we could learn from them and try to avoid the same outcome. Lately, though, cave diving fatality analysis wasn't a thing. The cave diving community was small enough that news of the fatalities always made it around the social media sites quickly. The causes were never discussed though. At least, not by anyone who knew what the causes were. There was plenty of speculation. Too much speculation. And people would get pissed off about that and chastise others for speculating. What else could they do? If the actual cause wasn't going to be revealed, people were going to speculate. It was human nature.

Some people claimed there was nothing new to learn from the recent cave diving fatalities. The cause was the same as always. One of the rules of cave diving was violated and that resulted in someone dying. I disagreed with that. There was always something to be learned. And sometimes, people needed reminders. They needed the rules reinforced, even if the cause was the same old cause for dozens of other fatalities. If that wasn't the case, we wouldn't continue to have cave diving fatalities that were the result of the same causes.

Besides, there were plenty of new cave divers that weren't familiar with the previous fatalities and the lessons learned from them. Sure, the information was available online in the various forums and social media groups. Who was going to take the time to search out those discussions and read through them? Very few people, if any.

The same people that claimed there was nothing new to learn referred us to the rules of cave diving:

- Be trained for the dives you're doing
- Always maintain a continuous guideline to the surface
- Use proper air management when diving
- Use the appropriate breathing gas mixture for the depths you will be diving
- Maintain your equipment in good condition to minimize failures.
- Live a healthy life and only dive when you're feeling 100%

An acronym was even created to make it easier to remember – Thank Goodness All Divers Live Healthy. Training, Guideline, Air management, Depth, Lights/Equipment, and Health. They were simple rules, and they covered all the causes of cave diving fatalities. With the exception of Parker Turner's death in a cave, every single cave diving fatality could be attributed to one of those six rules.

Parker Turner's death was a freak accident caused by a *sandvalanche*. The sand on a steep slope at the entrance to the cave he was diving in, Indian Springs just outside of Tallahassee, Florida, came loose and slid down the slope. It wasn't just a little sand. It was a lot. It was so much that it blocked the way out. Parker and his teammate, Bill Gavin, were trapped inside. Turner's efforts to dig out an exit and get to his decompression tank saved Gavin's life that day. Unfortunately, Turner breathed all of the air in his tanks before he made it to his other tank. He drowned only fifteen feet away from it. To complicate the situation, the visibility in the cave had gone from crystal clear to less than five feet so Turner probably didn't even know his decompression tank was only fifteen feet away. It was a horrible way to die.

So I gave Joey some slack. If he had taken the death of someone he only knew online badly, losing someone who he was good friends with, probably even best friends, would really affect him. Having been on the dive with him only made it worse. I hoped Joey could do this safely. I was concerned that his mental state might jeopardize his safety. And maybe even mine.

I knew there was no use in trying to talk Joey out of going to look for Gary. He was too stubborn to sit on the sidelines and hope Gary would come out on his own. Would he be disciplined enough to turn the dive when he reached the pressure we agreed upon? Would he exit the cave even if we didn't find Gary? I wish we had discussed the plan more. It was too late for that now. Joey was already inside the cave.

I followed behind him. Surprisingly, he wasn't swimming as fast as I knew he could. He was finally learning that slower usually meant farther in terms of penetration distance and air supply. If you didn't overexert yourself, your air would last much longer. I was able to easily keep up with him this time.

We got to our primary reel at the beginning of the main line faster than we had earlier. It helped that we were following the line and not setting it into place, having to stop to place tie-offs every time we changed our direction of travel. Gary's line marker was still on the line where we had left it. Alone. A solitary reminder of what we were doing. I watched Joey place his marker back on the line next to Gary's. I placed mine next to Joey's as I swam past it. We headed to the right, along the main line and up into the halocline. I had to make contact with the line to make sure I followed it in. The visibility had become so blurry from Joey swimming through it that I couldn't even see the illumination from his dive light.

A couple of minutes later I was below the halocline and back in clear water. Joey was about twenty feet ahead of me maintaining an even rhythm of finning and breathing. I continued to look around hoping Gary had made it out to this area somehow and was maybe still looking along the perimeter of the tunnel for leads. If he was, he could be certain I would kick his ass. At this point, he should be making a quick exit from the cave, not looking for leads. We had been separated from each other for more than an hour. Certainly, Gary wouldn't be going along on his dive like nothing was out of the ordinary. *Would he?*

I saw the ceiling of the cave dip down close to the guideline. It came within a couple of feet of the silty floor below it. The silt I had likely stirred up just moments earlier had settled back to the floor. You wouldn't even know we had been here. Joey shifted to the right, so I shifted to the left side. That would allow us to get a good look on both sides of the dip. We both moved back toward the line after passing the dip. Our jump spool line was another fifty feet in.

Joey sped up when he saw the jump line. I watched him cut the corner and turn toward the right, to head back into the tunnel where we were when we last saw Gary. I didn't see any lights coming from that tunnel, but the halocline ran right through its center, and it would be difficult to see any light more than ten feet away. I followed Joey around the corner. Even with our powerful three thousand lumen dive lights, the tunnel we were heading toward was black. It swallowed our light beams into its void. Strangely, it seemed like it was darker than it had been when we first went into it almost three hours earlier. It also appeared smaller. I felt the walls closing in around me. I felt my anxiety rising.

Three hours. Had it really been that long since we began this dive? I glanced at my dive computer and confirmed it. Two hours and fifty-eight minutes. I began to feel beyond hope that we were going to find Gary alive, if at all.

I instinctively reached down and brushed my fingers over the line from the jump spool and wrapped my thumb and forefinger loosely around it. It gave me comfort to feel the line. It gave me a sense of safety. No matter what happened to the visibility in the cave, we would be able to exit as long as we had that continuous guideline leading out to the cenote.

Joey stopped for a couple of seconds at the jump spool to place his line marker on the line. I reached the jump spool just as Joey was swimming onward. I watched him being swallowed by the halocline. I looked at the line and saw Gary's marker was still there. I added mine to the line of markers, formed a circle with my thumb and forefinger around the permanent guideline, and followed Joey into the halocline.

28

Joey

Gary's markers were still on the lines. I expected the line marker at the primary reel, but I was hoping he had at least made it out to the jump spool. I was hoping his marker would no longer be on the line. But there it was. I placed mine next to Gary's and took off into the halocline. I was moving fast enough that the mixture of the fresh and saltwater layers wasn't affecting the visibility for me. I thought about moving off the line and trying to preserve some of the visibility for Lindsey, but I decided she would just have to deal with it. It was more important to find Gary than to be careful moving through this tunnel. Besides, the tunnel was narrow enough that I doubted I could move through it without disturbing the visibility.

Where could Gary be??

I glanced at my dive computer. It had been almost two hours since we last saw him. Well, since I last saw him. I wasn't sure when Lindsey last saw Gary. I should have asked her when we were on the surface. But all I wanted to do was get back into the cave and look for him. I didn't bother looking around as I swam farther into the tunnel. It wasn't that big. I could touch both walls at the same time and there were only a couple of offshoots about midway through the tunnel. I doubted Gary would have gone into either one of them.

Or would he? Maybe I should check?

No, we had last seen him much farther back inside the cave. He had been going in, not heading back out, according to Lindsey. He wouldn't have swum all the way out to this point and gone to check out those tunnels. In Florida, we always checked for leads on the way in. We would look on the way out and note any potential leads we saw, but we wouldn't do any more than that. We wouldn't go off the line to look at them. Those leads were saved for another dive on another day.

Except our dives and days in Cozumel were limited. Would Gary have gone off the exiting guideline to look at those tunnels? I wasn't so sure anymore.

I saw the line ahead and to the right leading to the first of the two tunnels. It was probably connected. It was probably just a loop from that location to the next. Not even worth putting line in. Although I would have loved to have been the one to have found it. And what if it did do more than loop? As I swam past it, I looked into the tunnel. I couldn't see much. The halocline was already distorting the visibility. I could tell it was deeper than the tunnel I was in. Both the floor and the ceiling dropped down. All I could see was a dark, blurry hole below me. I quickly shielded my light to see if there was any illumination coming from it. Nothing but black.

Even if Gary had gone in there, I probably wouldn't be able to see any sign of him. I might check it out on the way out, though. I would just stick my head inside for a peek. Just in case.

About thirty seconds later, I saw the other line disappearing into another hole to the right. This line almost looked like it intersected with the line I was following. It had to be the blurriness of the halocline. I didn't recall an intersection. This offshoot looked a little bigger. It also dropped deeper down than the tunnel we were in. They had to be connected to each other. We would have to check it out. It was fairly close to the entrance to the cave but didn't look like it was traveled much. I looked at the pressure in my tanks. Time to switch regulators. I had breathed half of the air in the tank with 800 psi. That meant I had 400 psi left to breathe from the other tank, then I would have to turn around and exit.

Maybe…

If we hadn't found Gary by that time, then he obviously wasn't going to be needing my stage tank. Maybe I would breathe some of the air in there and keep looking for him. Between Lindsey and me, we would have enough air to share with Gary if he needed it.

Lindsey!

I shielded my light and looked for the illumination from her light behind me. I didn't see anything. I dropped my head down so I could look back between my legs. Nothing but darkness. Had I gotten that far ahead of her?

Just as I was about to slow down to wait for Lindsey, I saw her dive light pop around a corner. It looked like she was about thirty feet behind me. It was difficult to tell through the disturbed halocline. I brought my head up and it happened again. I smacked my head into a wall. It really hurt! The pain was almost overwhelming. The goose egg on my head from hitting it earlier was where I took the brunt of this hit. The area was already tender. Hitting it again made me feel like I was going to throw up.

I stopped, put my hand on the wall in front of me, the one I had smacked my head on, to steady myself and concentrated on not throwing up. I was stunned by the impact. I slowly shook my head, careful not to make the nausea worse. I eased my eyes open and waited for my vision to clear. The blurriness remained. I felt panic rising inside me thinking I had done severe damage to myself. I blinked several times to try to clear my vision. There was no improvement. Then I remembered the halocline. I allowed myself to descend to the sandy floor, below the brackish water and into the undisturbed clear saltwater layer below. My vision cleared immediately.

Thankful I hadn't done significant damage, at least not that I could tell, I looked around the area where I had stopped. It was the same formation I had hit my head on about thirty minutes earlier, only from the other direction. Lindsey swam up beside me and gave me the okay light signal, asking if I was alright. I held out my hand, palm down and rocked it back and forth. *Kind of but not really.* I reached up and felt the goose egg on my head. It felt even larger than it had earlier. I was going to have to wear a hat the rest of the trip. If I could even get a hat over that bump.

I felt Lindsey's hand on my arm. She was holding onto me. I pushed it off, signaled to her that I was okay, and began to slowly swim around the offending column. It seemed to have it out for me. I was going to have to remember that thing from now on. That was twice it got me. Three times would not be a charm.

I moved a little more slowly this time. Lindsey was easily able to keep up. She kept sending me the circular okay signal with her light. I was certain she was concerned about me. I went from swimming like a bat out of hell to barely creeping along. Well, I probably wasn't swimming that slowly, but I was swimming much slower than I usually did.

A couple of minutes later we arrived at the Y intersection. I looked back at the other tunnel to my right that headed toward the main tunnel. The other tunnel was on both maps, so I knew it went back that way. I still hadn't found where it came out in the main tunnel, though. We spent a little bit of time the day before looking but didn't have any luck. We found the tunnel we were currently in and decided to use it to get back to this area.

Was it possible that Gary left that way to try to find the other end of the tunnel? Maybe he went out that way as we were going in this way. This place was such a maze! There were so many places Gary could be. We had so little air in our tanks. Not nearly enough to conduct a decent search for him. We could go get full tanks and come back, but by that time, if Gary was in trouble, he would be dead. No! We had to look now. We had to do everything we could now.

I looked at my pressure gauge. Only 300 psi left before I would have to turn according to the plan we had made. The plan Lindsey had made. I might just have to push it a little longer. After all, I had 2000 psi in the stage tank I was carrying. It wouldn't do Gary any good if we weren't in the cave to give it to him. I kept glancing at the line below me waiting for it to transform from the thicker yellow line to the thinner white cave line. The tunnel was much bigger. It was getting deeper as well. Not that deep. Only forty feet. But that was significantly deeper than the twenty feet of depth of the halocline tunnel. Which meant we were breathing twice the amount of air.

I looked back at my pressure gauge. Two hundred psi left until I was supposed to turn around and exit the cave. To leave Gary behind. I was going to have to stretch this out somehow. We still hadn't seen any sign of Gary.

I started doing the skip breathing thing again. Holding my breath for several seconds before exhaling and inhaling. It wasn't good. It could give me a headache. Well, it would make the headache I already had from smacking my head twice even worse. I shouldn't be skip breathing but my air supply was quickly being depleted.

Still no Gary.

Lindsey was keeping up with me. I saw her light sweeping from side to side, looking for any sign of Gary. We could have been so much more effective if we had split up. I should have looked in those offshoots or gone back down the other tunnel at the Y while Lindsey kept going this way. We weren't doing Gary any good by staying together. There wasn't any point in splitting up now, though. I looked at my pressure gauge. Only 100 psi remaining until I was supposed to turn.

100 psi.

That was maybe three minutes, four at best with the skip breathing I was doing. I only had 400 psi in the other sidemount tank.

I kept looking for Gary. Looking for any sign that he had been in this area of the cave. Silt hanging in the water. Bubbles on the ceiling. The line from his explorer reel tied off to the line in this tunnel and heading into a whole new section of cave that no one had ever found. That would be the only acceptable excuse for Gary taking off without us. I could forgive him for that. Anything else, I wasn't so sure about.

Suddenly, I noticed some bubbles moving on the ceiling not too far ahead of us. I focused my light on the bubbles and followed their trail. I watched the trail and moved my light in the direction they were coming from. They led right back to Lindsey and me. Those were our bubbles.

I took a breath, but the air stopped coming halfway through it. My tank was empty. How had I breathed it empty so quickly? I had to turn around. I didn't want to. I wasn't ready to give up on Gary. I thought about switching to my stage tank and continuing just a little farther. I looked back at Lindsey. She was right behind me. She would notice me switching to my stage tank regulator. The valve was closed, and I'd have to open it before I could breathe from that regulator. There was no way I could do that on the sly. Would Lindsey try to stop me? Would she try to make me turn around and head out?

I was about to find out.

29

Lindsey

I lost sight of Joey as we were swimming through the blurry tunnel. Only seconds earlier, he had been about twenty feet ahead of me. The tunnel must curve ahead. I couldn't remember. A few seconds later, I was coming around a bend and Joey's light came into view. The mixture of the halocline water made it difficult to see Joey. All I could see was the glow from his dive light. And it was not moving.

That was strange.

Why would Joey stop? Did he find Gary?

I sped up and was beside him about twenty seconds later. He was holding his head and appeared injured. At least, from what I could see in the blurriness that had enveloped us. I asked him if he was okay by circling my light beam in front of him. I expected him to circle back okay. Instead, he held his hand out and rocked it back and forth.

He wasn't okay!

I had no idea what had happened. A million thoughts raced through my mind. The main one that kept coming back was that Joey had found Gary and Gary was dead. I scanned the area expecting to see a yellow fin sticking out of the blurriness surrounding us.

Joey brought his hand to his head and seemed to be pressing against it. I looked around again and saw the large formation that stood in the middle of the path of this tunnel. Joey must have smacked his head into that column. I grabbed Joey's arm, fearful that he might lose consciousness. I had no idea how hard he had hit the formation, but I did know that he had been swimming fast.

A moment later, Joey pushed my arm away, circled his light, and began swimming around the column farther into the cave. He must be okay. At least I hoped he was okay. If he wasn't feeling well, we needed to head out. Gary would have to figure things out for himself. I would leave him my stage tank in case he needed extra air.

Joey continued to swim away from me. I pushed the thoughts I was having aside and followed behind him. I kept up with him this time. He wasn't swimming nearly as fast as he had been. I swept my light back and forth in the tunnel looking for signs of Gary while at the same time keeping a close eye on Joey. We really shouldn't be in the cave if he hit his head so hard it stopped him in his tracks. Not only stopped him but dazed him long enough to keep him from moving for almost a minute.

I continued to follow Joey into the cave. I checked my gauges for my air pressure. I had already switched regulators a few minutes earlier and was breathing the last of my planned usable air. Joey should have done the same. I still had 600 psi. This meant Joey only had about 500 psi left. Not much. Not for forty feet of depth more than one thousand feet from the cave opening.

Joey wasn't going to want to turn around and head out before finding Gary. I didn't want to either. But one victim would be better than three victims. What good would we be doing by also dying in this cave? It was bad enough that one body would have to be dragged out of the cave several thousand feet. I couldn't imagine having the task of dragging three dead bodies out. We couldn't risk our own lives. We couldn't do it to ourselves. We couldn't do it to our families. We couldn't do it to the person that would be tasked with removing the bodies from the cave.

Joey's parents already didn't like the fact that he was a cave diver. And they really didn't like him coming on this trip for a week of cave diving. If something happened to him while he was in Mexico, they would not cope with it well. They might even blame me.

My parents wouldn't cope with it well, for that matter. But at least they were much more understanding about my diving. They knew it was my passion and had accepted it long ago.

I watched Joey check his gauge. He must have been getting close to turn pressure. I waited for him to switch to his stage tank. I knew that thought was going through his mind even though we had agreed to reserve that for emergencies. Joey would have a difficult time turning around without finding Gary. He would have a difficult time exiting the cave without knowing what happened to Gary. I watched and waited.

It would be tough for me, too. Gary was a good friend. But he and Joey were really good friends. They had gone through a lot of similar experiences with their cave diving. That was how they first became friends. They had shared a horrible experience. Different dives, but similar outcomes. Those experiences created a bond between them.

I watched as Joey checked his gauge again. I noted a hesitation in his movements. He must have reached his turn pressure. He looked at his gauge again. He was still swimming farther into the cave, but I could tell he was struggling with himself over whether to turn and exit or keep going. I had seen him behave that way before when we were close to turning during a normal dive. This time it was different. This time the stakes were much higher. I couldn't let him put himself in danger. Put both of us in danger.

Our best option was to remove our stage tanks, clip them to the guideline, and make our way out of the cave. At least if Gary was alive, and he was heading out of the cave low on air, he would find our stage tanks and be able to use them to get himself out. How did I convince

Joey of this? How could I make him understand that endangering himself wouldn't help Gary at all if Joey ended up dead in the cave? How could I do this without being able to talk to him in the environment we were in?

As I followed Joey, I pulled my wetnotes out of my pocket. I wasn't going to be able to communicate what I needed to by using light or hand signals. I was going to have to write it down.

Hopefully, Joey would understand.

Hopefully, he wouldn't be resistant to my efforts to keep him alive.

Hopefully, I wouldn't have to turn around and leave him in the cave to die with Gary.

30

Joey

I opened the valve on my stage tank and heard the air in the tank rushing to fill the hose that was connected to it. I grabbed the second stage regulator and pulled on it, releasing the hose from where it was being held against the tank by hose retainers. The hose retainers were just loops of elastic material positioned around the tank so the hose could be tucked into them and held in position when not in use. I placed the regulator in my mouth and filled my lungs with air.

I noticed Lindsey's light getting brighter and larger as she swam up next to me. I had fully expected that. She wasn't going to be happy with the change in plans. She would want me to turn and leave. Leave Gary behind in the cave. How could I do that? How could I leave one of my best friends in the cave to die? How could I tell Jim I had left Gary to die? How could I tell Gary's parents I had left him to die? Or his sister?

I was having a difficult time dealing with it. How would they deal with it? Would they think I sentenced him to his death by leaving the cave without using every bit of air I had to look for him? Would they blame me for inviting Gary on this trip? I blamed myself so how could they not. I certainly felt like I was sentencing him to his death if I turned around instead of continuing to look. I didn't understand how Lindsey could be so willing to turn and leave. How could she leave

Gary behind? This wasn't like the situation with Jack Johnson in Jackson Blue in Florida last year.

Gary was our friend. He was like a brother.

Lindsey's wetnotes appeared in front of my face from my left. Lindsey was swimming beside me and had shoved them in front of my mask. I pushed them aside without reading them. I wasn't going to turn back yet. It didn't matter what the notes said.

I brought the regulator from my stage tank around my head, rested the hose on the back of my neck and swapped the regulator with the one in my mouth. I clipped the regulator I had been breathing from onto a D ring on the right side of my chest. I kept swimming farther into the cave, scanning the cave for Gary.

Lindsey shoved the wetnotes back in front of my face. I brushed them aside again. Lindsey grabbed my hand and pulled me toward her. I pulled her along beside me. The additional drag slowed me down, but I kept going.

Why couldn't she understand I had to do this? Why couldn't she understand I had to find Gary. Even if he was already dead in this cave. I had to know. I couldn't just turn around and leave him without knowing.

She pulled back on my hand and tried to slow me down even more. Tried to stop me. I kept swimming farther into the cave dragging Lindsey along. I tried to shake her off so I could go faster. She kept a tight grip on my wrist. She kept trying to get my attention.

I kept swimming.

I looked at the pressure gauge on my stage tank.

1800 psi.

Dragging Lindsey along was causing me to breathe faster than I normally would. I tried to shake her off again, but she wouldn't release her grasp on my wrist.

I kept swimming.

I swept my light back and forth. I tried to cover it to see if I could see Gary's dive light anywhere around us. Lindsey didn't shield her light though, so that was pointless. She was making things difficult for me. She was making things difficult for Gary.

I tried to fin with more force while also focusing on keeping my breathing rate down. I concentrated on skip breathing to make my air last longer. I tried to get Lindsey to release her grip on me. She tightened it.

I looked at my pressure gauge again.

1600 psi.

My air was going quickly. I started breathing from my stage tank with 2000 psi in it. I should reserve at least one third of the air I had for any additional emergencies. Six hundred psi in reserve. Actually, 666 psi even though the gauges weren't quite that accurate. Wasn't that ironic? Or was it a foreshadowing of what was to come with this dive. The image of the grim reaper sign found at the entrance of many of the caves in Florida flashed through my mind.

Six-six-six.

The number of the beast. The beast being this cave.

I began to have second thoughts about what I was doing. I should have stuck to Lindsey's plan. I should have clipped the stage tank to the line and begun to swim out rather than using it to continue looking for Gary. It wasn't too late. I could turn around and swim back to the spot where I started breathing from the stage tank and leave it for Gary with 1200 psi in it. That would be better than nothing. That would be better than breathing it to 1400 psi, turning and having to use it to exit the cave and not leaving anything for Gary. Not leaving him any kind of fighting chance.

It didn't feel like I was exerting as much effort to move forward. It didn't feel like Lindsey was dragging me back so much. I looked around. It wasn't that Lindsey wasn't trying any harder to stop me. I had slowed down. Having second thoughts had slowed me down without realizing it.

I looked at my gauge.

About 1500 psi.

I had to make a decision within the next minute. By then the pressure gauge would read 1400 psi. I would need 600 psi to get back to where I had started breathing from it. I could then leave the stage tank with 800 psi for Gary. It wasn't much. It wasn't what we had planned. But it was better than leaving him nothing at all.

Maybe I should look at Lindsey's wetnotes. What if she had seen Gary or evidence of where he had gone? No. If that was the case, she would be trying harder to stop me.

I looked at Lindsey. She was still holding onto my left wrist with a death grip. That might not have been the best choice of words. She was holding onto me very tightly. She wasn't looking at me, though. She was looking around the cave, as if she was still looking for Gary. So she probably hadn't seen him. She was just trying to get me to stick to the plan.

I tried to see the words she had written on her wetnotes. They were too far to read and at an unfavorable angle for me to see clearly. I reached across with my right hand and grabbed her right hand, the one holding onto my left wrist. She pulled back but didn't release her grip. She didn't look at me either.

I moved my hand up her arm and grabbed her forearm. I squeezed it several times, trying to get her attention. Lindsey finally looked at me. I could see a mixture of sadness and anger in her eyes, both directed at me. I pointed to her wetnotes. She ignored me or didn't understand. I looked at my stage tank pressure gauge again.

1400 psi.

I had to make a decision.

31

Lindsey

I quickly jotted a short message for Joey onto a blank page in my wetnotes. I kicked my fins hard and caught up to him. I shoved my wetnotes in front of his face open to the page with my hastily scribbled note. Joey shoved the wetnotes aside. He didn't even read them. He couldn't have. He didn't have time and didn't illuminate them with his light.

I shoved the notes in front of him again. I had to convince him to turn around. Continuing into the cave was a death sentence. Instead of one possibly dead diver there would be two dead divers. Three if I didn't turn around soon myself.

Joey shoved the notes aside again.

I grabbed his wrist and tried to turn him toward me. He kept swimming. He was too strong for me to overpower. I hung onto his wrist as he continued to swim forward dragging me along. He wasn't moving as quickly as he had been, but I could tell from the exhalation bubbles coming from his regulator that he was breathing faster. He wasn't going to get very far at this pace.

Would he ever turn around? Was he thinking logically enough to know he would have to turn around soon if he was going to make it out alive? At this point, it wasn't a matter of matching the pressure needed with the pressure used to penetrate the distance we had. Stress levels were up. Exertion levels were up. We were both breathing faster than we usually did. Joey was going to need more than what was in his sidemount tanks to swim back that distance. Especially with the water current working against us in that four-hundred-foot section of cave with the halocline.

Was he planning on breathing exactly half of his stage tank, or would he leave some in reserve? He was going to need that reserve at this point.

I tried pulling him back again. He tried to shake me off. I wasn't ready to let go. I wasn't ready to leave him behind like Debra Reeves' boyfriend had left her behind in Orange Grove cave in Florida so many years ago.

I didn't know how he did that. How had he come to the decision to leave his girlfriend to die in the cave? Someone he supposedly loved. I wasn't there and didn't know the exact circumstances they were facing. I was here, though, and I was having a very difficult time with the decision facing me. I didn't know what to do.

I set a plan. We were supposed to turn, not switch to breathing from our stage tanks. Joey blew the plan off and switched anyway. I should have left him behind. I should have turned around and saved myself like Debra's boyfriend saved himself. But I couldn't just leave Joey in the cave to die. Even if it meant risking my own life.

Joey covered his dive light to try to see if he could see any sign of Gary's light. I didn't cover mine. I wasn't going to encourage him. We had to turn and head out of the cave. The do or die decision was coming upon us. I watched Joey check his pressure gauge again. He had to be getting close to needing to turn or deciding he would die looking for Gary.

How could Joey do this to me? It's one thing to put himself in danger, but to drag me along with him. Okay, to be fair, he wasn't holding onto me. I was holding onto him. But he didn't even acknowledge me. He refused to look at my note to him.

The next breath was hard to pull in. I glanced at the pressure gauge on the tank I was breathing from. It was almost empty. The needle was pointing at the zero. The air in it wasn't even enough to register on the gauge. I switched regulators so I was breathing from my other sidemount tank. There should still be 700 psi in that one. I looked at the gauge to confirm that.

Breathing one tank empty and about to breathe the other tank halfway. That was 1800 psi of air used to get to this point. I hadn't bothered to switch to my stage tank. That still had 2200 psi of air in it. If we turned at this moment that would leave me with 900 psi in reserve. Did Joey have enough to get out on his own? He started with 700 psi less than me, 200 psi less in his stage, 200 psi less in one of his sidemount tanks, and 300 psi less in the other. And he was breathing faster than me. There was no way he would make it back to the surface with just the air he had in his tanks.

If I turned to leave without Joey, I would be sentencing him to death. But if I didn't turn, I would be sentencing us both to death.

32

Joey

I looked at my stage tank pressure gauge again.

1200 psi.

1200 psi?!?

How had that happened?? I just had 1400 psi in it a minute earlier. I looked at my dive computer. Actually, that was three minutes earlier. What happened? How had that much time passed? That meant I would have 400 psi left in my stage tank after using 800 psi to get back to where I started breathing from it. And I hadn't given myself any buffer in my sidemount tanks. I couldn't leave the stage tank for Gary. I needed it to get myself out of the cave. *What had I done?!?*

Lindsey must have more air than me. She could leave her stage tank for Gary. Had she balanced out her breathing among all three tanks?

I turned toward Lindsey and grabbed the gauge on her sidemount tank. It was empty. A big fat zero. 0. Nada. Zip. Zilch.

Useless.

She must have kept breathing from her sidemount tanks. Her stage tank must still have 2200 psi in it. That should be plenty for her to get out of the cave, but not enough to leave it behind for Gary. Maybe she could swap it out with her left sidemount tank and leave that one for Gary. Was there enough time for her to do that?

Gary, Jim, and I had practiced removing our sidemount tanks and clipping them back onto our harnesses several times back home in Florida. It was practice for penetrating into small restrictions that wouldn't allow us to pass through with the tanks positioned on our sides. Lindsey wasn't into diving small tunnels, though. She was a little claustrophobic when it came to those things. Could she swap tanks efficiently enough so we didn't waste a bunch of time doing it and breathe through whatever little air was left in them? If not, there wasn't any point in swapping tanks at all.

If we turned at this moment, we might have enough air to get back to the cenote and make it to the surface. We might have a couple hundred psi each left in our tanks. I should have listened to Lindsey. I should have followed her plan. I continued to push farther into the cave hoping to find Gary. Hoping he would be around the next corner, and we would all reunite and quickly exit the cave. Everyone a little stressed, but everyone alive.

I was too stubborn. Look where that had gotten us.

The note! What was Lindsey trying to tell me? I reached across and snatched the note out of her hand.

Must leave now! 2 late 4 Gary

She had given up on Gary. Or had she seen his body? If she had, why wouldn't she tell me? Why wouldn't she have brought me to it?

I looked at the note again.

2 late 4 Gary

Did Lindsey know something I didn't know? Had she found him when I was in that tunnel surveying? We had been on the surface, though. She would have told me then rather than have allowed us to come back into the cave looking for him.

Wouldn't she have?

2 late 4 Gary

Too late for what?!? Gary had to be alive! There still had to be a chance to find him! There still had to be a chance to get him out of this cave.

2 late 4 Gary

33

Lindsey

Gary was probably already dead. Even if he wasn't, I doubted we would be able to find him. I didn't think Joey had enough air in his tanks to make it out of the cave. We might both make it out together. I would have to monitor my breathing and reserve some air for him. If we didn't both turn in the next sixty seconds, we definitely wouldn't have enough air to make it back to the surface. We would both die in this cave.

* * *

When I started my cave diving training, I never considered the possibility of dying in a cave. I was younger then, still a teenager. Okay, I wasn't that much older now, but I had a lot more experience.

As an eighteen-year-old I thought I was invincible. Who was I kidding? This morning, I thought I was invincible. There was no way I was going to die in a cave. I was better than that. I followed the rules. I planned conservative dives. I didn't put myself into precarious positions.

The more I was around the cave diving community, the more conservative I became. It happened about three months after getting my full cave diving certification, the pinnacle of certifications, the one that said I was trained and qualified to do safe cave dives. The first cave diving fatality of a person I knew happened. I didn't know that person well. We had crossed paths at cave diving sites over the previous couple of years since I had started my training.

The cave diving community was small and close, at least within the various regions around the world. Cave divers in Florida knew other Florida cave divers in person or from social media. Cave divers in Mexico were the same way. Except they were more likely to know each other in person because the caves weren't as spread out in distance as they were in Florida. Based on social media posts, it seemed the community wasn't much different in France. Except there, the cave divers came from all over the continent. Australia also had caves, but I didn't see a lot posted about those. Australia did have its own cave diving organization, so that said something.

Those were the big three, four if you count the land down under, as far as cave diving was concerned. Sure, there was cave diving in many other places. But Florida, Mexico, and France seemed to be the major hubs of cave diving. Lots of training happened in those locations and lots of cave divers traveled to them to cave dive.

Weekends at the Florida springs were typically packed with cave divers getting their fix in after a hard week at work. I had even come across some Texas cave divers that got off work Friday and drove to Florida through the night. They would arrive Saturday morning and head straight to one of the caves. After diving all weekend, they would drive back Sunday night so they could go to work Monday morning. Those guys were crazy.

I wasn't out every weekend because I had to work every other weekend, usually teaching open water classes. But I did get to do some cave diving at least once a month. When I was still training, before I got my full cave diver certification, I was out cave diving more often.

I had heard of fatalities in the caves while I was in the process of getting trained. But those incidents were far removed from me. The first one happened in Mexico. It was an incident involving three people consisting of a guide and his two clients.

I didn't know the guide. He was one of dozens, maybe hundreds of cenote guides living in Mexico. He took his two clients, a couple on vacation from Brazil, on a cenote dive. The three never made it out of the cave. The bodies were recovered the next morning much farther inside the cave than they should have been considering the Brazilian couple weren't trained cave divers. They weren't even trained to dive in the cavern zone where there was still daylight. They were entry level open water divers with very little experience. They were only supposed to be doing a cenote tour in the daylight zone of the cave.

No one could figure out exactly what had happened. No one knew what had caused them to die. All we knew was that they had gone where they shouldn't have. There was a lot of speculation, as usual, but no hard evidence, at least not that anyone talked about.

It was the first cave diving fatality that had occurred after I embarked on this journey, so I'll always remember it even though I didn't know any of the people involved. How horrible would it be to be on vacation, doing a fun dive in one of the most beautiful places in the world, and then run out of air knowing there's nothing you can do to save yourself. You're too far from the cenote. Too far from the surface. You might not even know what direction to go to get to the surface. And your next breath was going to be a mouthful of water.

I couldn't imagine how they must have felt at that moment. What they must have been thinking about. It was one thing to face death after you had lived a full life and were ready to move on to whatever awaited you beyond. It was one thing to die suddenly from a car accident or falling from a high place. You might know for a second that you weren't going to survive but there wouldn't be enough time to really think about it. No time to build up any fear over it.

But underwater in a cave, watching the needle on your pressure gauge dropping with every breath you took. The panic inside of you growing because you have no idea how to escape the cave. Knowing that death was coming for you. Trying desperately to find a way out of your situation but deep down knowing that it was beyond hope.

You were too far inside the cave. There was no way out. It would almost be better to remove the regulator from your mouth and take in that breath of water. Just end it. End the psychological suffering. End the torture. But you were too scared to do that. You were too hopeful that a miracle might happen. So you kept trying to find the exit to the cave. You looked for an air pocket above you that might let you live just long enough for someone to come in and see you and help you escape death.

Then you took that next breath and there was nothing there. All hope disappeared. All hope was gone. The next breath would come with searing pain as the water rushed into your mouth, past your vocal cords, and burned the mucosal membranes of your lungs.

How long would the pain last before you lost consciousness? How long would you suffer? How much would it hurt?

Not long after the three fatalities in Mexico, the death of a cave diver in Florida happened. This was someone I had met a few times while out gaining experience on the weekends. This happened at Ginnie Springs in High Springs, about a three-hour drive from where Joey and I usually went cave diving in Marianna. We liked to go over there every now and then to see something different. Joey liked to refer to it as the slum caves. The Marianna caves were a lot prettier.

I didn't know the person that died in Ginnie Springs that well. He was from out of state. Many of the cave divers we were used to running into visited from out of state like those crazy Texans. There were underwater caves outside of Florida, but they were either not easy to access or the conditions in them weren't suitable for most cave divers.

So Florida saw a lot of cave diving tourists in High Springs, Luraville, and Marianna, the three main hubs for cave diving in the state. The really dedicated out of state cave divers would visit three or four times a year. They weren't so much tourists. They just weren't fortunate enough to live in Florida.

This guy was one of those. He was in Florida regularly. He was active on social media. Lots of people knew who he was. Unfortunately, it seemed that not many people were very surprised by his death, at least based on the gossip on the social media sites following his death.

His death was a quick one. He had a stage tank that was marked as containing oxygen. Contrary to all the news articles about scuba diving, divers don't breathe oxygen underwater, at least not any more oxygen than we breathe on land. We typically breathe air, twenty-one percent oxygen, seventy-nine percent nitrogen, and a bunch of trace elements mixed in for good measure.

Sometimes we'd enrich the air with a little more oxygen. The typical mixture we used contained thirty-two percent oxygen and sixty-eight percent nitrogen. This allowed for less nitrogen uptake into our bloodstream so we could stay underwater longer. The issue was the more oxygen we had in our tanks, the shallower we had to be. We could breathe twenty-one percent oxygen to one hundred and thirty feet of depth. Actually, we could go much deeper with standard air, but one hundred and thirty feet was the accepted limit for recreational divers. If we went any deeper, we would need to decrease the amount of oxygen in the mixture and replace it with helium. That required more training.

If we enriched the air, such as when we used a thirty-two percent oxygen mixture, our maximum depth became one hundred and ten feet. Going any deeper exposed us to the risk of having a seizure from breathing too high of an oxygen concentration at the greater pressures.

Breathing one hundred percent pure oxygen limited us to twenty feet of depth. And that was only allowable for decompression stops in which we weren't moving very much and exerting ourselves.

So this guy had a stage tank that had the number *20* on it in three-inch tall numbers indicating it was only good to a depth of twenty feet. He covered the *20* with duct tape and proceeded to rig up the tank to use as a stage tank. It was rumored that one of the other divers diving with him asked if he wanted to analyze the air in that tank. He responded that he had analyzed it back home and it contained air. Back home was in another state.

Unfortunately, it didn't contain air. At least the tank he had brought to Florida didn't contain air. Maybe the one he had analyzed did, but that wasn't the one he brought on the dive with him. That was why you should analyze the air in all of your tanks right before your dive.

About three hundred feet into the cave, at a depth of eighty feet, while breathing from that stage tank, he had an oxygen toxicity seizure and drowned. That was a seizure caused by breathing too high of a concentration of oxygen too deep. This was confirmed after his body and equipment were recovered and the gas in the tank was analyzed. The tank contained one hundred percent oxygen. It didn't contain air. He had been four times deeper than he should have been and the oxygen hadn't taken long to cause him to have a seizure. This happened three hundred feet from the opening.

The good thing for him was that he never saw it coming. One minute he was swimming along in the cave, the next he was unconscious and having a seizure. The seizure didn't kill him. The regulator falling out of his mouth while he continued to breathe while underwater killed him.

While you were having a seizure you couldn't control your muscles. You didn't have the mental capacity or the physical control to do it. Either the regulator fell out of his mouth, or he was no longer sealing the regulator with his lips. Either way, water got into his lungs, and he drowned. But he didn't see it coming. He was saved from that horror at least.

His dive buddies weren't though. They witnessed it. They saw him having a seizure. They watched him die. Helpless and unable to do anything about it. Then they had to pull him out to the surface. What a horrible experience that must have been.

* * *

I snapped myself out of my thoughts and looked at Joey. I couldn't watch him die and I didn't want to be dead either. I shook his arm, desperately trying to get him to turn around and leave the cave with me. I didn't want to leave him in the cave to die. That would be second only to having to watch him die. But I didn't want to become the next victim to an underwater cave either. He didn't acknowledge me.

I shook him harder and jerked his arm toward me, desperate to get him to turn and come with me. Joey snapped his arm away from my grasp. He looked at me. Looked in my eyes. My vision had become blurred. Not because of any halocline. This time it was the tears in my eyes that were blurring my vision. I couldn't wipe the tears away because I was wearing a scuba mask. I had to let the tears gather at the bottom of the mask. I felt their warmth as puddles formed and grew in size.

Joey turned away from me and continued swimming farther into the cave. I mumbled I love you through my regulator as I watched him swim off. I turned and started heading out, sobbing, my shoulders shaking. I had just lost the love of my life. My best friend.

34

Joey

2 late 4 Gary

It couldn't be too late for Gary. He couldn't be gone. He couldn't be dead. I couldn't give up on him.

Lindsey grabbed my arm and shook it. I kept swimming. I had to find Gary. I had to make sure he left the cave with us.

Lindsey shook my arm again. This time she jerked it back toward her. I pulled my arm away from her, her grasp on it released. I looked at her, into her eyes. They looked wet, like she was crying. I didn't want to leave Lindsey. I didn't want to die in this cave. I knew we should turn around and leave. Deep down I knew it was probably too late for Gary. I just wasn't ready to admit that to myself. I wasn't ready to concede. I needed to keep looking for him.

Lindsey looked so sad. If I didn't turn, we would probably both die in this cave. Could I do that to her? Could I leave Lindsey to die by not turning around? We should both go. There was nothing more I could do. It probably was too late for Gary.

Then why couldn't I turn around and go? Why couldn't I give up on him?

I looked back toward the tunnel in the direction we had been going. It bent around to the right. Maybe Gary was just around the next corner. Maybe if I swam just a few more feet, I'd see him, and we'd all be able to get out of this cave alive and safe.

I needed to check. I needed to go look. Just one more corner. Then I'd turn around.

One more.

Lindsey turned away from me and started swimming in the opposite direction. I watched her body shake. I swore I could hear her crying through her regulator.

Just one more corner then I'd turn and catch up to her.

I turned back to that corner and finned as hard as I could. It was only about forty feet away. I could get there in less than a minute.

I glanced back at Lindsey. I could still see her. She wasn't swimming very quickly. I could easily look around this corner and turn to catch up to her. She always swam slowly.

2 late 4 Gary

Just one more corner.

I got to the corner and looked around. I didn't see anything. No Gary. No lights. I shielded my light to see if I could see Gary's light coming from one of the offshoots. Complete darkness.

I unshielded my light. I saw another corner about twenty feet ahead. Should I go look? I promised myself just one more corner, but this one was so close. I glanced back and still saw Lindsey.

Just one more corner.

I swam the twenty feet to the next corner. About fifteen seconds later I got to it and looked around it into the tunnel that continued into a void. Still no Gary. I shielded my light again. Still complete darkness.

I knew I had to turn around. If I had any chance of catching up to Lindsey and getting out of this cave alive, I couldn't go any farther into it. I looked down the tunnel one last time hoping to see Gary coming around the next corner, the one that looked like it was about fifty feet away, too far for me to go check without sentencing myself to dying in this cave. I didn't see him.

I said a silent goodbye to Gary. I felt a tear escape my eye and roll down my cheek until it was stopped by my mask. I turned to follow Lindsey out.

I didn't see Lindsey, though. She was no longer in view. I tried to picture the cave passage in my mind. Had she gone around a corner? Or had I wasted too much time looking for Gary and she had gotten too far for me to catch up?

I looked at my gauges. I quickly calculated how much time I had left.

Not enough.

Had I just guaranteed my own death?

35

Lindsey

I was in total disbelief. How could Joey have done that to me? How could he have kept going into the cave knowing he wouldn't have enough air to make it back out? How could he leave me like that? Did Gary mean more to him than I did? Or was he so overwhelmed with losing a friend on a dive that he wasn't thinking logically?

Should I have stayed with Joey? Was there anything else I could have done that would have convinced him to turn and exit the cave with me?

I reconsidered my decision to leave Joey. Maybe I should turn around and go find him. Try harder to convince him to come with me. It was too late for Gary. There was nothing either one of us could do to save him. Why couldn't Joey understand that?

I hesitated.

I slowed down.

I looked back behind me hoping I would see Joey's light in the distance, swimming to catch up to me.

Nothing but darkness.

I thought about turning around again. Going to find him. I didn't do it. I didn't even have to look at my gauges to know I barely had enough to get out of the cave alive without turning around. If Joey had come with me, we would probably be surfacing with no air in any of our tanks.

I continued to swim toward the exit. This was the most difficult decision I ever had to make in my life. A decision I would have to live with for the rest of my life. I not only lost a friend, but I lost my soulmate. I started to cry even harder. My body almost convulsing from the sobs escaping through my regulator.

Every breath I took came with a little bit of water. I was crying so hard that I couldn't maintain a seal around the mouthpiece of the regulator. I couldn't overpower the urge that was turning the corners of my mouth down, making it impossible to form a seal. With every breath I took, water seeped in between my lips and the mouthpiece.

At first it wasn't enough to make a difference. I was able to breathe around it and exhale the water easily. But the harder I cried, the more water came seeping in. Eventually, it was enough to start flowing back into my throat. When the water hit my vocal cords, I began coughing. First, it was short, gagging coughs. It quickly turned into violent coughs when the amount of water that was entering my mouth was more than the amount of air coming in through the regulator.

I stopped swimming and reached out for a large boulder that was directly beneath me to stabilize myself. I coughed the last of the water out of my airways and focused my attention on getting dry breaths of air into my lungs. I forced my lips to close around the mouthpiece and form a seal. Then I started bawling again and my lips opened, and the water came rushing in. Followed by another coughing fit.

If I didn't gain control of myself, I would end up dying in this cave, too. Alone, after having abandoned Joey and Gary. I pushed the thoughts of Joey and Gary out of my mind and concentrated on what I had to do. First, on my breathing. I had to get that under control. If I couldn't breathe from my regulator without taking in water, I was never going to make it out of the cave. My air supply was already dangerously low. The coughing wasn't doing anything to help conserve it.

After a minute or so, my breathing was slowing down. I had a proper seal around the mouthpiece and was bringing only air into my airways. Thoughts of Joey and Gary began creeping back into my mind and I felt the crying starting to come back. I pushed the thoughts aside and focused on what I had to do. I had to stop thinking about the boys behind me and keep my focus on getting out of the cave alive.

Was this how Debra Reeves' boyfriend had felt? Had he gone through the same thing, the same emotions?

This cave was huge. More than four miles of tunnels that we knew about. Very much a maze. And it wasn't visited by cave divers very often. No one knew where we were planning to dive. Jose knew we were diving in this cave all week, but he didn't know where in the cave we would be each day. I had to make it out, if for nothing else but to let them know where to look for the bodies.

The crying came back full force with that thought. I focused and pushed it aside. I forced myself not to cry.

I aimed my dive light forward and found an area about forty feet ahead of me to focus on. I pushed off the boulder I had been holding onto and began swimming to that spot. When I was about ten feet away from it, I found another spot about thirty feet ahead to focus on. I continued this way for a few minutes, playing mental leapfrog with the spots I was finding to focus on.

I reached the junction in the tunnel, the area where I had to veer to the right and swim into the narrow halocline tunnel. This was where I would start to feel the current working against me. That was a good thing. It would give me something else to focus on. With the distorted visibility from the halocline, I wouldn't be able to find landmarks far enough away to make that work any longer. I slowed down and glanced back one last time, hopeful that Joey might have changed his mind and had begun following me out.

He wasn't there.

Nothing but a black void.

I turned back toward the narrow tunnel and continued to swim. Almost immediately, I felt the force of the water current against me, doing everything it could to impede my exit. It was like the cave wanted to keep me inside. It wanted to make me one of its victims. It wanted to kill me.

My next breath felt harder to pull in. I felt resistance. I quickly reached for my pressure gauge and saw the needle on the zero just as the next one stopped midbreath. That tank was empty. I promptly swapped regulators and began breathing from my right sidemount tank. Except I couldn't get a breath from it either. I grabbed the pressure gauge on that tank and looked at it. That needle was also on the zero. I remembered that I had breathed that tank empty right before I left Joey. All I had left was my stage tank.

I reached back to the stage tank that was positioned above my left sidemount tank. I found the regulator where it should be, held in place against the body of the tank by two hose retainers. I pulled on the regulator. It didn't budge. I pulled harder. It gave way a couple of inches then it stopped. Something was keeping me from being able to deploy my stage tank regulator.

I had no air in either of my sidemount tanks. The last breath I took was only half a breath. And now I couldn't get to the regulator attached to the only tank that had any air in it. If I didn't do something quickly, I was going to drown.

36

Joey

I swam as quickly as I could while still trying to keep my breathing under control. I felt my headache increasing in intensity. I had been skip breathing to try to stretch out the air I had left in my tanks. That meant I was getting carbon dioxide buildup in my bloodstream. That's what was making my headache worse.

I would have to suffer through it. I didn't have enough air in my tanks to make it out to the surface if I breathed normally. I wasn't sure I had enough air in my tanks to make it to the surface skip breathing. I had to try something, though. I had to catch up to Lindsey. She was my only hope.

I swam harder. Whenever I saw something I could grab onto, I reached out and grabbed it and pulled myself past it, pushing myself off of it. I didn't know if that was going to help or just make me need to breathe more often. But smaller muscles were supposed to require less oxygen. I was still skip breathing, but the seconds between inhalations and exhalations were decreasing as I exerted myself even more.

I shielded my light every thirty seconds or so, hoping to see Lindsey's light ahead. All I saw was darkness. I glanced at my dive computer. I had been swimming for at least five minutes. I should have seen her already. Had she taken a different route? Was there a different route to take? The only alternate route I could think of was at the junction right before the narrow halocline tunnel. We hadn't been to the left yet, but I doubted Lindsey would exit through an unfamiliar path.

We didn't know if there were restrictions in that tunnel or not. We didn't know if the line was intact or if it had deteriorated. On the map the passage looked like it was about the same length as the halocline tunnel we had been taking. It was supposed to come out into the main tunnel about one hundred feet closer to the exit than the halocline tunnel. That would only save a couple of minutes, a minute and a half if we were swimming fast. All other things being equal.

We didn't know if they were equal, though. We didn't know what the water flow was like in that tunnel. Based on the map I would assume the current wasn't as strong or could even be non-existent. Most of the water that was being directed into this tunnel should be coming through the halocline tunnel. There were too many unknowns about that route. Lindsey wouldn't go that way.

So where was she? I should have seen her light by this time. I tried to swim harder, faster, but that only increased my breathing rate. The exertion made it harder to skip breathe and made my head hurt worse. I glanced at my pressure gauges and took inventory of my air. One tank was empty. One tank had 400 psi. The stage tank had 600 psi in it. That meant I had less than 1000 psi total in all three tanks. Could I make it out on that? I tried to work the numbers in my head, but I was too stressed to focus. Too distracted.

I decided to switch to my sidemount tank and save the stage tank. I grabbed my other regulator and put it in my mouth after pushing the stage regulator out. I clipped the stage regulator to a D ring positioned in front of my right shoulder. I reached back and closed the valve out of habit.

I cautiously took a breath. I felt a little water rush into my mouth, but I was prepared for that to happen. I had bent my tongue up so the tip was touching the roof of my mouth and blocking any water from shooting directly to the back of my throat and into my airway. It worked. I got an almost full breath of air. I exhaled through my mouth to clear whatever water might have been left in the regulator and to expel the small amount of water that had gotten into my mouth.

I took another breath. This one was completely dry. Nothing but air. I glanced at the pressure gauge. Less than 300 psi left in that tank! How had that happened? I had 400 psi last time I checked. Then I remembered that tank was the one connected to my BC air bladder. Every time I pressed the button on the inflator to adjust my buoyancy, I was using air from that tank. I had to stop doing that. I should be orally inflating my BC to preserve the air I had left.

Maybe I should switch to my stage tank and close the valve on my left sidemount tank. I was likely to forget not to use the power inflator rather than orally inflating. I needed that air to get out of the cave alive. Especially if I couldn't catch up to Lindsey.

Why hadn't I listened to her? Why hadn't I turned and left with her? What had I been thinking? We had been taught never to worry about what was around the next corner. That's what got people in trouble. Cave divers specifically. We always wanted to see what was just beyond the next corner. It was to our own detriment.

For me it was usually when exploring cave passages I had never been in. I sometimes pushed the limits a little when there was a corner just ahead. I always wanted to look around the next corner and see what was beyond it. It was difficult to avoid the temptation. Until now I always got out of it okay. It meant using less than 100 psi and the exit was always quicker than the penetration side of the dive. That was under normal circumstances.

This dive was anything but normal. We had lost contact with Gary. We had overstayed our planned time for the dive. We had exited the cave and then came back to look for Gary again. And I had blown off the plan a second time. I shouldn't have gone to look around the next corner. Gary wasn't there and now I might not get out of the cave alive. I might be joining Gary in this water-filled grave.

How would Lindsey deal with that? All alone in Mexico, her two travel buddies dead in a cave. How would she deal with the authorities? How would she deal with arrangements for getting our bodies back to the states? How would she deal with the grief of losing us? How would she deal with telling our families and friends?

What had I done? What had I been thinking? I should have turned and exited with her. I should be there for her. We should be grieving for Gary together.

I tried to pick up the pace again, careful to keep my breathing as under control as I could. I thought I saw a light ahead. I quickly shielded my light to try to confirm it. Nothing but black. No light.

Was it Lindsey? Had I seen her as she was going around a corner? Or was it my imagination playing tricks on my mind? Was it just my hopes?

About a minute later I came to the junction in the passage. I looked to the left. I asked myself again if Lindsey could have gone that way. Would she have broken from her own protocol? Her own rules? I considered going that way but stopped myself from doing it. It was highly unlikely that Lindsey would have broken the rules. The distance of the two passages didn't look that different on the maps. The tunnel to the left had too many unknowns. I headed to the right, into the halocline tunnel.

Almost immediately the visibility became horribly distorted. It was so blurry I couldn't see two feet in front of me. Lindsey must have gone this way. She couldn't be too far ahead. It had been too long since we came in for it to still be stirred up so badly. Lindsey must have caused this distortion in visibility.

How long would it take for the fresh and salt waters to settle back into their respective zones and the visibility to clear? It had been clear on the way out earlier, but more than an hour had passed from the time we swam through that area to the time we were swimming back out. Had Lindsey gone through five minutes earlier, or twenty minutes earlier? It didn't matter. If I found her, I might have a chance. If I didn't find her…

At least my body wouldn't be too far from the entrance to the cave.

I remembered the formation I had hit my head on. Twice. I brought my left hand up in front of my head. My right one was already in contact with the guideline so I wouldn't get too far from it. My left hand would protect me from hitting that damn column again. A moment later that's exactly what happened. My left hand smacked into the column. My head followed closely behind. But at least my hand cushioned some of the impact. It didn't feel good, but I didn't see stars this time.

I moved around the formation and kept swimming as quickly as I could without getting myself out of breath. I felt a lot of resistance when I took my next breath. I grabbed the pressure gauge. Zero. I reached for my stage tank. I should have left the valve open and had it ready to breathe from. Now I was going to have to open the valve and switch to the stage tank regulator while maintaining contact with the line to my right so I didn't get lost. Could this dive get any worse?

37

Lindsey

I quickly reached down to my waist and felt for the bolt snap at the end of the bungee cord that was holding the bottom of my stage tank against my body. My fingers fumbled around looking for it. I was usually able to find it quickly and get it unsnapped in no time. When I really needed to do it, I couldn't find it.

My fingers finally stumbled over the bolt snap. I wrapped them around the body of the snap and my thumb found the gate latch. I put pressure on the latch to open it and pulled my hand away from my waist in one fluid motion. I released the bolt snap and felt it being yanked to the side by the recoil of the bungee cord. The stage tank rolled to my left side, but it didn't fall completely off my back. I reached back and searched for the bungee cord so I could pull it around in front to look at it and figure out the issue with the regulator.

It was getting more difficult to hold my breath. How much time had passed? Thirty seconds? A minute?

My hand found the bungee cord and I pulled it and the tank. Something was keeping it from coming around. I was able to stretch the bungee, but something was keeping it from releasing itself completely. I started to reach around my waist with my right hand, then quickly snapped it back to the cave line it had been holding onto. If I let go of the line, I could end up getting pushed away from it and lost in the cave. I could barely see two feet in front of me. This tunnel wasn't very big, but I had no clue if I was near those two offshoot tunnels or not.

I released the bungee and felt around my waist with my left hand. I found the bolt snap wedged between my hip and my sidemount tank. We used the large bolt snaps so they would be heavy enough to drop down when we put the stage tanks on. The disadvantage to that was when pulling the stage tank off the bolt snap sometimes got stuck. Unfortunately, this was one of those times.

I shoved the bolt snap up between the sidemount tank and my hip and felt the stage tank shift again. I reached back to grab the bungee so I could pull it around. The stage tank wasn't there. Where had it gone?

I felt panic start to creep in again. My lungs were about to burst from holding my breath for so long. I was going to die in this cave with more than 2000 psi of air in my stage tank because I lost it.

I started to exhale the breath I had been holding. I began to prepare myself mentally for the next breath I was going to take. A breath of water. I felt a strange calmness envelope my body. After what I had just been through in the past hour, death would be welcome. At least the suffering would end.

As the calmness overtook me, I suddenly realized the upper bolt snap on my stage tank must still be clipped to my chest D ring. I quickly moved my hand to the D ring and not only found the bolt snap, but also the valve of the stage tank. When I released the large lower bolt snap from its entrapment, the bottom of the tank floated up away from my body because it only had 2000 psi in it. It always started floating when the air pressure dropped to about 2500 psi.

I grabbed the valve and pulled the stage tank down and around my body. I quickly twisted the valve open and heard the whoosh of the air from the tank rushing through the first stage regulator and into the hose. I spit out the second stage regulator that was in my mouth and moved the stage tank toward my face, its second stage regulator mouthpiece pointing toward me. I took it in my mouth and quickly hit the purge button on the front. I had no air left in my lungs to blow out the water in the regulator. As I purged the regulator of the water that had settled into it, I took a huge breath. My lungs quickly expanded, and relief washed over my body. I remained in position for several seconds. Just breathing. Staying alive. Thinking about nothing.

Then I remembered I was breathing from my last tank. I needed to continue to make my way out of the cave. I tried to pull the second stage regulator from the hose retainers. It gave way a little more than it had when it was clipped onto me, but it still wouldn't release from the retainers. I traced the hose from the second stage down to where it was looped near the bottom of the tank and started to trace it back up when I found the problem. The bottom loop of the hose was stuck against the screw on the gear clamp that was holding the lower bungee connection onto the tank.

I was usually careful about where I positioned the screw so it wouldn't interfere with the hose or tear into my wetsuit. I moved my face closer to the tank so I could see it. The screw was in the proper position on the tank. The hose had somehow been pushed to the side from where I normally placed it and had jumped over the screw, trapping it inside the loop. The hose retainer was just above the gear clamp, so it was holding the hose tightly against the tank.

I slid the hose retainer up the body of the tank, away from the gear clamp and pulled the hose loop up and over the screw, moving it to one side. I tugged on the hose again and this time it easily slid out of the hose retainers and floated loosely in the water. I swung the stage tank around my sidemount tank and above me, dropping the large bolt snap in between the sidemount tank and my hip. At this point, I would usually grab the bolt snap with my right hand and pull it across my waist to clip it onto a D ring on my right side. But I was still holding onto the guideline to my right.

I dropped my right hand down alongside the guideline, to the outside of it, and wrapped my arm around it so the line was in the crook of my arm. I reached across and found the bolt snap, pulled it to my right, and secured it to the D ring.

With the stage tank back in place, resting in the crevice formed by my torso and my left sidemount tank, I pulled the second stage regulator out of my mouth and routed the hose around my neck, placing the regulator back in my mouth. I didn't want the hose hanging loose and getting caught up on anything. I took a couple more breaths, making sure my breathing was under control. I slid my arm back up and found the guideline with my thumb and forefinger again, forming a circle around it. I looked back one last time to see if Joey had decided to follow me. The visibility was horrible. I wouldn't have been able to see him if he was five feet away.

I thought I felt movement on the line. I waited a few seconds to see if I could feel it again. Nothing happened. I must have kicked the line with my fin and my mind made me think it might be Joey coming up behind me. I turned toward the exit and continued my swim out to the opening. To the surface. To the reality of having lost my boyfriend and my friend on a cave dive.

38

Joey

I reached across my body with my left hand and grabbed onto the guideline. Once I had a hold of the line, I let go with my right and reached across to open the stage tank valve. I could barely reach the valve. It had been so easy to close, but now when I needed it open, I couldn't get a grip on it. Usually, I used my left hand to pull the tank down and to my side and my right hand to rotate the valve. I was stuck having to do this one handed, something I had never practiced.

I managed to find the knurled knob of the valve with the tips of my fingers. I tried to rotate it but didn't have enough leverage on it using just my fingertips. I tried to pull the valve around to my side, but I didn't have enough reach with my right arm to make that happen. I pulled the valve up to try to get it higher and easier to reach. The stage tank only moved a couple of inches before being stopped by the bungee cords holding it in place.

I slowly released a few bubbles of the breath I had been holding as I contemplated how I was going to do this without losing hold of the guideline and getting separated from it. Without any visibility in this tunnel, there was no way I would find my way out quickly enough to survive. It was a narrow tunnel, but there were those two areas with the offshoots. Two that I was aware of. There might be other areas I hadn't noticed. The two I knew of were a bit larger, and they were not much farther ahead. I could have been right next to one and not known it because the visibility was so bad. If I lost contact with the guideline, I could easily get into one of those and start going who knows where.

I released the rest of the air I had in my lungs. With my lungs empty, I held my breath. I didn't know if I would get a full breath of air with the next inhalation, or if I would get anything at all. All I knew was that I didn't have much longer before I would drown if I didn't get that stage tank valve opened.

When I was just about at the point of having to take another breath, I had almost decided to let go of the guideline and take my chances with having to find it again. That would have been better than holding onto the line and drowning with a tank that still contained air. Then an idea suddenly came to me. I could unclip the bottom bungee from the D ring on my waist strap. That would allow the tank to move enough for me to open the valve one-handed. My hand shot to my waist and quickly found the bolt snap. I opened the gate latch and snatched the bolt snap away from the D ring, letting it go, and feeling it smack against my left hip as the bungee cord recoiled.

I reached back up for the valve, luckily finding it quickly. I pulled it around and down and began rotating the knob as I was pulling. I heard the air rush into the hose. I began to pull in another breath from the regulator in my mouth, but there was nothing left in my sidemount tank.

Quickly letting go of the valve, I found the secondary regulator clipped to my chest D ring. My fingers fumbled with the bolt snap. I should have put a breakaway connection on it. I finally managed to open the gate latch and release the regulator from the D ring. I pushed the regulator in my mouth out and shoved the stage tank regulator in, pressing the purge button at the same time just as I lost the ability to hold my breath any longer. I felt some water enter my mouth, but thankfully the regulator purge allowed me to get more air than water.

I had forgotten to use my tongue to block my throat and some water managed to sneak through to my vocal cords causing me to cough violently. I kept the regulator in my mouth and coughed through it.

When the coughing fit subsided, I relaxed and pulled in a few more breaths, feeling each one fill my lungs. I didn't bother to clip the stage tank back on in its position alongside my back. I didn't have time to mess with that with only 600 psi in the tank. Probably only 500 psi at this point. I had to get out of the cave.

I moved around the formation that kept ambushing me each time I tried to pass it and continued to swim through the halocline tunnel. Since I couldn't see anything because of the blurriness of the mixture of waters, I closed my eyes. It was much more relaxing than trying to follow a blurry light out. With my eyes closed, my brain didn't expect me to be able to see. With my eyes open, there was an expectation that I should be able to see and not satisfying that expectation only created confusion. It also caused me to feel duress. Duress could lead to panic. I was already on the verge of panic and didn't need to be pushed over the edge.

It was much easier to move through zero visibility with closed eyes. I had learned that a few years earlier when I was in my first siltout in a cave and I couldn't see anything. It was only because I had closed my eyes that I had been able to make it out of that situation alive. Somehow, I had a knack for finding myself in these situations.

I had about a five-minute swim to the end of this small tunnel where our jump spool was tied onto the end of the line. At that point I would be able to open my eyes and look around again. I quickly moved forward with my right thumb and forefinger forming a circle around the guideline against the right wall and focused on keeping my breathing rate slow. It was much easier to do with my eyes closed. I felt calmer and less stressed that way.

I knew there was a very good possibility I might not make it out of this cave alive. I screwed up when I didn't listen to Lindsey. I found myself coming to terms with it, though. There was nothing more I could do except try to conserve the little remaining air I had left in my stage tank and swim as far as I could. At least that way, it would be easier to find my body and recover it if I didn't make it. When I didn't make it.

Strange. Somehow those thoughts didn't bother me. I always thought if the time came that I was going to die while cave diving that I would be in full panic. I would be thrashing around trying my damnedest to get to the surface. I wasn't panicking. I had accepted that death could happen. I finally understood how Steve Berman had been able to clip his body to the line right before he died. He must have known and just accepted it. Maybe I could even be as brave as he had been and clip myself to the line.

I also understood how bodies could be found so close to stage tanks that still had air in them. How they could be found so close to the exit.

I always wondered how they could get so close yet not make it all the way. The tank was right there. How could they not go that extra fifty or one hundred feet? When you run out of air, that's it. You can hold your breath for as long as possible but eventually you can't hold it any longer. And when that happened, you drowned. It didn't matter if you were one thousand feet from your stage tank or ten feet from your stage tank. When your body told you it was time to take another breath, even if there was no air to breathe, it would be nearly impossible to resist that physiological command.

Maybe if you were within sight of that stage tank, or within sight of the daylight streaming in from the sun outside. Maybe then you might find that little extra something within you to push through. Maybe you could pull from deep inside and manage to hold your breath just a little longer. Maybe you could overcome that involuntary urge.

Maybe.

Maybe not.

39

Lindsey

I eventually made it out of the halocline tunnel and into the main passage. I didn't remember most of the swim. It was all a big blur. And not just the visibility. Although that was a big blur as well. I looked at the three line markers on the line next to the jump spool. All of them were still there just as we had left them on our way into the cave. All untouched.

Mine.

Joey's.

Gary's.

I reached down and pulled my marker off the line and secured it on its pigtail holder in my thigh pocket. I looked at the remaining two markers on the line and started bawling. The clear visibility of the main tunnel turned blurry again. This time from my tears.

I looked back into the halocline tunnel one last time hoping to see a light coming from beyond. All I saw was blurry darkness. I didn't know if the blurriness was from my tears or from the mixture of the freshwater and saltwater. It didn't matter. There was no light. No Joey behind me. No Gary coming my way.

I turned back toward the exit and began to swim again. I could have cut the corner created by our jump line and the permanent main line. I should have cut the corner to save time and get out more quickly. I didn't. I followed the line, swam directly above it, reached the intersection of the two lines and turned right to continue out of the cave. I looked to my right, back toward the halocline tunnel. I was still hopeful that one of the boys, or even better, both, would swim out from the tunnel at any moment. It didn't happen.

I was no longer in a rush to get out of the cave. If I swam at a normal pace, I would be at the surface in less than ten minutes. That meant in less than ten minutes I would be all alone on the surface. No one else around. Joey and Gary wouldn't be there talking excitedly about what they had seen on the dive. They wouldn't be smiling and laughing. They wouldn't be teasing each other about the imaginary silt clouds they accused each other of making while calling each other silt monsters. They wouldn't be there at all. Only the memory of them would be on the surface with me.

What was the point in this? What was the point in continuing out of the cave? I should have stayed with Joey. I should have continued on with him until he breathed all of his air and let him breathe the last remaining air from my stage tank. We could have taken our last breaths together.

I continued to regret my decisions as I slowly moved through the tunnel. I recognized offshoot tunnels we had explored two days earlier, tunnels that became smaller the farther we went. Joey and Gary loved those. They loved the small, silty tunnels. I wasn't very enthusiastic about them. I preferred the larger areas where we had plenty of room around us. I followed them into those tunnels anyway. It made them happy. And it made me happy to see them happy. Even if it made me a little uncomfortable. I could deal with it. For them I could go beyond my comfort zone.

I couldn't deal with losing them, both of them, at the same time. Why had I let Gary swim off without me? Why hadn't I signaled him with my light and stopped him? Why hadn't I chased after him? We would all be alive and on the surface if I had just done things differently. If I had made different decisions, we would all be alive. Their deaths were my fault. I was the one who did this to them. I should be back there with them. I should be about to meet the same fate as they were about to, or as they already had.

I looked at the pressure gauge on my stage tank. I still had 1200 psi left in it. Maybe I should head back and look for Joey. He likely hadn't gotten very far before he…

Well, he just likely hadn't gotten very far.

I could find him. I could be with him. I could take my last breath with him.

I stopped swimming and looked around the cave. I was so lost in my thoughts I wasn't paying attention to the tunnel or where I was. I didn't recognize my surroundings. None of it looked familiar. Had I swum off the main line and into an offshoot without realizing it? Was I now lost in the cave somewhere?

I looked at the line below me. It was the same orange colored guideline that we were used to seeing in the main tunnel. We had only seen that line in the main tunnel. Where was I?

I shined my light around hoping to find a familiar sight, a familiar formation. Everything looked strange. Everything looked different to me. I should be in a wide room not a narrow corridor. I should be seeing that area where the ceiling dips down right over the guideline.

I started to swim again in hopes of reorienting myself to my location in the cave. I was still swimming along the orange guideline, so I had to be in the right place. The first day here we had swum the entire length of the orange line. In the subsequent days we hadn't seen this same line in any other location. I had to still be in the main tunnel. But nothing looked familiar.

I stopped again. I turned around. I looked at my dive computer. I looked at the time on it. I couldn't remember when I had arrived in this tunnel. So knowing the current time didn't make any difference. I couldn't be that far from where we had put our jump line from the main guideline to the halocline tunnel line. It was only about five or six minutes of swimming from the beginning of the main guideline to that point.

I still had air in my tank. I could swim back and find our jump line. Even if I didn't recognize the tunnel, at least that would be familiar. I began to backtrack. I swam faster. I needed to see something familiar. I needed to see something I recognized. I paid more attention to the guideline I was swimming above, only taking my eyes from it for a second or two at a time to look around the cave in hopes of seeing a familiar sight. I didn't see anything I recognized, but I remained above the line.

Then I saw a couple of line arrows on the line. The larger permanent line arrows that marked offshoots from this tunnel. The line arrows were pointing in the direction I was swimming. They were pointing the way that should be heading farther into the cave. But they were supposed to be pointing toward the exit.

Had I turned in the wrong direction at the intersection of the jump line and the main line? Had I gone deeper into the cave instead of out toward the cenote? I could swear I had turned in the right direction. But then why would the arrows be pointing the opposite direction? It didn't make sense.

My training kicked in despite the immense grief I was experiencing. It had been drilled into my head to always trust the line arrows. No matter what your brain tells you, always trust them. Especially the permanent ones. They would always lead you out of the cave. A part of my brain was screaming at me that the arrows were wrong. It was telling me that the direction they were pointing couldn't be the way out. The logical part of my brain was telling me not to listen to the emotional part. It was telling me to follow my training.

I always thought having to trust the line arrows would be an issue I'd face in zero visibility when having to make contact with the guideline and follow it out. I never thought I would be questioning the direction I was traveling with perfect visibility. Visibility in which I could see as far as my light beam allowed.

About three minutes after I turned to swim back, I saw the jump line intersection. It was forty feet ahead of me. The jump line to the left disappearing in the darkness. That was strange. It should be going to the right. It always went to the right. Did someone come in and move the jump line? Did someone use it to go into another tunnel off this main one? Was that even our jump line?

There was another tunnel to the opposite side of the orange line in the main tunnel. It headed away from the halocline tunnel. Did Joey or Gary come out and head in that direction using our jump spool? Why would they do that?

I arrived at the jump line and examined it. It looked just as it had when I last saw it. Could I really have turned in the wrong direction? I decided to turn left and follow the jump line to the spool. I wanted to see if it was still secured to the guideline in the halocline tunnel. I had to see if Joey's and Gary's line markers were still on it.

Less than a minute later I was hovering over the line markers. They were there. The jump spool was secured to the halocline tunnel line. That meant I had somehow turned the wrong way. I had overlooked the two large line arrows on the main guideline on either side of the jump spool line that was secured to it.

I looked at my stage tank pressure gauge again. 900 psi. I thought about continuing back into the halocline tunnel. I thought about trying to find Joey. I wanted to see him again. I wanted to be with him. I couldn't do it though. I wasn't brave enough to commit myself to a certain death, even if it was to be with Joey. I turned around. This time I made contact with the line below me by circling my thumb and forefinger around it. I reasoned that if I was tethered to the line by my arm, it would be more difficult for me to make another mistake navigating out of the cave.

I looked back behind me one last time. The visibility in the halocline tunnel had started to clear. The freshwater and saltwater were separating and getting back onto their respective sides, forming a clear delineation between them. As I was watching the different waters claiming their own domains I saw it. A flash of a light far back in the tunnel. It was brief but I swear it was there. It had to be there. It had to be real. My mind couldn't be fooling me this time.

40

Joey

I opened my eyes briefly every thirty seconds or so to see if the visibility had cleared. It hadn't. It remained blurry so I closed them again. It was much easier to move through the cave without the confusion of the halocline blurriness. I didn't understand why it was so blurry. Why were the freshwater and saltwater layers mixed together ahead of me? I hadn't seen Lindsey in a long time. She had left me a while back. She should be out of the cave.

I tried to look at my pressure gauge, but the water was too blurry to read the small numbers. I couldn't get the gauge close enough to my eyes to make out where the needle was pointing. I continued to swim and focus on my breathing. I focused on skip breathing so I could stretch out the little bit of air I had left in my stage tank. By this point, it had to be well below 300 psi. It might even be below 100 psi. I had no idea if I was going to make it out of the cave. I kept swimming. It was all I could do. It was all I would do.

During one of my cave diving classes, my instructor told me a story of a diver who got lost in a cave and couldn't find his way out.

"Years ago, an instructor was doing the final dive for a cave diving class. They were in Peacock Springs in the Peacock III system in Luraville, Florida. One of his good friends, who was only trained at the intro cave diver level tagged along."

"If he was his buddy, why hadn't he finished his full cave certification yet," I asked.

"Well, you see, he was diving a single tank configuration. He hadn't saved enough money yet to buy double tanks and all the gear that goes along with that."

I nodded.

"So anyways, the intro cave diver was tagging along. Apparently, the cave instructor and his intro cave diver buddy had done full cave dives together before, but it had always just been the two of them. This was the first time the buddy was tagging along with the instructor during class dives."

"Is that allowed?"

"No, not in that way. I could have someone who is qualified to do the dive tag along with us during training, but only if it doesn't upset the student to instructor ratio. But I can't have an intro cave diver tagging along on a full cave diver class, especially if he's only in a single tank. Ya understand?"

"Yessir."

"Now, the instructor did bring along an extra tank, what we call a stage tank. Apparently, he usually did this whenever he and his buddy went on their cave dives together. The stage tank was for the buddy to breathe from whenever they were heading out of the cave. The buddy wasn't used to carrying a stage tank, so the instructor always carried it for him. Besides, it would be against standards for the intro cave diver to be using a stage tank, so the instructor thought by him carrying it, he would still be within the rules."

"But the intro cave diver was still diving beyond his training limits."

"Yes, he was! That's one of the points of this story. The other is that during one of the drills for the class, the instructor was busy paying attention to his student and not his intro buddy. The buddy, probably bored, decided to poke around the cave while he waited and ended up getting too far from the instructor and his student. They got separated. Well, not being trained on how to do any kind of navigation off the main line in a cave and not using a line spool to do his little bit of exploration, he ended up out of the main tunnel, off the main guideline."

"Holy crap!"

"Holy crap is right! Best we could tell, he tried to find his way back, but he kept going farther and farther into the cave and away from the main guideline. And all he had was the one tank on his back. Remember, the instructor had the stage tank for him clipped onto his BC. The instructor looked for his buddy as long as the air he had on him permitted, which wasn't long considering he also had a student with him whose breathing rate was not the greatest. He had to bring his student to the surface and go back in to look for his buddy. He eventually found the intro cave diver buddy, but it was too late."

"Where did he find him?"

"He found him back in some dead-end tunnel. The sad part is the buddy had given up on his search to get out. He was found with his wetnotes out. He had started to write a letter to his parents apologizing for getting himself into that situation and allowing himself to die. It must have taken him a good ten minutes to write that letter. Ten minutes he could have used to keep looking for a way out of that darned cave."

It was a lesson that stuck with me. Never give up. Never give in. Never stop trying. Even when circumstances look completely dire and dismal, keep pushing yourself because it might make all the difference. I didn't know if that intro cave diver would have survived if he hadn't stopped to write a letter to his parents. I did know I wasn't going to stop. I wasn't going to give up. No one was going to find my body with a half written letter in my wetnotes.

I opened my eyes again to see if the visibility had cleared. It didn't look any less blurry, but I thought I saw a light flash ahead. It was difficult to tell through the blurriness. I shielded my light and looked again. All I saw were popping stars as my eyes tried to get accustomed to the darkness.

41

Lindsey

There it was again! Another flash of light. Could that be Joey? Or maybe Gary? Maybe it was both of them. Maybe Joey finally found Gary. Or did Joey decide to turn around and try to make it out? How had he made it this far? There hadn't been much air left in his tanks. He couldn't have enough air to make it out of the cave.

I shielded my light and waited a few more seconds to see if I would see the flash of light again. If it was Joey, I would have to wait for him. There was no way he would make it to the surface without the air in my stage tank. I had to be here for him.

There was one problem. One big problem. My stage tank was the only one with air left in it. I had already breathed my sidemount tanks empty. We would have to buddy breathe from the single regulator on my stage tank. That would complicate things. That would slow us down. It was difficult enough to buddy breathe when you remained in one location facing each other. That was how I taught my open water students. We practiced the skill a couple of times in class for about twenty seconds each time. Then the students did it again during the checkout dives, but usually only for about ten seconds.

That was the extent of most diver's experience with buddy breathing, if they got to experience it at all. It used to be a required skill to learn, but one never utilized. I still taught it because it helped boost confidence. Equipment had come a long way since the open water scuba diver course was created. With the exception of vintage equipment divers, most scuba divers had two second stage regulators on their tanks. This made buddy breathing obsolete. A diver could donate a second stage regulator to an out of air diver, and both divers could breathe from a single tank at the same time.

I saw another flash of light. I shielded my own light to help me see through the darkness.

The problem was when divers moved onto technical diving, the type of diving that required more than one tank and decompression stops, that alternate second stage regulator was placed on a second tank so there was more redundancy. Each tank ended up with one second stage regulator instead of two.

With manifolded backmount tanks, each regulator set was attached to its own tank, but the two tanks were connected through a manifold that allowed the air from both tanks to equalize between each other. Divers sharing air were breathing from two tanks, but the air source was the same, just double the volume.

With sidemounted tanks, the tanks were completely independent of each other. There was no equalization of air between them. Well, except with that manifold system someone created. But that never became popular. Most sidemount divers ridiculed it. It might have been useful in a situation like I found myself in at the moment. Maybe. I wasn't sure how that manifold system worked. Except in this situation, both of my sidemount tanks were empty. And the manifold system didn't include connecting stage tanks to its manifold as well. So even if I had one of those special manifolds, it wouldn't be of any use.

More light in the distance. Could it be Joey?

Buddy breathing was reintroduced in technical dive training courses. It was a mandatory skill. For some, it was the first time buddy breathing since their open water scuba class. For most, it was the first time buddy breathing ever. It was also a required skill for the divemaster course. In that course, not only did we have to buddy breathe, but we had to buddy breathe as we removed our dive equipment and swapped it with our buddy's.

Yes, all of our dive equipment – BC with the tank on it, fins, and mask. I was surprised they didn't also make us strip our wetsuits off and swap those. That would have been quite comical as the person I was partnered with was about twice my size. It would have been very entertaining to watch him try to squeeze into my wetsuit while I was swimming around in his. Literally swimming inside his wetsuit.

We got a lot of practice in divemaster class doing this task. It was probably the one skill we practiced the most, since it was the one skill we were all terrified of failing. We didn't understand why we even had to do it. Why would we ever exchange dive equipment underwater while sharing a single regulator?

As it turns out, it wasn't about the skill itself as much as it was about problem solving and dealing with unusual situations that may present themselves while you were underwater. It was especially important for dive professionals, such as divemasters and instructors to learn because of the unpredictability of the students they might have. Maybe that problem solving skill would get us out of this cave alive.

A quick flash. This time it looked much closer.

During our decompression diving classes, we revisited buddy breathing during decompression stops. The premise was that one of us had lost our decompression oxygen tank, or the regulator was malfunctioning, or all of the oxygen had somehow leaked out. If the decompression obligation was a short one, we could decompress using the air mixture we had in our main tanks. If the decompression obligation was on the long side, or if the water was unusually cold and extending the decompression stop would create higher risk, then it was better to share the decompression tank and buddy breathe.

Buddy breathing involved taking two breaths from the regulator and handing it to your buddy. While your buddy took two breaths, you slowly exhaled your second breath. By that time, your buddy should have been handing back the regulator.

More flashing lights. The light was getting closer. I thought about moving toward it. I didn't. It was better to wait in the clear water. The visibility was too distorted in the halocline tunnel. I waited and watched.

As an open water diver, both divers held onto the regulator together, facing each other, and pushing the regulator back and forth between each other. During decompression dive training, it was handled similarly. During decompression stops you were hovering at a specific depth and when your obligation at that depth was done, you slowly ascended ten feet shallower. Slowly as in an entire minute to ascend those ten feet. So it wasn't much different than what was done in the initial open water scuba class other than being midwater.

That was the only experience Joey had with buddy breathing outside of his initial open water scuba training. During divemaster class, because we had to remove our dive equipment and put on our partner's, it was a little less disciplined. My buddy and I tossed the regulator back and forth to each other. Anyone observing would have thought we were playing a game of catch underwater. We needed both hands to undo the fasteners and straps on the BC and fins and to remove our masks. We needed both hands to put all of our buddy's equipment back on and get it situated properly. Because of this, holding onto the regulator the entire time was out of the question.

The light was no longer flashing. It was almost constant now. Only a few more seconds.

The problem was Joey wasn't a divemaster. He had no experience doing a task-loaded buddy breathing exercise. But that was the only way we were going to make it out of the cave with the little bit of remaining air in my stage tank. We both had to be swimming toward the cenote. We couldn't face each other. Joey would have to be to my left because that was the side my stage tank was on. I would route the hose in front of me instead of around my neck, take two breaths, then hand the regulator to Joey, who would be swimming alongside me to my left. He would take two breaths, then hand it back to me.

We wouldn't be able to look at each other because we would be swimming and have to focus on the tunnel and the guideline leading out. We wouldn't be able to both maintain a grip on the regulator at the same time. We would have to begin the exercise, get a routine established, then start moving.

The light looked like it was only seventy-five feet away.

Before we did any of that, before we could begin sharing air, I had to communicate to Joey that I only had one usable, breathable tank available, and we would have to buddy breathe. The only thing going for us was that there were no single file restrictions between where we were and the cenote. We could remain side by side as we swam out.

All of these thoughts rushed through my mind in a matter of seconds as I kept my light shielded and watched the light from the halocline tunnel coming toward me. That light began moving side to side. It wasn't just moving. It was moving fast. It was Joey. He was sweeping his light rapidly back and forth. I unshielded my light, aimed ahead of me, and returned the signal. I prayed that it was Joey and not my mind playing tricks on me.

As I swept my light back and forth, I pulled my wetnotes out of my thigh pocket with my other hand and flipped them open. I stopped shining my light into the tunnel long enough to jot a note to show Joey.

1 tank left – must buddy breathe

Then I waited. I again considered heading into the tunnel to meet him but thought better of that. The visibility in the halocline tunnel wasn't clear enough. And even if it was, two people in the halocline facing each other trying to communicate would only make the visibility worse. We would have a difficult time seeing each other. It would be almost impossible for Joey to be able to read my note.

So I waited.

Impatiently.

I glanced at my dive computer then at my pressure gauge. The light in the distance disappeared. The tunnel turned black. Had he breathed through the last of his air? Had he drowned only fifty feet away from me? Did I just kill Joey by not going to meet him?

42

Joey

My eyes finally adjusted to the darkness. Or at least, the small pops of light I was seeing had decreased enough so I knew the lights were being created by my eyes and not dive lights in the distance. I kept my light shielded, though. Maybe Lindsey was also shielding her light looking for me.

If she was looking for me, maybe I should unshield my light and point it directly in front of me. Rapidly sweep it back and forth to try to get her attention. I gave it a few more seconds. After not seeing anything definitive, I closed my eyes to not eliminate the adjustment to the dark they had just made and unshielded my light. I rapidly swept the beam back and forth a few times. I shielded it again and opened my eyes.

A few seconds passed and then I saw it. I distinctly saw a light moving back and forth. It was faint. It looked far away. But it was there. I picked up my pace and swam toward it as fast as I could. It had to be Lindsey. If it wasn't her, it would at least be another diver. Hopefully a diver with lots of air.

I swam as fast as I could. I no longer cared about conserving the air I had left in my stage tank. There was someone ahead that had more air. Air I could breathe to get out of the cave. Air I could use to keep myself alive.

I gave up on doing the modified frog kick, a finning technique we were taught at the cavern diver level to minimize disturbing the silt found on the floors of most caves. A modified frog kick involved bending our knees so our feet were above them and clapping the bottom of our fins together. Sort of. We didn't actually clap our way along. It would be annoying to hear a bunch of clapping as we swam through the cave. The fin bottoms never touched each other. But the motion directed the force of the fins and the water they moved into each other and back behind us rather than down. This meant visibility in the cave was preserved because the fin movement didn't disturb the silty floor. It was an efficient kick when done while slowly moving through a cave taking in the sights around you. But it wasn't moving me fast enough.

I reverted to the flutter kick, which was the finning technique I learned in my open water scuba class. I just moved my fins up and down, much like swimmers do with their legs on the surface. This allowed me to do more kick cycles, and hopefully to get to the diver I had just seen much more quickly. Hopefully, it would get me to the diver before he or she left.

It meant my breathing rate was going to increase. The air in my tank would be used up much more quickly. But there was another diver ahead. A diver with more air I could breathe.

I tried to fin faster. I was getting tired. I was getting out of breath. It was getting more difficult to breathe.

Then, just as suddenly as it had appeared, the light in front of me disappeared.

Wait!!!

Come back! Don't leave me!

Did the diver take off? Did I just breathe through the little air I had left only to be abandoned by what I thought was going to be the thing that got me out alive?

I stopped and tried to regain control of my breathing. I tried to hold my breath between inhalations and exhalations. I couldn't hold it very long. My lungs were aching for air. My muscles were starving for oxygen. It was getting harder to pull a breath from the regulator. I grabbed the pressure gauge and looked at it. I could finally see the face of the gauge and the numbers along the perimeter. The needle was on the zero. After all this effort, I was about to drown. So close to the exit, yet too far to make a difference.

43

Lindsey

The light reappeared a moment later. I let out the breath I didn't realize I was holding. I watched as the light appeared to be moving closer. It was difficult to tell through the blurriness of the halocline. At times it looked like it was getting brighter. Other times it almost disappeared completely. I kept shaking my head to make sure I wasn't staring too hard and seeing things that weren't there.

Then the light stopped moving completely. It was still too blurry to see anything but the light. I also couldn't tell exactly how far it was. Maybe forty feet. Maybe a little less. Why wasn't he moving??

I waited a few seconds longer, hoping to see the light begin to move again. The anticipation was too much. When it didn't move, I decided to swim in toward it. Bad visibility or not, I had to find out what was going on. I formed a circle around the line with my thumb and forefinger and began swimming toward the light as quickly as I could. It shouldn't take more than a minute to close the distance between us. I held onto my wetnotes with my left hand as tightly as I could. If Joey was out of air, would I make it to him in time? Or would I find him unconscious?

Drowned?

Dead?

No! He couldn't be dead. I swam even harder, faster, trying to cut the time to get to him to only seconds. I felt the sharp coral growths on the guideline as it quickly glided by in between my fingers. The hard, sharp coral that had started to grow along it was slicing into the soft skin on my palm, creating razor thin cuts. It felt like I was getting a million paper cuts at once. The saltwater burned as it penetrated into the newly formed lacerations.

The back side of my hand was scraping against the hard, uneven limestone wall that was just to the right of the guideline. There were several areas where the line was up against the wall. I tried to pull it away from the wall to minimize the scraping, but there was too much resistance. This was the thicker, yellow line that lacked elasticity. It was pulled too tightly between the tie-offs. Pulling it toward me only caused the coral growth to cut even deeper into my palm.

I took my chances and let go of the line. I just swam toward the light. The irony of that struck me. And made me sad. I pushed the thought out of my head. The only light we would be swimming toward would be the sunlight penetrating through the surface of the cenote into the cave. I had to make it to Joey.

The light was getting brighter, closer. I couldn't be more than thirty feet away from it. If it wasn't for the light shining toward me, I could probably see Joey's outline, even through the blurriness.

Twenty-five feet to go.

I could see the light moving. It wasn't moving toward me. Just moving around in place. That meant Joey had to still be alive and breathing.

Twenty feet.

Unless it was the current moving the light. No, it wasn't random motion. It had to be Joey.

Fifteen feet.

Almost there. I kicked harder and grabbed onto the wall next to me to help pull and push myself faster. I felt the sharp edges of the rock poking into my palm, creating a burning sensation in the lacerations made by the coral. I didn't care. Those would heal.

Ten feet.

I could finally see Joey through the blurriness and the light. He was looking at his pressure gauge. I didn't see any bubbles coming from his regulator. I watched intently, hoping to see some sign that he was still breathing.

Five feet.

I could almost touch him. He was looking at me. I couldn't see the expression on his face. It was much too blurry for that. But I could tell he was looking at me. Or at least he was looking toward me. I reached out and grabbed Joey's arm with my left hand, the wetnotes squeezed between my fingers and his forearm. I reached for the regulator in my mouth, ripped it out, and thrust it toward Joey. I watched as he spit his own regulator out and heard the air rushing through the hose routed next to my left ear as he took a breath. I slowly blew tiny bubbles through my pursed lips so I wouldn't be holding my breath. Not a full exhalation. Just enough, as if I was blowing through one of those tiny straws used to stir coffee.

With my right hand, I reached for the wetnotes in my left hand. I didn't want to let go of Joey's arm. The hose tethering us to each other was only forty inches long. If we moved too abruptly the regulator at the end of it that he was breathing from could get ripped from his mouth. I shoved the wetnotes in front of Joey's mask, hoping the water was clear enough for him to read what I had written. He must know I needed the regulator back because he could see I didn't have one in my mouth. Was that registering in his mind. Did he realize I didn't have a regulator in my mouth?

I continued to blow out small bubbles as Joey looked at my note, as he processed what I had written. I was nearing the end of the air I had in my lungs. In a few seconds I would have to hold my breath.

Then maybe thirty seconds after that I would drown. Maybe sixty seconds.

I had done some breath hold diving before and could usually only hold my breath for about half a minute. I practiced it over and over and my time had increased. My best time was forty-five seconds. But that was months ago, almost a year. I wished I had kept up with it. Being able to hold my breath longer would have been useful now.

There were breath hold divers that could hold their breath for several minutes. The world record was something like twenty-four and a half minutes. I didn't quite understand how that was possible. I knew he had breathed pure oxygen prior to the attempt. It was also a static breath hold, meaning he was floating at the surface in place, not exerting himself. It still seemed impossible.

The records for exertional breath hold diving were much more reasonable, but still far out of my reach. And without any practice in almost a year, I doubted I could hold my breath very long. The only thing that might help prolong it was the adrenaline I was feeling and knowing that when I could no longer hold my breath, death would be certain.

Fortunately, it didn't come to that. Joey must have been able to read my note. He must have understood. He pushed the wetnotes aside and I let them drop to the floor of the cave below us. I wouldn't need to write anything else to him. We didn't have time for any more notes. Joey grabbed the regulator hose. He thrust it back in front of me, directly in front of my mouth. I quickly grabbed it back and took a couple of shallow breaths. I needed just enough to refresh the oxygen in my lungs. I knew the air pressure in the tank was low. It wasn't going to last long, especially with two people breathing from it.

I pushed the regulator back toward Joey. He pushed it back at me and tried to back away. I tightened my grip on his arm and held onto him. I pushed the regulator toward him even harder. He couldn't refuse it. I wouldn't let him.

We remained in the blurry halocline, face to face, in a standoff. Joey had to give in. I couldn't watch him die. And I wasn't going to take the regulator back until he took a breath. He was being obstinate. I didn't know what to do.

44

Joey

I continued to stare at my pressure gauge, willing the needle to move. Thinking somehow it would pop up a few hundred psi. Just enough to get me out of the cave.

It didn't move.

I saw a flash of light ahead again. It was much closer this time. And it looked like it was moving toward me. Apparently, Lindsey, or whoever had been at the end of the tunnel, hadn't left. The light must have been pointed in another direction and I couldn't see it through the bad visibility. I looked at my pressure gauge. Still on the zero. I tentatively took another breath. It was hard to pull air through the regulator, but I still got a breath.

The light coming toward me was getting closer, moving faster. I looked back at the pressure gauge. Still no change. Then the light was directly in front of me. It was Lindsey! She grabbed my arm with a death grip. I had never felt her hold me so tightly. I didn't think she was that strong. She shoved her regulator in front of my face. She was donating air. Somehow she knew I was almost out of air. I spit my regulator out, letting it drop below me and took her regulator. I took a deep breath. It came easily and filled my lungs.

I looked at Lindsey and noticed she didn't have a regulator in her mouth. I knew she had donated the regulator she had been breathing from, but she should have replaced it with one of her other regulators. She should have a regulator in her mouth to breathe from. Yet, she didn't.

Lindsey shoved her wetnotes in front of my mask. I tried to make out the writing on the page through the blurry water. I moved my face closer to the notes to try to make the letters on the paper clear but then I had no light on them. I pushed them back a couple of inches so I could shine my light on them. Then I saw it.

must buddy breathe

Three words.

This had to be Lindsey's stage tank. Her sidemount tanks were empty. Just like mine. I wondered how much air she had left in her stage tank. Would it be enough for both of us? Was there enough air in it to get both of us back to the surface?

I doubted it.

I didn't know if she even had enough for one of us to make it out of the cave. Why would she do this? Why would she come back if she knew it meant both of us would die in this cave?

I pushed the wetnotes aside and grabbed the regulator. I handed it to Lindsey and watched her take a couple of quick breaths. There was no way we would make it out of here both breathing from that one tank. I thought about trying to look at the pressure gauge to see how much air was left, but it would be difficult to do that. The pressure gauge was on the end of a six-inch long hose that was attached to the first stage regulator that was screwed into the tank valve. The gauge was directed down alongside the body of the tank, which was positioned on top of Lindsey's left sidemount tank. I would have to practically climb on top of her to get close enough in this halocline to see the small needle and numbers on the gauge. In the process, I would disturb the visibility even more and not be able to see anything.

I decided I wouldn't take the regulator back. Lindsey needed to get out of here. She needed to go. She needed to leave me behind. Only one of us could be saved and it should be her.

Lindsey pulled the regulator out of her mouth and pushed it toward me. I pushed it back. She pushed it toward me even harder. How was I going to communicate to her that she had to leave me and just go? What could I do to convince her?

I didn't want her to watch me drown. I didn't want her to try to drag my body out of here. I had experience doing that a few years earlier when I found that dead body beyond the grate. I was a new diver then, but I didn't imagine it would be any easier three years later, even with all the experience I had gained as a cave diver in that time. I also didn't know the diver. I didn't know the person. He was an inanimate object to me. It would be much more difficult to have to drag out of a cave the body of someone you knew, someone you loved.

Lindsey didn't take the regulator. I didn't want to take the regulator. I didn't know what to do. How could I convince her?

My lungs were starting to hurt. I could feel a burning deep inside my chest. I wasn't going to be able to hold my breath for much longer. I didn't want Lindsey to watch me drown, but she wouldn't leave. I tried pushing the regulator back toward her. Her arm was extended, and her elbow was locked. She was holding onto my right arm tightly. I couldn't push her hand away and I couldn't push her away.

I finally gave in. I needed a minute to sort things out and devise a plan. I needed to figure out how to get her away from me so she didn't have to watch me die. I took a breath. The burning in my lungs immediately subsided. I pushed the regulator back toward Lindsey as I slowly blew small bubbles through my lips.

We had to start moving. Remaining in this location wasn't going to get either one of us out of the cave. I reached for Lindsey's BC with my right hand to try to get her to rotate so we could begin our swim out. Maybe I could figure out a way to get her to continue without me before we breathed through too much of the air left in her stage tank.

Lindsey rotated herself so she was to my right. This was going to be interesting. I had only buddy breathed twice before. I did it once in my open water class and another time in my decompression diving class. Both times we were face to face. In the open water class, we remained stationary, kneeling on the bottom of the pool. In the decompression diving class, we did it during a simulated decompression stop. The only movement we made was when we ascended to the next shallower stop depth. We remained facing each other.

In my cave diving class, we discussed the possibility of buddy breathing, but we never practiced it. The discussion was mainly focused on drilling into our heads how important it was to always have enough air in our tanks to get out of the cave. Buddy breathing would be possible but very difficult to do while moving and would likely prolong our exit.

Yet, here I was with Lindsey having to buddy breathe from her stage tank side by side while swimming out of the cave. To make things even more interesting, we were in a narrow tunnel swimming through a halocline that had caused the visibility to be so blurry we could hardly see each other.

We were both going to die.

45

Lindsey

Thankfully Joey finally accepted the regulator and took a breath. He handed the regulator back to me and grabbed my BC. He started pulling me to his right while also rotating my body. He was ready to begin swimming out. I wasn't sure I liked this. I knew we had to get out, but I also wanted to keep an eye on him to make sure he was still breathing. That would be difficult to do in the diminished visibility while side by side.

I reluctantly moved myself to Joey's right and we began to swim. We moved forward for a few seconds before getting wedged shoulder to shoulder between the walls. I moved up slightly so I was hovering just above Joey's right side, and we squeezed through the narrow area. The guideline was adjacent to the left wall, so Joey was the one who had to remain in contact with it. The visibility was too poor for me to see it. I had to trust him to not lose sight or feel of it.

Putting that trust in him wasn't a big deal. Not after risking my life by swimming back into the halocline tunnel to help him. The people who said one fatality was better than two when it comes to cave diving were never in a situation like Joey and I were in. At least Joey and I were together.

We came to another narrow area in the tunnel, and I had to ascend above Joey again. We didn't have far to go before we broke out into the main tunnel, where it was thirty or forty feet wide and the visibility was back to normal. If we kept having to slow down to negotiate these narrow areas, we wouldn't make it there with enough air to get out.

I decided to remain above Joey. Then an idea came to me. I could swim above him, holding onto his shoulders and sharing my stage tank regulator over his left shoulder. The tunnel we were in was tall enough to accommodate this. Swimming out in this manner would remove the issue of the narrow sections of the tunnel and allow me to keep an eye on Joey to make sure he was breathing from the regulator and not just taking hold of it to appease me.

I shifted to my left and grabbed Joey's right shoulder. After taking a breath, I handed him the regulator over his left shoulder, positioning it in front of his mask so he would know to expect it from that side instead of from his right like we had been doing when I was next to him. Joey took the regulator and took a breath. He handed the regulator back to me and I watched small bubbles escape around his head as we continued to move toward the main tunnel of the cave.

The rest of the swim in the halocline tunnel went much more smoothly and quickly than it had initially gone. We had only moved about forty feet, but it seemed like four hundred. We made it to the end of the permanent line. I could finally see more than just a few inches in front of me. And there was room for us to be side by side again. I decided to remain above Joey. From that position, I could watch him.

Joey hesitated when we got to the jump spool. I looked at the line and saw our three line markers lined up next to the spool. I watched as Joey pulled two of them off. He handed one to me. He then touched the remaining line marker. Gary's line marker. I watched him close his hand over it and squeeze it tightly. A few seconds later, he pushed off the rock toward the main guideline about forty feet away.

We cut the corner toward the left. I recalled going to the right only minutes earlier when I was by myself. I didn't know why I had done that, why I had gone that way. I knew the exit was to the left. I knew the way out of the cave. I was thankful I had gone that way, though. If I hadn't, I wouldn't have turned around and I wouldn't have found Joey coming out. I wouldn't have been able to help him. He would have died in the halocline tunnel. A higher force must have made me do it. That force made me go right so I would have to turn back. It made me be here for Joey. Maybe I was supposed to sacrifice myself for Joey.

A few seconds later the orange guideline was to our right. A few feet ahead the ceiling dipped down right above the line. The passage was too low there for us to remain in the position we were in. Either Joey would have to swim around the ceiling dip to the left or I would have to reposition myself to his right. I didn't want to move. I liked being above him, watching him, holding onto him. It was comforting. It was nice. It was the way I wanted to spend my last moments with him.

Joey kept swimming along the orange guideline. I didn't know if he had noticed the ceiling dipping down or if the thought had occurred to him that we wouldn't fit under it in the profile we were in. I tried to push him to the left so we could go around the ceiling dip. Joey shifted slightly but not enough to avoid it. I pushed harder. If he didn't adjust his course of travel in the next couple of seconds I was going to swim right into the ceiling.

I pushed again but Joey didn't respond. He kept swimming straight for the ceiling dip.

46

Joey

We started swimming out of the halocline tunnel. The narrow tunnel became narrower, and Lindsey was forced to move above me for us to be able to pass through. After getting past that section, she moved back to my right side. A few seconds later, we encountered another narrow segment of the tunnel. Lindsey moved again.

Then I felt Lindsey's hand on my right shoulder and saw the regulator appear in front of my face from my left. It seemed she was going to stay above me for the exit. That was probably for the best. It would have taken us far too long to exit this tunnel if we kept having to slow down every time the walls squeezed in.

We finally arrived at the jump spool. The three line markers were there. Gary was still somewhere behind us. He was most certainly dead at this point. I removed Lindsey's and my line markers and handed hers up. I felt her grab it from my hand. I tucked mine into the sleeve of my wetsuit. There was too much going on to properly stow it away on the pigtail holder in my pocket.

I placed my hand on Gary's line marker. I had no intention of removing it. He was still in the cave somewhere. The line marker would remain in his memory. I knew it would eventually be removed, probably in the next day or two when his body was found. But for now it would stay. I squeezed my hand around the marker until I felt its edges digging into my palm. I felt the edges creating an indentation on my hand. I felt a tear escape my eye.

I pushed off the wall to my left at an angle toward the main line so I could cut the corner again. Even though the cave from this point on was wide enough to accommodate Lindsey and me side by side, she remained positioned above me. It didn't matter where she was. It made no difference. Her position above me made it easier to buddy breathe, but the air wouldn't last. I wondered how much air she had left in her tank. I wondered how much farther we would get before the air was completely depleted. I wondered what it would feel like to breathe water and drown.

I saw the ceiling dip ahead next to the line. The space below it was not tall enough for us to get through stacked like we were. It only dipped in that one area near the line. I wondered why the line had been placed there instead of routing it around the dip.

Then an idea came to me. I continued to swim directly toward the dip. I felt Lindsey push on my shoulder to the left. She wanted me to swim around the dip. I moved slightly but not enough to completely avoid it. She pushed harder. I stayed the course. I knew that once I got to the dip Lindsey would be forced to let go of me and move to the side or behind me. That would be my chance to take off. That would be my chance to save her life by letting her have the rest of the air in her stage tank. There was no way we were both going to make it out of this cave alive. I had to give her a fighting chance.

I swam directly for the dip. I finned harder, faster. I wanted to create some momentum so I could get Lindsey away from me and I would have enough time to get away from her before I drowned. There was an offshoot to the right just after the ceiling dip. I had noticed it the day before. I pictured the maps in my head and saw the outline of the tunnel. There were more offshoots off that tunnel not too far from the main tunnel. And then more offshoots after that. It would be easy to get lost in there. I hoped Lindsey wouldn't follow. I had to get enough momentum to get in there and lose her. If she did follow me, it wouldn't matter if she had her stage tank all to herself. She would breathe the air in it before being able to make it out of the cave.

I began having doubts about my plan. If Lindsey followed me in there she would die. Maybe my plan wasn't so great after all. I tried to stop before I got to the dip. I was too close, though. I was only a couple of feet from it and moving much too fast. I felt Lindsey's hand slide off my shoulder. I felt her grab onto my BC and tug back on it. I felt her grip on me release. I coasted under the dip and came out on the other side of it. I watched the beam from Lindsey's light get dim as my actions put distance between us. I stopped and rotated so I was facing Lindsey. She was under the ceiling dip holding her head with her right hand and the regulator with her left hand.

What had I done? Had I caused Lindsey to slam her head on the ceiling? Had I hurt her? Was she going to pass out because of my thoughtless actions? The thought of escaping her quickly vanished. I swam back to Lindsey, reaching her in only a couple of seconds. I grabbed her left hand and pushed the regulator in front of her mouth. Lindsey seemed fazed. She seemed confused. How hard had she hit her head?

After a few seconds Lindsey finally took a breath from the regulator. A feeling of relief washed over my body. A new sense of survival overcame me. We had to figure out a way for both of us to get out of this cave alive.

47

Lindsey

My head slammed against the ceiling. I immediately saw a burst of lights in front of me. Only the lights weren't in the cave. They were in my head. I had just taken a breath and was in the middle of handing the regulator back to Joey. It was still in my left hand.

Why did Joey suddenly take off like that? I grabbed his harness and tried to pull him back. He moved faster. And then I hit my head. I looked at my hand and saw the regulator again. I couldn't think of what to do with it. I placed my right hand over my head where I had just hit it on the ceiling and hovered in place, dazed. Suddenly, I saw a very bright light in front of me. I shook my head but that only caused the pain to intensify. The light seemed to get brighter. I realized this light wasn't in my head. It was Joey's light. He was coming toward me. He was coming back.

Had he done that intentionally? Did he not realize the ceiling dipped there? Why did he start to swim faster as we got closer to it? I tried to react, but it was too late. I slid my hand down his back, grabbed onto his BC, and tried to stop him. Then I felt my head slam against the ceiling. I thought I was going to pass out.

I started to do something, but I wasn't sure what to do. Then Joey grabbed my hand and pushed the regulator against my lips. I tried to push it back, but I was too weak. I felt my lungs begin to burn. I realized I had been holding my breath and I needed to take another breath. I scrambled to get the regulator into my mouth so I could breathe. The burning in my lungs subsided as the air rushed past my vocal cords. My thoughts became clearer. How long had I been holding my breath?

I handed the regulator back to Joey and watched as he breathed from it. He handed it back to me and then moved toward me and slightly above. I didn't know what he was doing. We should be getting out of here. I felt Joey grab something above me. It felt like he was trying to remove my stage tank. Was he trying to take it from me? This was the only air we had left. Why would he take it?

Was he trying to take it and leave me for dead? I started to struggle against him. I tried to get away. He couldn't have my stage tank. I was fine with sharing the air with him, but he couldn't have it all to himself. I tried to push Joey away from me, but he didn't budge. I felt him moving the stage tank even more. I reached down to the bolt snap on my waist D ring that was holding the bottom of the stage tank against me. Joey would have to get underneath me to let that loose. That's when I could get away from him. Underneath me he would be vulnerable.

Only he didn't move underneath me. Instead, he moved back away from me. I was moving with him. Joey was holding onto my BC and pulling me with him. He wasn't trying to get away from me with my tank. Maybe he wasn't going to leave me for dead. I was so confused.

I saw Joey's left hand move in front of my face. He was holding it open as if expecting me to hand him something. I had no idea what he wanted. Then I felt him tugging on the hose of the regulator in my mouth. He was trying to steal my regulator. No, that wasn't right. Joey wouldn't do that. He just needed to take a breath. How long had I had the regulator? How many breaths had I taken?

I removed the regulator from my mouth and cautiously handed it to Joey. I was suspicious of his intentions. I wasn't sure why. Joey had never done anything to me to cause me to think he would want me dead. For some reason, I couldn't help but have those thoughts. I tried to rationalize them away, but they wouldn't leave. Something was wrong.

A couple of seconds later the regulator was back in front of my face. Joey must have taken a breath. He was giving it back to me. I grabbed the regulator and took another breath. Then another. This time I remembered to hand it back to Joey. Something wasn't right in my head, but I knew I had to trust him. He refused to take it. I held it out for him for several more seconds until my lungs started to burn again. I took a third breath to relieve the pain. I gave the regulator back to Joey. This time he took it.

I looked around the cave. None of it looked familiar. Was Joey leading me out of the cave? Or were we heading back to look for Gary again?

Gary! Where was Gary? I couldn't remember the last time I had seen him. We needed to go back and look for Gary!

I tried to get Joey's attention to let him know we had forgotten Gary. Joey ignored me. He kept swimming. He pulled me along beneath him. Maybe we were already going to get Gary. I looked around the cave again. I still had no clue where we were. I looked at the orange guideline below us. It looked familiar but I couldn't place it. What was happening to me? Why couldn't I remember anything?

48

Joey

I quickly ascended above Lindsey. I had to see how much air was left in her stage tank. I had to know if there was a chance for us to get out of the cave alive. Once above her, I pulled at the stage tank to get to the gauge. The tank was rotated so the valve opening was pointing forward toward Lindsey's back. That made it easier for her to reach back and pull the pressure gauge forward to see it, but it made it more difficult for me to get to it from above her.

I rotated the stage tank counterclockwise, bringing the pressure gauge around so it was facing me. I looked at the position of the needle. I blinked a couple of times to make sure my eyes weren't deceiving me. I refocused on the needle.

500 psi.

That was all the air we had left between the two of us. 500 psi.

I might have been able to get back to the surface with that much air. I might even have been able to do it with 400 psi. But there were two of us. Lindsey didn't breathe as much as I did, but she would still need at least half of that 500 psi to get out of the cave. Probably more than half.

We had to be at least 200 psi short of what it would take. We would be those cave divers whose bodies were found less than one hundred feet from the opening. Lifeless. Why hadn't I stuck to the plan? Why had I insisted on looking beyond the next corner?

I pushed those thoughts aside and focused on what had to be done. The longer we remained where we were the more certain our deaths would be. I wasn't ready to give up quite yet. I felt the burning in my lungs returning. Lindsey still had the regulator in her mouth. I moved my open hand in front of her face and waited for her to place the regulator in it. She didn't move. I gently tugged on the hose to communicate to her that I needed to take a breath.

Lindsey slowly removed the regulator from her mouth and placed it in my hand. It almost seemed like she didn't want to give it to me. I rapidly drew it to my mouth before she changed her mind and pressed the purge button just enough to clear the water out of it before taking a breath. I felt the burning subside. I took a second breath.

As much as I wanted to take in a full breath and fill my lungs to capacity, I didn't do that. I kept the breaths shallow. There was only 500 psi left and more than five hundred feet to travel before we could make it to the surface. I gave the regulator back to Lindsey and watched her place it in her mouth and take a breath. I dragged Lindsey along below me as I continued to swim toward the opening. I checked the pressure gauge again.

400 psi.

The air was going fast. We weren't going to make it.

Lindsey pulled the regulator out of her mouth and tried to give it to me. I pushed it back toward her and continued to hold my breath. My lungs were beginning to burn, but I had to try to conserve our air. I had to try to get us to the surface before the tank ran empty.

Lindsey continued holding the regulator out for me. Finally, she took it back and took a quick breath before trying to give it back to me. I took it. My lungs were burning too much. The drive to breathe was getting too intense. I wasn't going to be able to hold my breath for much longer than a few more seconds.

This time I took a full breath. I couldn't stop myself halfway like I was able to the last time. My lungs needed the air too much. My muscles needed oxygen. I started to feel lightheaded. I also started to feel pain in my head. This time it wasn't over the goose egg that had formed at the top of my forehead. This had to be from skip breathing.

That meant the carbon dioxide level in my blood was increasing. That meant the drive to breathe would also increase. I wanted to take a second breath, but I resisted the urge. Instead, I gave the regulator back to Lindsey.

I looked ahead and could see a large mound rising off the floor about fifty feet ahead. We were so close. The beginning of the guideline was less than a hundred feet from that mound. Then we only had another two hundred and fifty feet or so to the cenote.

Two hundred and fifty feet. It might as well have been a mile.

49

Lindsey

The fuzziness started to fade away. I began to recognize the cave around us. I remembered hitting my head hard on the ceiling. Joey swam so fast, and I was holding onto him for dear life. When my head smacked into the ceiling, I felt the darkness closing in on me.

Suddenly, what was happening to us came rushing back in. Joey and I were breathing from one tank. Buddy breathing from that tank while having to swim out of the cave. How far were we from the opening? How much air did we have left?

The regulator appeared in front of my mask from above. I hadn't realized I didn't have it and that I was holding my breath. I took the regulator from Joey and exhaled the air I was holding. I took another lungful of air from the tank. I handed the regulator back to Joey. I looked around the cave and tried to orient myself to our location. It didn't look familiar. Nothing looked right. Had I hit my head that hard?

I watched the brittle sea stars scattered about the floor, retracting into their holes as we passed over them. There seemed to be dozens of them. There was only one place in the cave that I knew had so many in one area. That was not very far from the opening, near the beginning of the guideline. But this tunnel didn't look familiar. Things didn't look right.

I continued to sweep my light beam around the cave trying to find a familiar sight. A familiar formation. I looked for anything I could recognize. A large mound came into view ahead just inside the top boundary of my light beam. I moved my light up and watched as the mound became illuminated and came into view. I finally recognized something. We were almost back to the beginning of the guideline. We were almost out of the cave.

The regulator appeared in my view again. It hadn't been very long since I handed it to Joey. Why was he giving it back so soon? Had he even taken a breath? I started to push it back toward him but changed my mind. I could feel my lungs beginning to burn again. I needed to take another breath. I took a quick breath and handed the regulator back. I felt Joey push it back down.

Why wasn't he taking it?

Suddenly, my vision became blurry. We had just passed over the mound I had seen and were moving over it when I could no longer see clearly. I worried that I was about to pass out. I must have hit my head hard. I couldn't recognize anything. I was having trouble remembering what was going on. And my vision was no longer clear. I began to doubt whether I would make it out of the cave alive. I was going to lose consciousness and drown. I thought about Joey having to drag my lifeless body the last remaining bit through the cave and to the surface.

No! I couldn't let that happen! I couldn't die like this and leave him alone. I concentrated on clearing my vision. I blinked my eyes several times to try to shake the blurriness out of them. I shook my head back and forth. Nothing was helping. I couldn't even see the guideline. I didn't know if it was below us or next to us. If it wasn't for Joey, I probably would have drowned by this time.

I realized I still had the regulator in my mouth. If I was going to pass out, I'd rather Joey have the regulator. It would fall out of my mouth when I lost consciousness. I pulled it away from my mouth and held it over my head. I expected Joey to refuse it again. Only this time, he didn't. He took the regulator, and I heard the air rush through the first stage that was positioned just above my left ear.

Then just as suddenly as my vision had become blurry, it cleared. We were descending on the other side of the mound, and I realized we had just gone through the halocline again. How could I have forgotten about that short stretch of halocline we had to swim through? We should be seeing our primary reel in a few seconds. We only had another three hundred feet to go before we were at the surface.

The regulator appeared back in front of me. My lungs weren't hurting that badly yet, so I refused it. Joey held it in place in front of my face. I wondered how much air was in the tank. I thought about checking the pressure gauge but decided against it. What was the point in knowing? It wouldn't change anything. Either we had enough to make it to the surface, or we didn't. Neither of us was going to leave the other in the cave to save ourselves. No point in looking at the gauge. It was better to keep focused on swimming out. It was better not knowing. Knowing would only cause anxiety. I had to believe we had enough air in that tank to get us both to the surface.

With a renewed determination, I began to kick faster and harder. We had to make it to the surface. We had made it too far to not make it to the surface. I took a quick breath from the regulator and handed it back to Joey. We swam around a bend in the wall and the primary reel came into view fifteen feet ahead. There were still three line markers on the line. I told myself that didn't mean anything. I wasn't planning on retrieving my line marker. My focus was on making it to the surface. Hopefully, Joey was thinking the same thing.

As we approached the primary reel, I extended my right arm out and brushed the palm of my hand across the three markers. I felt the hard edges of the markers skip over the lacerations from the coral on my palm. I didn't pull away. I felt as each of the three markers skipped over the cuts. The pain made me feel more alive. The pain also

represented what I felt at the loss of Gary.
Then I felt Joey pulling back on me.

50

Joey

I saw the primary reel come into view as we rounded that last bend with the orange guideline below us. I had never been so happy to see it at the end of a dive as I was at that moment. Usually I hated to end our dives. I could stay in the caves forever if I had gills. But our limited air supply meant we had to surface at some point. Lindsey held the regulator above her head for me to take a breath.

We usually exited the cave with a lot of air remaining in our tanks. The past couple of days we had been surfacing with 1200 to 1300 psi in each one. That was more than the third we kept in reserves. It seemed we always used less air during the exit than we did during the penetration part of the dive. It was probably the excitement of heading into the cave versus the sadness of having to exit the cave.

I took a breath and passed the regulator back to Lindsey.

I was never happy exiting with so much air. That was almost half of the air that each tank could hold. We could have stayed another five to ten minutes each time. Maybe longer. We always turned at our agreed upon air pressure, but I didn't understand why we couldn't push it another hundred or two hundred psi if we were coming out with so much extra air.

Lindsey passed the regulator back to me.

Lindsey wouldn't budge on the plan. She insisted we turn at the more conservative air pressure. At the moment, I was wishing we had done that on this dive. I wished we had been even more conservative. I finally understood.

I watched as Lindsey reached out for the line markers. I glanced at the pressure gauge. Only 200 psi left in her stage tank. We didn't have time to retrieve our markers. Even a couple of seconds of delay could mean the difference between life and death.

I passed the regulator back to Lindsey. This time she didn't take it. She was too focused on the line markers. I pulled at Lindsey's BC as I reached out to swat her hand away from her marker. Just as my hand was about to touch hers, I noticed she wasn't trying to remove her marker. She was just brushing her hand along all three markers as we went by them. The visibility turned blurry again, this time because of the tears that were welling up in my eyes.

I felt the regulator being pulled from my hand.

We continued past the reel and markers, around the next wall to the right, heading for the natural bridge over the stop sign. We weren't that far from the opening. We would begin to see thin rays of sunlight penetrating into the darkness of the cave. As my vision cleared, I saw the regulator in front of my face again. I grabbed it and took a shallow breath.

Lindsey and I had developed a rhythm in our buddy breathing. I was no longer thinking about it as we passed the regulator back and forth. It hadn't taken long for me to build muscle memory of the movements required to buddy breathe as we were quickly moving through the cave, desperately trying to make it to the surface before we breathed the last of the air from Lindsey's stage tank.

I passed the regulator back to Lindsey.

I looked at the pressure gauge again. The needle had dropped below 100 psi. I glanced down at the top of the stop sign that came into view as we swam over the natural bridge. We were still about two hundred feet from the cenote. Two hundred feet from being able to surface and not rely on pressurized air inside of an aluminum can.

The regulator reappeared in front of my face.

Less than 100 psi.

Two hundred feet to go.

Two people needing that air to survive.

We weren't going to make it.

51

Lindsey

My palm slipped past the last marker. I felt it slipping away along with my hopes of finding Gary alive. We had tried everything we could. We had spent far more time in the cave looking for him than we should have. We had risked our lives. I still wasn't sure whether we would make it to the surface before breathing the stage tank empty. I was surprised every time I took a breath and the regulator delivered. I didn't know how Joey and I had been able to make the little air that was left in my stage tank last this long.

We were almost three hundred feet from the cenote. We still might not make it. I remembered hearing a story about a cave diver in Florida who had been doing a solo cave exploration and survey dive. He failed to resurface from the cave. The next day, a diver went into the cave to search for his body. It was a small cave with low ceilings. While body recoveries are usually done by teams of divers, that body recovery was best done by a single diver because of the restrictive tunnels of the cave. It was safer done alone.

The body was found three hundred feet from the opening.

Three hundred feet.

That was about how far we were from the opening.

They say it looked like he was darting for the exit. His arms were extended in front of his body. Both of his tanks were empty.

Would that be how Joey and I were found? Less than three hundred feet from the opening, maybe only one hundred feet, rushing to try to get to the surface.

I passed the regulator back to Joey.

We swam over the natural bridge. We still had about four minutes to go until we could begin our ascent.

Four minutes.

It didn't seem like a long time. It also seemed like forever.

Would we make it? Would we be able to stretch out the small amount of air left in that one tank long enough to get to the surface?

I wanted to look at the pressure gauge. I wanted to know how much air we had left. I wanted to know if I should take a breath from the regulator when Joey passed it back to me or if I should refuse it. Joey wouldn't let me refuse it though.

Maybe I could fake taking a breath. That likely wouldn't work. Joey wouldn't see bubbles coming from me and he would know. I would need to take a small breath so I could have some air in my lungs to blow out. Or I could just take a breath of water right this minute. Open my mouth and inhale deeply. The suffering should be minimal and short-lived. I'd feel my lungs burning for a moment and then hopefully pass out quickly. Or would I?

I had no idea. I didn't know how long it would take to lose consciousness. It probably wouldn't be that fast. I would have to focus on getting through the pain and not thrashing around until that happened. Could I do that?

What about Joey? The suffering might be short-lived for me, but he would spend of the rest of his life reliving this moment. He would live the rest of his life watching me thrashing around beneath him as I drowned. Could I do that to him? Even if it was the only way he could survive this dive?

The regulator appeared in front of me again. I pulled it into my mouth and took a breath. I wasn't ready to end it. I was too scared. Not so much for myself, but for Joey. I didn't want him to have to witness me die thrashing in front of him. I didn't want him to suffer through losing two people on the same dive.

There was another way! I might be able to stretch out our air supply and make it to the surface. There was a risk. I could lose consciousness. If that happened, there was no way I would survive. But I would also go much more peacefully. Joey wouldn't have to witness a violent death. We were so close to the surface. It might just work.

I passed the regulator back up to Joey and prepared to implement my plan.

52

Joey

I took the second stage regulator from Lindsey but didn't take a breath from it. Less than 100 psi. I had to conserve every last bit of the remaining air for Lindsey. I had to make sure she could get out of the cave alive.

She couldn't see me from her position beneath me. She wouldn't know I wasn't taking breaths. Hopefully, she wasn't listening for the sounds of air moving through the first stage regulator and the louder sounds of exhaling that breath. That was the only thing that might give me away.

I handed the regulator back down to Lindsey without breathing from it. I saw her hesitate as she reached for it. Did she know I hadn't taken a breath? Was she listening that closely? Or was she thinking the same thing I was thinking? Was she going to try not to breathe from the regulator either? I watched her closely. She brought it to her mouth. I continued to hold my breath as I listened for the sound of air rushing through the first stage regulator and the hose toward Lindsey's mouth and lungs.

I didn't hear anything. Did I miss it? Did Lindsey not take a breath? Was the tank empty? I grabbed the pressure gauge and turned it so I could see the numbers on its face. The needle was still hanging just below the 100 psi mark. That didn't mean a whole lot. These gauges weren't the most accurate pieces of equipment. I knew that one of my own sidemount tank gauges was off by a little more than 100 psi. The stage tank pressure gauges were even less accurate.

I had noticed the air pressures in my sidemount tanks were always off by 100 psi or so. It happened regularly. The tanks were always filled at the same time and to the same pressure. I almost always ended my dives with nearly identical pressure in the two tanks so a differential in the heating of the tanks as they were being filled wouldn't account for the variance. Not a variance of 100 psi.

The more air that was pressurized into a limited space, the more the temperature would increase in that space. Higher temperatures resulted in higher pressures. Once the temperatures dropped back down to the ambient temperature, the pressures also dropped. If one tank required more air, the pressurization of the additional volume of air would cause the temperature to be higher. So if the tanks began with a 500 psi difference and both were filled to 3100 psi hot, the tank that started off with less pressure would get hotter. Once they cooled down, the hotter tank might only have 2700 psi while the not so hot tank only cooled to 2800 psi. I rarely had that much of a difference in the tank pressures at the end of a dive.

One day I decided to swap the regulators on my tanks to see if the pressure gauges gave me the same pressure in each tank. The pressures were the opposite of what they had been. Or rather, the pressure gauges read the same as they had, but on different tanks. It was the gauges that were not accurate. At least one of them wasn't.

After that I took all of my regulators and Lindsey's regulators and checked the same tank with each one. Lindsey thought I was being obsessive, but I had to find out. No two readings were the same. I found a difference of up to 500 psi between the lowest reading gauge and the highest reading gauge. I had no idea which gauge was providing an accurate reading.

I performed the same test of our gauges with a tank after a dive to see if the difference remained as high or if the gauge readings were closer to each other at lower pressures. The differences weren't as significant. The highest difference was 300 psi between the lowest reading gauge and the highest reading gauge. That was still a lot.

Unfortunately, I never bothered to compare the gauges with a tank pressure less than 500 psi.

Not that it would have mattered. I had no idea whether the pressure gauge on Lindsey's stage tank was one of the higher reading gauges or one of the lower reading gauges. I had marked the back of the gauges when I performed this test. That was more than a year ago. The marks had since worn off from the constant exposure to water.

I flipped over the gauge just to make sure. There was no mark. I had no idea what kind of reading I was getting from this gauge. It could be accurate, and we had less than 100 psi, or the tank could have 200-300 psi in it. I wouldn't know until one of us took that last breath.

By that point, it might be too late.

53

Lindsey

I grabbed my BC inflator and placed the end of it in my mouth as if I was going to orally inflate the air bladder. I was about to inflate it, but that wasn't my reason for doing this. I didn't need to get positively buoyant. I needed to put the air in my lungs some place where I could reuse it.

I slowly exhaled the breath I was holding into the bladder through the inflator. Once my lungs were empty, I quickly refilled them with the air I had just exhaled. The recently expelled air that I had just pulled back into my lungs wouldn't have the usual twenty-one percent oxygen that we found in ambient air. Exhaled air from our lungs only contained sixteen percent oxygen. The breath I had just taken from my BC inflator might have a bit more than that.

I handed the unused regulator back to Joey, hopeful that he hadn't noticed that I hadn't breathed from it.

The BC bladder was filled through a hose connected to the sidemount tank on my left side. The air that had been in the bladder had twenty-one percent oxygen. That meant the air I exhaled with only sixteen percent oxygen would mix with it and the two concentrations of oxygen would equalize producing a concentration somewhere in the middle. Hopefully. It depended on how much air was in the BC bladder compared to how much air I exhaled into it. Unfortunately, I didn't think there was much air in the bladder before I exhaled into it. Regardless, the higher percentage of oxygen wouldn't last long.

Joey handed me the regulator and I exhaled into my BC bladder and quickly inhaled it again.

Eventually, the mixture of air in the bladder would drop to sixteen percent. It would continue to drop even lower as I continued to rebreathe the air from it. Our bodies only released sixteen percent oxygen in our exhalations if we were breathing air with twenty-one percent oxygen. Anything less than eighteen percent was considered hypoxic. Hypoxia led to confusion and then to unconsciousness. Eventually, the oxygen percentage would continue to drop. Anything less than ten percent was deadly. That is if I didn't pass out before that.

I had the regulator again but again used the BC bladder to exhale and inhale.

I was slowly letting out a tiny amount of air, careful to direct it to where I thought Joey's head was. I needed him to see the bubbles so he wouldn't get suspicious about what I was doing. I only had to do this for a couple more minutes. If I could make the air in my BC bladder last that long, we would both make it to the surface. The risk was that once the oxygen concentration dropped below eighteen percent, it wouldn't take long for the hypoxia to make me lose consciousness. I had to maintain focus enough to continue to breathe from my BC inflator. I had to be aware enough to take a breath from the regulator if I had to so I could replenish the oxygen content. A breath of normal, oxygenated air should be enough to clear my head and prolong things. I had to remain alert enough to do that. My ability to think could get severely impaired. It was risky. It was our only chance.

Joey handed the regulator back to me again. I took it but didn't use it. Instead, I exhaled into my BC bladder again and quickly sucked the air back into my lungs. I started to feel funny. Things started to look hazy. I had to maintain my focus. One more breath from my BC bladder before I would take another breath from the regulator. Just one more.

I pushed the regulator back toward Joey. The movement felt awkward. My arms felt weak. It felt like the water had gotten thick.

I moved my head to look around the cave. The walls looked distorted. The floor looked so far away. It looked like I was seeing everything through a telescope. The view was getting smaller. I felt like I was getting swallowed by the darkness.

The regulator came into my field of vision and blocked everything else out of sight. I could no longer see the cave walls or the floor. All I could see was the regulator hanging in the water in front of my face. I wondered how it was hanging there. How was it being suspended in midwater? It was too heavy to have any positive buoyancy.

I reached for the regulator. It was time to take a breath. I was losing focus. I was losing my grasp on reality. I raised my hand and tried to grab the hose. My hand appeared to pass right through it. It was as if the hose wasn't there. It was just an apparition. I shook my head slightly to try to clear my vision and the regulator disappeared. Had it even been there? Suddenly, the cave began spinning around. Or maybe I was spinning.

I couldn't hold my breath any longer. My hand fumbled for the BC inflator that was clipped to the chest strap on my harness. After what seemed like several minutes I found it. I grabbed it and placed it against my lips. I tried to blow the air from my lungs into the inflator, but I met resistance. The air wouldn't escape my lungs. I realized I hadn't pressed the button to open the valve that would allow me to blow air into the bladder. My fingers searched for the button. It seemed like several more minutes before I found it. Everything was moving so slowly. My lungs were starting to burn. My chest was aching. I squeezed the button with all my might as I forcefully blew out the air that was in my lungs. I felt instant relief as the pressure that had been building inside my chest was released.

The cave stopped spinning, but my field of vision continued to get smaller. I was looking though a pinhole. All I could see was a small area of the cave tunnel directly in front of me. Then I saw rays of light shining down. The heavens had opened up and were awaiting my arrival. I thought of Joey one last time. I hoped he would make it to the surface. I watched the rays of light disappear as the pinhole shrunk and completely closed me inside the darkness.

54

Joey

Lindsey handed the regulator back to me. I hesitated before taking it. Had she taken a breath? Was there even a breath left in the tank to take? It was becoming more difficult to continue holding my breath. I skipped taking a breath the last time I had the regulator in my hand. It had to have been close to thirty seconds since I had taken a breath. I didn't think I could hold it for much longer.

If there was no more air in the tank, I would have to continue holding it. That or drown. I focused on holding my breath and handed the regulator back to Lindsey unused. If there was any air in the tank, I wanted her to have it.

My chest burned. My lungs screamed. It was getting harder to resist the urge to exhale. But if there was no more air in the tank what would happen? We were still two hundred feet from the opening. Swimming as fast as I could, that would take me at least three minutes. There was no way I could hold my breath for three minutes. I couldn't do that if I was hovering still in the water, never mind swimming as quickly as I could to get to the surface.

I began to slowly exhale, letting out tiny bubbles through my pursed lips. Maybe I could extend this exhalation long enough to get us out of the cave. Lindsey pushed the regulator back toward me. I hadn't noticed if she had taken a breath or not. I was too busy concentrating on holding my breath and swimming toward the opening.

Then it happened. The urge to exhale overtook my body and all the air I had left in my lungs came forcibly out in a violent cough. With that came the irresistible urge to inhale. I snatched the regulator from Lindsey's grasp, shoved its mouthpiece into my mouth, and sealed my lips around it. In the brief millisecond between sealing my lips around the mouthpiece and sucking in a breath, I wondered if there was any air left to breathe in. I wondered if I would get another breath or just meet resistance.

I began to inhale.

At that moment, time seemed to stand still. At the risk of sounding cliché, I watched as my life played out in front of my eyes. Things like that do happen in those final moments before death. The air seemed to take forever to come. I began to think there was no air left in the tank. That was the end. Lindsey hadn't taken a breath because there was no breath to take. We were both going to drown in this cave, less than two hundred feet from the opening.

Then I felt it. I felt the rush of the cool, dry air from the scuba tank bursting out of the regulator, drying out the top of my tongue, tickling that thing that hangs down in the back of my mouth as it rushed into my throat and down toward my vocal cords. I felt my lungs begin to expand as the air filled the empty spaces. I felt an immense sense of relief at being able to get one more breath.

Just as suddenly as the air had started to fill my lungs, it stopped. The regulator stopped working. Or rather, there was no more air in the tank to make the regulator work. I felt the mechanism in the regulator slam shut as the last of the air in the tank travelled through it. I sucked in harder, trying to get any last bit of air that might still be residing in the tank to come through.

I got nothing.

That was it.

Six tanks.
All empty.
No more air.
Less than two hundred feet from the surface.
It might as well have been two hundred miles.

55

Joey

I pulled the regulator out of my mouth and let it drop. With the mouthpiece in my mouth, the urge to breathe was too great. Without it there, I could fool my brain a little longer. I noticed the regulator was hanging just below Lindsey's head. I yanked it back up by the hose. I didn't want her to take it and try to get a breath from it with nothing left in the tank. I held the hose up with the regulator just above Linsdey's head, thoughts rushing through my head trying to figure out a way to get us out of this cave.

Only one hundred and fifty feet from the opening.

We couldn't die so close to the surface. We had made it this far. I had nothing. No ideas. No air. No chance for survival.

Beams of light suddenly appeared in front of me coming from the right side of the tunnel. I looked in the direction they were coming from. They appeared to be coming through the ceiling of the cave. Were they real? Or was this just my imagination playing tricks on me again? Was I hallucinating from the lack of oxygen? If it was real, was the opening large enough for us to pass through?

I changed my heading and started to go directly toward the light. As I got closer, the beams grew in size and brightness. What had begun as a few narrow beams of light that could have come from a dive light now filled the area of the cave we were approaching. I continued to look up at the ceiling where the light was coming from but couldn't determine its source.

Lindsey began to slow down. I tugged at her and tried to get her to speed her pace. I had to see where the light was coming from. If it was a diver, that meant tanks with air in them. If it was an opening, I could only hope it was large enough for us to get through and get to the surface. Either way, those rays of light might have just given us our only fighting chance to survive.

Lindsey stopped moving. She was no longer finning. Her light was pointing at the floor below us. Her arms were extended below her, hanging from her shoulders, no movement. Was she looking at the light beams? Had she dropped her hands so the beams wouldn't have to compete with her dive light? I refused to believe it could be anything else.

I shook Lindsey by the shoulders. Her arms swung flaccidly below her. She didn't respond. I shook her more violently. Still no response. Her dive light slipped from her hand, a mushroom cloud of silt appearing as it hit the floor.

Why wasn't she responding? Why was she doing this?

Mad thoughts rushed through my head. I refused to believe something was wrong with Lindsey. I refused to believe she had drowned. I grabbed onto her harness tightly and changed direction for the source of light. I knew there was no way I would make it another one hundred and fifty feet to the opening where we had entered the cave. That source of light was our only hope for survival.

I kicked as hard and fast as I could. My lungs were burning. My chest felt like it was about to explode. I concentrated on releasing a tiny amount of air to try to relieve some of the discomfort. I couldn't do it. All the air that was left in my lungs came out with hurricane force. My lungs were empty, and we had no more air from which to breathe.

I looked up toward the ceiling, toward the source of light. During the time I had been distracted by Lindsey's lack of movement, the light had grown significantly. I could now see that it wasn't a diver above us on a decompression stop. It wasn't just a small crack in the ceiling letting in some ambient daylight. It was a large passage through the ceiling that led to another opening. I could not only see the light, but I could see the surface of a cenote about fifty feet away from us.

I glanced at my dive computer display. We were twenty-one feet deep. I looked back at the source of light. We weren't directly beneath it. We still had to swim a horizontal distance of forty feet or so to get to where we could ascend to the surface.

I shook Lindsey again. Still no response. I pulled back on her head to maintain an open airway like I had been taught in my rescue diver class. If it was just forty horizontal feet, Lindsey had no chance for survival. But because we also had to ascend, any air that was in her lungs would expand and might keep water out. If she was unconscious, it hadn't been for very long. Maybe a few seconds. There was still a chance for both of us to make it out of this cave alive.

I swam as hard as I could, making sure to keep Lindsey's airway open so the air in her lungs wouldn't be trapped in them as we ascended. After all we had gone through, she didn't need to get a lung overexpansion injury. Better than drowning, but not much. It wasn't likely to be survivable on an island with minimal medical treatment options.

As I swam, the opening grew in size. This opening was much larger than the one we had been entering and exiting through. When we were about twenty-five feet from it, I recognized its shape from the many photos and videos I had seen online. It was the main opening that was located on the small end of the cenote. This was the opening we were able to see from the surface.

Twenty feet to go.

I looked down at Lindsey and saw small bubbles escaping around her mask. My vision became blurry. I felt tears rolling out of my eyes down to the mask skirt below them. I was hopeful the bubbles I saw might mean Lindsey still had air in her lungs. I knew the air in her mask would also be expanding with the drop in pressure as we got shallower. Those tiny bubbles might not mean anything.

Fifteen feet to go.

Through my tears I thought I saw a small bubble escape from Lindsey's mouth. I tried to shake the tears away and focus on her lips as I swam even harder to get us to the surface.

Ten feet.

More bubbles escaped from between Lindsey's lips. This gave me more hope. There might be a chance. I swam even harder, oblivious to any discomfort I might have been experiencing from holding my breath for so long.

Five feet.

The pain in my lungs was beginning to break through the adrenaline. I didn't know how long I had been holding my breath. I didn't know how much longer I could hold it. But we were almost there.

We had almost cleared the overhead. We were five feet from the edge of the rocky overhang and five feet deep. I prepared myself for having to get Lindsey's head above the surface and hold her face up into the air. I thought back to my rescue diver class and having to do rescue breaths in the water while towing an unconscious diver back to shore. It was the hardest task we had to do. And here I was about to have to do it for real.

We finally cleared the ceiling.

The urge to breathe had grown immense. I squeezed my lips tightly together much like little kids do when threatening to hold their breath when they don't get their way. I felt the mask squeeze tighter on my face as I involuntarily tried to take a breath through my nose.

Fortunately, the mask was clear of water. It didn't relieve the intensity of the urge to breathe, though.

Our heads broke the surface!

I immediately opened my mouth and sucked in a large breath of air. I let that out and took in another breath of air. I did this over and over as I tried to get control of Lindsey's lifeless body. I rotated it so her face was up and out of the water and frantically kicked in an effort to keep us both floating at the surface. My hand reached for Lindsey's BC inflator and pressed the button to inject air into the bladder. Nothing happened. Then I remembered there was no air in any of our tanks so nothing to inflate with.

I frantically looked around and saw that this part of the cenote wasn't a large area. It only measured about twenty feet in diameter. I had less than ten feet to tow Lindsey. There was also a large boulder just below the surface near the edge where I could prop her body and give her rescue breaths much more easily. It was only five feet away.

I tried to direct my kicks so we moved closer to that boulder while I struggled to keep us both on the surface. That five feet might as well have been fifty feet. Unable to float easily, there was no way I could do rescue breaths without being on the boulder. I quickly evaluated my options. I could keep trying to kick toward the boulder or I could try to inflate both mine and Lindsey's BCs. Getting to the boulder would be quicker and allow me to give rescue breaths much more easily. I continued to kick.

I felt something under my feet and yanked them up. Could it be the crocodile? Jose had said they removed it, but what if it came back? What if another crocodile had taken up residence in this cenote? We began to sink below the surface. Crocodile or not, I had to keep us at the surface. With no air in our tanks, we would be no match for a crocodile underwater. I wasn't sure having air in our tanks would make a difference. I extended my legs out to resume kicking and felt something underneath them. Something hard and not moving. It wasn't a crocodile. It was a shallow ledge about four feet below the surface. I planted my feet on the ledge and pushed up.

With my newly found stability, I was able to pull Lindsey to the boulder next to me. The top of the boulder was just below the surface. I orally inflated her BC to get her positively buoyant, while keeping her face up in the water. I pulled her next to me so her head and shoulders were on top of the boulder. The boulder was shallow enough I was able to rest her head on it. I pulled her scuba mask up to her forehead and pinched her nose as I tilted her head back. I took a deep breath, leaned over Lindsey, and released the air from my lungs into her lungs. I took another breath and repeated it.

I wasn't a religious person, but I prayed for Lindsey to survive. I prayed for her to live through this.

56

Gary
About 2 hours earlier

Joey had all the luck! I couldn't believe he found a tunnel without any line in it. One that had never been explored. A real virgin cave passage. I watched his fins disappear into the small hole he found as he went around a bend. The line from his explorer reel was trailing behind him. I was so envious.

Lindsey hovered over the intersection of lines created by the permanent guideline and the line from Joey's explorer reel. She looked like she was thinking about following him into the tunnel. I doubted she would. It was not very big, and Lindsey didn't like the small stuff.

I glanced around the cave trying to decide what to do. I thought about following Joey. What if the tunnel got larger around that bend? What if he had found a passage that led to a new section of cave? I didn't want to miss out on that. On the other hand, what if it didn't?

I watched Lindsey move toward Joey. Was she really going to follow him? If she was, I wasn't about to follow her. Two's company, three's a crowd. Besides, Joey and I had discussed this the night before. I was going to look for my own lead. I turned and continued following the guideline farther into the cave.

I just wanted to check out the next fifty or one hundred feet to see if there was anything else in the area. Chances were if there was one tunnel that hadn't been found, there might be another. I might even find one that connected to the tunnel Joey was in. I swam farther into the cave, sweeping my light beam along the wall to my right, then the wall to my left. It was solid rock. No holes screaming out at me to be explored.

A couple of minutes after I started out, I decided to turn around. I didn't want to get too far into the cave alone. We were already a couple of thousand feet from the opening. This was also my first time alone in a cave. My first time alone on a dive. I had always been curious about solo diving, but with Jim around, it wasn't necessary.

Jim and I had gotten scuba certified together. We had done our cave diving training together. We had done every dive together, until this trip to Mexico. We had planned on coming down together, but he couldn't get the time off from work. Even though Jim worked from home, he still had to be logged into the system eight hours a day. He still had meetings to attend and projects to complete. He couldn't bear to come to Mexico and have to work all week while we were out cave diving. I wasn't going to come down without him. He insisted.

I think it was more self-preservation on his part than really wanting me to go. He knew I would mope around the house all day while Joey and Lindsey were down here. I also worked from home, but my job was a little more flexible than Jim's. Jim was right. I would have been unbearable.

Here I was on a cave diving trip in Cozumel, Mexico with Joey and Lindsey. Funny thing is Lindsey was more of a third wheel than I was. Joey and I were so amped up over the diving we were doing and going to be doing that we didn't talk about anything else. Lindsey seemed to be enjoying the trip and the dives, but not as much as we were. And we were annoying her a little, as evidenced by the daily lectures at dinner over things we were doing that were not to her satisfaction. To be fair, Lindsey was right. We were so excited about the new cave we were seeing and the potential for finding virgin cave passage, that we had been bending the rules a little. Maybe more than a little.

We did better this time. Joey even deployed a line before he went to check out the passage he found. I would do the same if I found a passage of my own. That didn't look like it would happen, though.

I turned around, disappointed in not having found anything. I didn't know how long the tunnel Joey was in would turn out to be. I did know he would be in there for a while. He wasn't very quick with getting the survey data. It took him a good fifteen minutes the day before to survey the tunnel he found that wasn't on any of the maps he had memorized. It was only a couple hundred feet long. I had at least fifteen minutes to poke around, maybe more.

I passed the intersection of the permanent guideline and Joey's line. I looked in the direction the line was going. I couldn't see Joey or Lindsey. I shielded my dive light and saw a glow coming from around the corner. They were still in there.

I looked around the cave again, trying to decide what to do. I glanced at my dive computer. Joey had only been in there about five minutes. I had time. On the way in we passed an offshoot tunnel that looked interesting. It already had a guideline in it, but I still wanted to take a look. I reached down to retrieve my line marker from the intersection. It wasn't there. Dammit! I forgot to mark the intersection again!

No. Wait! This wasn't an intersection until Joey tied his line onto the permanent guideline. I swam past it as Joey was creating the intersection. Relieved that I hadn't forgotten to leave a marker, I turned to the left, back from where we had come, and began to swim along the line, looking for the tunnel I wanted to see. Five minutes later, I hadn't come across it. I thought it was closer to where we had stopped. Apparently not.

It couldn't be much farther, so I continued to swim, feeling much more comfortable being alone in a cave knowing I was going toward the opening and not farther away from it. Joey and Lindsey shouldn't be too far behind me. I had started my swim out about fifty minutes into the dive. Our agreed turn time was one hour. That gave them another five minutes before they would begin their swim out. I kept swimming, but slower than usual. That would make it easier for them to catch up to me and we could all exit together.

I looked at my dive computer just as the dive timer went from fifty-nine minutes to sixty minutes. They should be starting out about now. I continued swimming slowly, sweeping my light beam back and forth looking for any leads we might have missed on the way in. I was also looking for that lined offshoot tunnel I had seen on the way in. I should have gotten to it already. I swear it wasn't this far from where we stopped. I must have missed it.

I thought back to what it looked like as I was swimming in. It had been on the right, which would be my left now, and the line was tied to the corner of the wall coming from the offshoot. That meant I wouldn't see the line while exiting. I'd have to look back to see it. Maybe I had missed it.

I slowed my pace even more as I considered turning around to go look for the offshoot tunnel behind me. I decided against it. Lindsey and Joey had to be on their way out by this point. Even if I did find it before I ran into them, it wouldn't take them long to meet up with me and I'd have to exit with them. Maybe I could convince Joey to come back down here on the next dive and I could check it out then.

I watched as the thin white guideline below me transformed into the thicker yellow line we had been seeing in different tunnels in this cave. Had I made it this far already? I looked at my dive computer; I had been swimming for fifteen minutes. It seemed like it had been only a few minutes. I must have missed the tunnel I was looking for. Then I remembered. It was in an area that had yellow line in it. I hadn't yet passed it. I focused my search to my left as I picked up my pace. Maybe I could still find it and have a few minutes to check it out before Joey and Lindsey caught up.

A few minutes later, I arrived at the line intersection that was shaped like a Y. The yellow line continued to the right. A thinner white line was tied to it and continued to the left. When we arrived at this part of the cave on the way in, I stopped and asked Joey if I should put a marker on the line. Joey shook his head, probably thinking the same thing I was. The lines were different, easily distinguishable by color and size. We could tell the difference with or without visibility. There was also a line arrow on the yellow guideline pointing in the direction we had come from.

As soon as Joey shook his head, he turned and continued to head into the cave without leaving a marker. I didn't leave a marker either. But Lindsey had. It was positioned on the yellow line directly in front of the permanent line arrow. I hoped she wasn't upset at us for not leaving markers. I continued my swim to the right, following the yellow guideline.

The cave got slightly shallower at this point, rising from about forty-five feet to thirty-five feet of depth. It also got narrower. Still not narrow enough to touch both walls at the same time but narrow enough to be able to see both walls clearly with minimal shadowing. We hadn't seen any leads along this part of the cave while coming in. However, I did suddenly remember that the offshoot tunnel I was looking for was off of the halocline tunnel. Jim was always complaining about my memory. He had sticky notes up all over the house reminding me to do this or that. I was going to have to start keeping notes on my dives. I might have to buy one of those wrist slates so it would be easier to keep notes.

I looked at my dive computer. One hour and twenty-five minutes. Lindsey and Joey should be well on their way out. They were probably six or seven minutes behind me.

Remembering where the lined offshoot tunnel was and still wanting to check it out, I swam a little faster, hoping to be able to get close to ten minutes to look around. Once Joey and Lindsey caught up to me, there would be no lollygagging. While it was okay with Lindsey that we looked around during the exit, she had made it clear that exploration takes place during the penetration side of the dive, not the exit side of the dive. That meant we could look but not touch on the way out.

I saw the distinct delineation of the saltwater and freshwater about thirty feet ahead. At that point there was only about fifteen feet between the walls. The tunnel curved to the left. I thought I would be seeing the offshoot soon after that. Maybe. Damn my shitty memory.

I stayed below the halocline as close to the floor as possible. I didn't want to screw up the visibility for Lindsey and Joey. There were places where it was difficult to stay out of the halocline, almost impossible. I moved along carefully, hoping I wasn't distorting the clarity of the water very much.

About twenty feet ahead I saw the large formation on the left side that had caused me to rotate my right tank up a little to get between it and the opposite wall. I was pretty sure the offshoot tunnel was close to that. In fact, I knew it was. I was still thinking about the offshoot and trying to look back for the line I had seen when I came to the large formation and almost wedged myself between it and the wall.

I rotated my left tank up as I passed through the narrow restriction. I glanced up and saw that had I been a couple of feet shallower I would have been able to get through without having to rotate. I also would have been in the middle of the halocline and screwed up the visibility for the others.

Two minutes later I found the offshoot tunnel. I looked back behind me. Complete darkness. No Joey or Lindsey yet. I had time to poke around for a few minutes. I retrieved a jump spool from my thigh pocket and looped it around the yellow guideline over a permanent line arrow. I deployed a couple of feet of the jump spool line, down along the wall and wrapped it around the thinner white guideline that was leading into the offshoot. I clipped the spool back onto its line and tucked the line in as close to the wall as I could to make sure it was out of the way.

I shielded my light and looked behind me in the direction I had come from. Still no lights. I checked my dive computer. One hour and thirty minutes. Wow! This was closer to the opening than I thought! I gave myself ten minutes to look. I had until one hour and forty minutes into the dive. That should be plenty of time to see which way this passage was heading.

One last glance to my left, back to where Joey and Lindsey would be coming from. Still nothing. I flicked my fins together and dropped out of the halocline tunnel into the offshoot tunnel.

Ten minutes.

57

Gary

This tunnel was fantastic! It did a little serpentine the first three minutes before it continued straight. A couple of minutes later, it dropped down to fifty feet into a low, wide room with a silty floor. I looked to my left and watched the ceiling and floor come together about twenty feet away. I looked to my right. It looked like it continued on forever. It got very low to the right, though. Low enough I didn't want to venture over there. But it kept going. I wondered if it got bigger beyond where I could see.

The floor of the tunnel leveled out at fifty feet of depth. The ceiling was low but not too low to pass through comfortably. Someone with backmounted tanks could fit easily. Maybe not as comfortably as someone diving with sidemounted tanks, but it was tall enough to fit. The guideline didn't look like it was in the best shape, but it was intact. I pulled on it and it felt strong. It was not at all brittle. We had come across a couple of tunnels with guideline so old that tugging on it just a little caused it to break and disintegrate. We replaced the line the first couple of times, then opted not to go into those anymore. We didn't want to waste the line from our explorer reels replacing lines.

I looked at my dive computer. One hour and thirty-seven minutes. I had three minutes to go. I continued to swim farther into the cave. I wasn't sure if it was really farther. I didn't know the maps as well as

Joey did. I did know that we had come in and turned right at the beginning of the permanent guideline. The permanent guideline seemed to veer to the left a little. But we jumped off that line to the right into the tunnel we had gone down. This offshoot tunnel was a right turn from there while heading into the cave. I was in a big square. At least I thought I was. Maybe this tunnel would end up back near the opening to the cave.

Just as that thought occurred to me, I saw a line arrow. Only this arrow was pointing in the direction I was swimming, not back behind me. The picture of the cave I had in my head must be right. I was in a big square. I was heading back to the opening. I looked at my dive computer. One hour and forty-five minutes. What had happened??

I should have turned back ten minutes earlier! How had I lost track of the time?? I started to turn, but that line arrow told me the opening was closer going the direction I was going than it would be if I turned around. The tunnel was also getting taller. I had a lot more clearance between the floor and the ceiling. I looked back behind me. Holy crap!! What happened to the visibility? Had I messed it up that badly?

I couldn't see anything behind me. There was silt hanging from floor to ceiling. I could barely see my own fins on my feet. I had somehow kicked up a lot of silt. If Joey saw this, he'd really be ripping into me about being a silt monster. I looked back at the line arrow in front of me. I stared at it. I looked behind me at the silt cloud I had created. The line arrow below me was pointing into crystal clear water, away from the silt cloud that had enveloped the entire tunnel behind me.

I wondered how long I had been stirring up the silt. Was it just a few feet, or was the entire tunnel blown out? I really didn't want to go back through it. I had been in decreased visibility before. Just last year Lindsey, Joey, Jim and I had to swim through zero visibility to get out of Jackson Blue when the ceiling collapsed. But that was different. We had no other option, and we were all scared out of our minds.

I looked at the clear passage in front of me and the line arrow pointing in the other direction.

What about Joey and Lindsey? They were certainly waiting for me by now. At least they should be. Dammit! I forgot to leave a line marker at the jump. They might not even know I went down this tunnel. When I got back to Florida, I would need to tell Jim we needed to start using individual markers rather than team markers. I needed to build the habit and muscle memory of deploying markers. Especially, if we were going to be coming down to Mexico more often to dive.

There was no line marker to see, but Joey and Lindsey should see my jump spool. That would let them know I had gone down this tunnel. What if they didn't see it? The jump spool was in the halocline tunnel. They might not even feel it. I had tucked it in out of the way behind the wall.

I looked back at the silt and decided to continue swimming forward. The silt behind me was freaking me out too much. It would be better to continue toward the exit in clear water than to turn back into the silty mess I had created. I wasn't comfortable in those types of conditions. Going forward seemed like the best option. And the arrow was telling me that was the quickest way out.

I continued farther into the tunnel, but back toward the opening of the cave. We had been taught in class to always trust the line arrows. The line arrows were always supposed to be right. But I hadn't been this way before. What if the line arrow wasn't right? What if the guideline this way wasn't continuous to the opening? What if it did lead back, but there was a long gap in the line, and I couldn't find the other line? What if the line was brittle or broken?

I should turn around and go back the way I came. I had enough air to make it back that way. I would be way overdue, behind schedule, but that would be the smart thing to do. I glanced behind me. I was still disturbing the silt on the floor. It looked even worse than it had before. It looked even scarier. I felt a shudder move through me. I felt anxiety. I kept swimming forward. I would turn around if the line ended before I could see daylight, or if it gapped with another line. I would have no choice then. But at the moment I had a choice and being able to see seemed like the better of the two options.

I looked at my dive computer again. Two hours!! I should be surfacing now! Lindsey was going to be pissed. If Lindsey and Joey had seen my jump spool, they might have followed me into this tunnel. Would they have continued into the silt cloud I had created? I doubted it. Joey might have tried, but Lindsey would have stopped him. She wouldn't want to go into a new tunnel without being able to see anything.

I doubted they had seen my jump spool. Thinking back to how I had run my jump spool line between the two lines, it wouldn't be easy to see. Even if they were coming in from the other direction, the halocline would make it difficult to see.

I could turn now. I should turn now. I would be at least thirty minutes behind them if I did that, maybe longer; I was no longer certain of anything. If I continued forward, I had a chance of meeting up with them on the way to the opening. This tunnel had to cut back into the main tunnel of the cave.

I continued forward toward the opening. I sped up a little. It was probably too late, but just in case Joey and Lindsey got delayed looking for me, I didn't want to miss them wherever this line intersected with the main guideline. Maybe this was that tunnel we had been looking for that was supposed to be about one hundred feet before the halocline tunnel. We thought it joined up at the Y intersection, but maybe we were wrong.

Come to think of it, we hadn't passed any line intersections on the way in on the main guideline. These line arrows pointed out, but this line wasn't likely to be a continuous guideline to the opening. At least, it wasn't likely to be continuous to the opening we had entered. Could there be a second opening? If it did go back toward the main guideline, I should be able to see it. I should at least be able to recognize the main tunnel.

What if I couldn't see another line? What if I didn't recognize the tunnel? Should I turn around then, or should I deploy another jump spool and try to look for another line? I looked back over my shoulder again. The silt cloud was getting bigger; it was following me. What had I gotten myself into?

I was beginning to regret my decision to explore this tunnel. It was a bad idea. I was alone, thirty minutes from my jump spool, which meant I was more than one thousand feet from it, and heading toward an opening I wasn't certain was even the same one we had entered. I had no idea whether Joey and Lindsey would see my jump spool or if they would continue heading out. What if they remained in the cave trying to find me? They wouldn't do that. I kept swimming, hoping to find the main guideline or an opening soon.

Two hours and twelve minutes.

I was more than forty minutes from my jump spool. What had I gotten myself into? I looked at my pressure gauges. I had breathed past turn pressure on both of my sidemount tanks. And not just a little past turn pressure. I hadn't breathed from my stage tank on the exit yet. I would save that.

I felt uneasy to have breathed past my turn pressures on my sidemount tanks and not turned around. But the arrows told me the opening was closer if I kept going straight instead of turning around. I should turn around. I should head back the way I came.

But the arrows told me the exit was closer this way.

I kept following the arrows.

58

Gary

Two hours and thirty-nine minutes. More than an hour from my jump spool. How was time passing by so quickly? This tunnel was turning out to be a lot longer than I expected. I saw a line intersection about thirty feet ahead. I could either go straight or go left. Or I could turn around like I should have done long ago. I had really gotten myself in deep.

About a minute later I arrived at the line intersection. My heart sank. This was bad. I should have turned back long ago. The line intersection had two line arrows on the lines, one pointed straight ahead and the other pointed to the left. I had no idea which way to go. I put a non-directional marker on the line where I was coming from. If I had to go back the way I had come, at least I would know which way to go. I hoped I wouldn't have to go back. Did I even have enough air to get back? I looked back. The silt was still following me.

I looked at my pressure gauges again. 900 psi in each sidemount tank. I still hadn't breathed from my stage tank on the exit, so it still had 2100 psi of air in it. If I had to turn around, there might be enough air to make it out the way I had come. Hopefully. I wasn't sure. I wasn't sure about anything. If I did turn, I had the silt to contend with. I didn't know if I could do it. I didn't know how much that would slow me down. There were too many unknowns, and it kept getting worse.

I decided to turn left at the intersection. That way led me up a sandy slope to a shallower section. At least I would be breathing less air. It looked like the floor was going to meet the ceiling. I couldn't see where the guideline was going. What if the line was buried at the top of the slope? What if the slope had once gone all the way up to an opening but it had filled with sand? What if there was a similar incident as had happened to Parker Turner and Bill Gavin and I couldn't get through?

I tried to convince myself I had enough air. I could swim back. I checked my gauges again to make sure. I wasn't feeling confident about it. I should have turned around long ago. My chest started to feel tight. My body started to feel restless. Why hadn't I turned around? Why had I kept going? Lindsey and Joey were going to be pissed. Especially Lindsey.

I looked back again. I still couldn't see anything. The silt kept following me. I felt like Pigpen from the Peanuts cartoon. If Joey saw this, silt monster wouldn't be the only thing he called me. He'd start calling me Pigpen. I felt my anxiety getting worse. I was trying to hold it back. I didn't want to go into a full panic. I continued up the slope hoping for the best. Hoping it didn't pinch down to an unpassable restriction, or no opening at all. This had to get me to the surface.

At twenty-two feet of depth, I came to the crest of the slope and saw that the floor leveled out and continued onward with plenty of clearance. It hadn't caved in. I wouldn't have to turn around.

Yet.

I was also almost thirty feet shallower. That meant my air would last a lot longer. I had more time to deal with the situation. As long as I didn't have to turn around and head back to the fifty-foot-deep tunnel I would have plenty of air.

Suddenly, it got harder to draw a breath. I looked at my pressure gauge and saw the needle pointing at the zero. Where did the air go?? I quickly swapped regulators. I looked at that gauge. Only 800 psi left in that tank. I still had my stage tank, but there was no turning back. It was too late for me to do that. I decided to switch to my stage tank rather than wait. I could then ditch it if I had to and keep my sidemount tanks with me. I grabbed the second stage regulator and pulled it forward. I then reached back and opened the valve. I swapped regulators and clipped my sidemount regulator to the D ring on the right side of my chest.

I continued to swim forward, hopefully toward an exit. There had to be an opening ahead. I saw something shiny. I aimed my light on it and saw trash on the floor. It was an old glass bottle. Then I saw a lone shoe. It was the left shoe. More unidentifiable bits. I felt a sense of relief wash over me. I was close to an opening. Where there was trash, there was access to the surface. I should see daylight streaming into the cave at any moment. I swam faster as I scanned the ceiling.

Two minutes later I still hadn't seen daylight. And I had come to another intersection. The line arrow at this intersection pointed to the left as well. I looked in that direction expecting to see beams of light penetrating the darkness. It was nothing but a black void. There was more trash scattered about the floor of the cave. The tunnel of this other guideline was also big. So big I couldn't see the wall on the other side from where I was located.

The water was also hazy. While I could see about forty or fifty feet in front of me, I couldn't make anything out. All I could tell was that there wasn't a wall within that distance. This was a really wide room. I looked to the right on the chance that the arrow was pointing in the wrong direction. No light coming from there either. There was more trash strewn about the floor. I couldn't believe the amount of trash I was seeing in this tunnel. Someone had been using the opening nearby as a dump site. It couldn't be the same cenote where we had entered. There wasn't any evidence of people dumping trash there.

Sure, there was trash around the cenote, but most of it was

concentrated around a wooden post near the road and among the trees that surrounded the cenote. There was no trash in the cenote. At least, none that we had seen. This had to be a different cenote I was close to.

What if it was in the middle of the jungle. What if I couldn't find my way back to the main cenote? More regret over the decisions I had made over the past…I looked at my dive computer – total dive time was two hours and fifty-three minutes…over the past hour and twenty-three minutes. If I had to turn around and swim back, I'd have to add another twenty to that for the swim from my jump spool to the opening. Another hour and forty-five. The realization that I didn't have enough air to turn back fell upon me.

I felt panic fighting its way into my mind. Almost two hours of swimming back the way I had come. An hour and a half of swimming through a tunnel in which I had blown out the visibility. Two hours swimming back with the air in my tanks dwindling away. How had I been swimming for that long? How had so much time gotten away from me?

I could skip breathe but would that be enough to stretch it out. My chest felt tighter. My breathing got faster. I frantically looked around. I had to find the way out. I had to get to the surface. I was going to have a panic attack if I didn't get out of this cave soon. But there was no light other than what was coming from my dive light. There was no sign I was close to an opening other than trash strewn about the floor of the cave.

I swept my light beam erratically back and forth looking for something, anything, that would tell me where I was. I was breathing so fast. My regulator was having trouble keeping up with my demand for air. The sound of the bubbles escaping the regulator as I exhaled was continuous. I put my hand down on the floor…through the floor…into the deep silt to steady myself. My light got buried and I was swallowed by darkness. I immediately snatched my hand up, bringing with it a mushroom cloud of silt. The situation continued to get worse.

I saw something shiny a few feet away from me. It was small but bright and it caught my eye. Something about it looked familiar. Something drew my attention to it. I felt my respiratory rate slow down a little. I was still breathing fast, but at least my regulator could keep up. I could hear brief pauses of silence between exhalations. I moved toward the bright, shiny object. It was partially buried in the silt. Once I was hovering over it, I reached down, grabbed the edge, and slowly tugged on it. I wanted to get it out of its underwater grave, but I didn't want to create more of a silt disturbance than I already had. The silt slowly released its grip on the shiny object and it broke free. I pulled it up in front of my mask so I could get a better look at it.

Chokis. That was the word written in blue on the wrapper. The bright, shiny object was a chrome-colored cookie wrapper. Not just any cookie wrapper, but a wrapper from Joey's favorite Mexican cookies. I thought back to when Joey and Lindsey had returned from their first trip to Cozumel. Joey had brought back a few boxes of Chokis. They were just small chocolate chip cookies. They came packaged six cookies to a sleeve in these bright, shiny wrappers.

I'll admit, they were pretty damn good cookies. Better than the stuff found in US grocery stores. I didn't know if I would have brought back a few boxes of them, though. Joey had, and he shared some with Jim and me. We sat in his living room while he told us all about diving in Cozumel and his plans for returning to dive the caves while we nibbled on Chokis.

I stuck my finger inside the wrapper I had unearthed. It was empty. Of course, it was empty. I was underwater. Even if it had cookies in it when it was discarded into the water, they would have disintegrated within minutes. I still had to check.

I noticed my breathing had returned to normal. I no longer felt anxious. The Chokis had calmed me. The thoughts of Joey and his excitement about Cozumel and the Chokis had relaxed me. This Chokis wrapper may have just saved my life. I carefully folded the wrapper and tucked it inside the sleeve of my wetsuit. I was going to frame it when I returned home as a reminder of this moment. It would serve to remind me about the stupid decisions I made to get to this point. It would serve to remind me to always keep calm in these situations. Maybe it would even serve to calm me down whenever I started to get anxious at home. Jim would appreciate that. Panicking never accomplished anything.

I looked at my pressure gauge on my stage tank. 900 psi. How had I breathed that much already? I still had the one sidemount tank, but there was no way I could turn around. I had to find the opening nearby. I glanced at my left wrist and saw a piece of the Chokis wrapper sticking out. Everything was going to be fine. I just had to go a little farther and I would be able to surface.

I placed another non-directional marker at the intersection on the guideline I had just come from. I turned left and continued to follow the direction the marker indicated was the opening. I saw old thick ropes covered in sand on the floor. At first, I thought they were large snakes or eels. Then I saw the twisted braid of the strands that made up the rope. I poked at one with my dive light. When it didn't move on its own and attack, I knew it was either dead or inanimate. I waved my hand back and forth over it to clear away the silt that had settled on it and confirmed it was a rope.

Next, I saw an old tire. I definitely had to be near an opening. I looked up at the ceiling hoping to see daylight. Tires were heavy. I imagined it must have been dropped into a cenote and landed directly below. Unless it landed on its tread and began rolling down the tunnel. There was a slight slope to the floor.

I looked at the depth reading on my dive computer. I was fourteen feet deep. I had to be close to an opening. What if I couldn't see the opening from the line and what if the line didn't go directly to the opening? What if there was a dark layer of tannins in the opening and daylight wasn't able to penetrate into the cave. I could be near a cenote and not know it.

Too many what ifs. I looked behind me. At least the water was clear now. Well, as clear as the rest of the tunnel. The silt cloud had stopped following me. I lost it somewhere along the way. I should have turned around and exited the way I had come in. I should have taken the confirmed route out of the cave. Our training told us to do that. Our training told us not to plan to exit in a location where we've never been. It was too late for that now. I didn't have enough air to go back the way I had come.

I shielded the beam coming from my dive light. Still no daylight streaming in. I unshielded the light. I looked around for the guideline I had been following. I couldn't find it. I stopped moving and searched frantically for it. I should have made contact with it before I shielded my dive light. Where had the guideline gone?

I rotated in place to look behind me. Maybe it had broken and I had passed the break while I was looking for daylight. Once I was facing where I had come from, I saw the guideline ten feet behind me. It disappeared into the sand on the floor. I flicked my fins a couple of times and headed back to the visible part of the guideline. I grabbed it and turned back to the way that was supposedly out. I pulled on the line and watched it slice its way through the sandy floor like a sharp razor slicing through butter. The line sliced through the sediment for about twenty-five feet before it was completely free. A thin indent remained in the sand where the line had been buried.

My only chance of making it out of the situation I had gotten myself into was to find the opening that was supposed to be nearby. I didn't remember another opening on the maps Joey had obtained. But I hadn't studied those maps like he had. Joey hadn't mentioned another opening either. He would have wanted to go check it out if there was one.

This could be an unmapped opening. It could have been found after the maps were published. It had been more than twenty years since that time. There was also that rumor about the team of divers that added forty thousand feet of line to the cave. Could this be the section?

The tunnel continued to get shallower. I was twelve feet deep. The water clarity was even hazier. I also felt a current. The current was pushing against me, not going with me. Could I be swimming in the wrong direction? The current should be coming from inside the cave not from an opening. Unless the opening was just a hole in the ceiling of a tunnel that passed beneath it. That would explain the direction of the current. I didn't understand why the visibility wasn't clear like it had been earlier.

I continued to swim, watching the depth reading on my dive computer get shallower every minute. The tunnel was getting a foot shallower about every fifty feet, maybe less. I was swimming slowly. The hour and a half mark since I had left my jump spool had passed long ago. I looked at my stage tank pressure gauge. I was down to 400 psi of air. It was going fast.

I felt my breathing get faster again. I felt my chest tightening. What had I done? What had I been thinking? I should never have gone off without Joey and Lindsey. I should have waited for Joey to finish his exploration and we should have stuck together.

I didn't know where in the cave I was. I had no clue if I was in a section of the cave that had been mapped. I hadn't left a marker at the jump. I had left a jump spool, but I couldn't remember if I had marked that one with my initials or not. If Joey or Lindsey saw it, they wouldn't know it was mine. They might think it was left behind by someone else.

I was going to die in this cave, and no one would be able to find my body. How would Joey and Lindsey take it? How would Jim take it? Would Jim blame himself for pushing me to go on this trip without him? Would Joey and Lindsey blame themselves for not keeping better tabs on me during our dives?

I had to find the opening. I had to get to the surface so I could figure out where I was. I had to get out of this cave.

59

Gary

I looked back at my wrist. I saw the Chokis wrapper peeking out. I felt myself starting to calm down. My breathing got slower. I placed a finger on the piece of the wrapper that was sticking out and flicked it back and forth. I tucked it farther into my sleeve. I didn't want to lose that wrapper.

I looked around the cave. I thought I saw a glimmer of light in the distance. I pulled my dive light into my chest and peered into the darkness. Was it just my imagination? Was I becoming so hopeful of seeing a way out of this cave that my mind was creating hopeful images? The lost underwater cave diver's version of a water oasis mirage in a dry desert?

I brought my dive light back up and saw the beam reflect off of something in the water. It was so hazy in this tunnel, and there was so much debris in the water. The debris wasn't trash. It was just pieces of detritus from the underwater environment. I wondered why it was so prevalent in this tunnel and no other part of the cave where we had been. The main tunnel did have some things in the water that made it look like we were swimming through shooting stars, but it didn't affect the visibility like this.

The glimmer of light I saw must have been caused by my dive light bouncing off the debris in the water. My mind had taken that and made me think I was seeing daylight. The situation was becoming more critical. I looked at my pressure gauge. This had to lead to a cenote where I could surface. If it didn't… I didn't even want to think about the consequences.

I stuck my finger in my sleeve and felt the Chokis wrapper. I continued to follow the line as I swept my light beam around the cave, occasionally shielding it to look for daylight. I hadn't seen any more trash in the past several minutes. The last piece of trash was the tire. I also hadn't seen any more line arrows. Had I passed the opening? Had I missed it? Was it behind me, somewhere near the tire?

I stopped swimming and assessed my situation. I could either keep going for a few more minutes to see where this line led, or I could turn around and swim back to the tire. Once at the tire, I could deploy line from one of my safety spools and search for an opening in the ceiling. If the opening was large enough for a tire to drop into it, it had to be large enough for me to get out of. At the very least, I could get my head above the surface and buy myself time to figure things out.

I decided to head back to the tire. The absence of trash concerned me. Where there was trash, there was an opening. No trash meant no access to the surface. It had been less than five minutes since I had seen the tire. It wouldn't take long to get back to it. I swam quickly and made it back to the tire in about three minutes. There was more trash in the area. The opening had to be nearby.

I pulled open my pocket flap and reached inside the pouch. I located my safety spool by feel and pulled it out, moving my fingers up the double-ender bolt snap to open the gate latch and release the spool from the small D ring that secured it inside the pocket. Transferring the safety spool to my left hand so I could free my right, I reached back in the pocket and searched for the pigtail holding my line markers. I found it and removed an arrow and a non-directional marker by feel. I would place the arrow on the line pointing in the same direction as the other arrows I had seen. The non-directional marker would go on the back side of the arrow to indicate the direction I had come from.

The non-directional marker seemed pointless at this time. I didn't have enough air to make it back out of the cave that way. My training had kicked in and I did what I had been taught, though. I got a little comfort doing what I had been trained to do, even if it was futile. Besides, if the visibility in this tunnel turned bad, I'd have that tactile marker telling me which way was which.

I secured the line from my safety spool on to the permanent guideline in between the arrow and the non-directional marker. I rotated until I was facing away from the permanent guideline and facing the direction of the tire. It was about fifteen feet away. I flicked my fins a few times until I was above the tire and looked around the cave. There was no indication on the silty floor to tell me where the tire had come from. Judging from the amount of silt on the tire, I surmised it had been there for quite some time, years, and any track would be filled in by this point.

I shielded my dive light and looked up, hoping to see even a sliver of light cutting through the darkness. Literally nothing. The ceiling of the cave was black. I unshielded my light and pointed it at the ceiling, looking for the brownish-yellow color associated with brackish tannic water. There was none of that either. I shined the light around the ceiling looking for a crack that might lead to an opening. The ceiling was solid rock. The tire hadn't dropped straight down.

I decided to swim to my left, the way I had been going along the line because that was where the current was coming from. The tire could have been pushed by the current before coming to its final resting place. It was possible I wouldn't be able to see an opening from where the guideline was located against the wall to my left, but I'd be able to see it from a more central location in the tunnel.

I swam for a couple of minutes, alternating between shielding my dive light to look for daylight and sweeping the beam across the ceiling looking for a crack or tannic water. I found neither. I felt a tug on my spool. I had let out all the line that was on it. I was one hundred and fifty feet away from where I had secured it to the permanent guideline. I turned around and spooled up my line, despondent.

I thought about Jim. I thought about Joey and Lindsey. I thought about my parents. How would they all react? How would they feel? Would anyone even be able to find my body? I was more than two hour's swim from the opening. Maybe less. I had been moving through the cave slowly. Divers could see the tunnel I went down once they found my jump spool, but would they swim that far to look for me? Would they know which way to go once they arrived at the intersecting lines?

I decided to swim along the permanent guideline in the direction the arrows had been telling me there should be an opening. I would follow the guideline until there was no more line. Hopefully, whoever placed those arrows hadn't placed them pointing in the wrong direction. Hopefully, I would find an opening beyond the end of the line. I removed the line from my jump spool from the permanent guideline and stowed the spool back in my pocket. I pulled my markers off the line and tucked them into the sleeve of my wetsuit, not the one with the Chokis wrapper, the other sleeve.

I began swimming along the guideline. I didn't bother looking around the cave this time. I would swim until I found daylight, or until I came to the end of the guideline. Hopefully, there would be daylight there. If there wasn't, I didn't know where else to look. If there wasn't, I was a dead man.

60

Joey

I continued to breathe air into Lindsey's lungs as I prayed for her to start breathing on her own. It hadn't been long between the last time I saw her moving underwater until the time we surfaced. A minute? Maybe less? During most of that time we had been ascending. Air should have been coming out of her lungs and not allowing water in. She had to survive. She had to come back to me.

I started unclipping her tanks from her harness in between rescue breaths. I gave her another breath as I watched her chest rise. I continued to pray. I reached behind her and pulled the zipper on her wetsuit down as far as I could so it wasn't squeezing her neck. I felt for a pulse. There might have been a faint one. I couldn't be sure. It gave me hope. I thought about doing chest compressions, but I couldn't get in a good position to do them. Lindsey was propped up on a slick, partially submerged boulder and I was standing on a ledge about four feet deeper.

I tried to climb on top of the boulder next to her to give me the leverage I needed to do proper compressions. It was too difficult. I hadn't removed my own tanks yet. I was too heavy and kept slipping off. I was better off continuing with the rescue breaths, especially if she still had a pulse. In between rescue breaths, I looked around frantically for someone that could call for help. I needed someone to call an ambulance. I screamed out in case someone could hear me.

"Help! Someone please help!"

The first day we had come to the cenote, we came back to this side of it and found a couple of locals hanging out, talking, and drinking beer. They finished their six pack, jumped on their motor scooter, and took off soon after we had arrived, leaving behind a pile of empties where they had been standing. Lindsey had gathered the trash into a sack and tossed it into the trunk of the car for proper disposal.

There was no one here this time.

I got Lindsey's left sidemount tank off first and pushed it to the opposite side of the boulder.

We also saw a couple of tour groups walk past us going to this side of the cenote as we were setting up our dive equipment. It wasn't constant, though. Groups were more common in the morning when we were setting up for the first dive. We hardly saw anyone at the cenote at the end of the second dive when we were tearing down the equipment and loading it into the car. It wasn't likely I would see anyone that could help me get Lindsey onto more solid ground or call for an ambulance.

I unclipped the stage tank and pushed it in the direction of the sidemount tank I had already released and started working on the right sidemount tank.

I gave Lindsey more rescue breaths, watching her chest rise and fall as I tried to breathe life back into her.

61

Gary

I thought I saw light in the distance. It was probably just another mirage. My imagination continued to play tricks on me. I kept swimming.

There it was again! This time it wasn't a flash of light. It was still there! I pulled my light back into my chest and shielded the beam. The light in the distance remained. I swam faster.

My next breath was cut off midway through the inhalation. I grabbed my pressure gauge and saw that the needle was pinned on the zero. I had breathed my stage tank empty. I quickly reached for my other regulator as I pushed the dead one out of my mouth. I found the regulator but couldn't get the bolt snap holding it in place on the right side of my chest off the D ring. My fingers fumbled, frantically trying to get it open.

I held my breath, hoping I could get the regulator free in time. After all this, to finally see light, only to drown with air in one of my tanks. Less than one hundred feet from an opening.

I gave up trying to get the bolt snap gate open and just yanked the regulator away from my shoulder. I felt the zip tie holding the bolt snap to the regulator hose break. I pulled the regulator away from the D ring and brought it to my mouth, pressing the purge button as the mouthpiece passed through my lips. I started to inhale, but it was too soon. I hadn't sealed my lips around the mouthpiece yet and I got a mouthful of water mixed in with the air that was being pushed through the regulator by the purge button.

I coughed violently as I tried to seal my lips around the mouthpiece. I didn't want to pull more water into my mouth as I was coughing. Coughing with my lips pursed around a mouthpiece was not easy, but I pushed through it until all the water was out of my throat and back into the environment around me.

I looked at the pressure gauge on my right tank, the one I was now breathing from. It had 700 psi in it. I had lost some air at some point. I should have switched regulators a while back. It hadn't occurred to me as I was searching for an opening to the surface. I was so focused on finding my way out I had forgotten to manage the air in my tanks. There was daylight less than one hundred feet ahead. I could make it there with 700 psi.

I swam as fast as I could toward the light. As I closed the distance the light spread across the passage. The opening ahead had to be as wide as the tunnel I was in. The tunnel was at least forty feet wide. The haziness remained. It gave the light a spooky look. It was almost like a fog, only underwater. Something moved to my right causing me to startle. I turned my light toward the movement and saw a fish swimming toward me. It was a decent size, maybe about a foot long. We had only seen tiny, guppy-like fish in the cenote over the past few days. What was such a large fish doing inside the cave?

I moved past the fish and continued toward the light. I watched it get brighter as I got closer. The outer edges of where the light was coming from were taller than the center. The opening looked like a giant frowning mouth. The cave was letting me know its disappointment in me for not following the rules. I advanced a few more feet and noticed there was a mound in the center of the opening causing the light to curve down around it at each end. The opening was the size of the tunnel I was in. There was a mound just outside of it. That must be where the cenote was. The ground had collapsed into the middle of the cave passage. I glanced at my dive computer and saw I was only twelve feet deep.

The line was tied to a large rock at the center of the mound. I looked up and saw I was just inside the cave. The ceiling above me extended another five feet or so. The line headed off to the left side. I could go straight, up over the mound, or follow the line to the edge of the opening. Following the line looked like the better option. I turned to go that way and noticed movement in the distance. I couldn't see what was moving. It could have been another fish. Or it could have been a crocodile. I looked at my pressure gauge. 300 psi. The air was going fast. I looked back up above me. The space between the top of the mound and the cave ceiling was small. I decided to keep going to the side of the opening. Fish or crocodile, I had to take my chances. I had to get to the surface.

62

Joey

I continued to give Lindsey rescue breaths as I fumbled through her tanks and hoses. I needed to get the tanks off her so I could pull her onto dry land. Just as I got the last hose pulled away from her, Lindsey started coughing. I quickly rolled her onto her side as I had been trained to do. She continued to cough violently, her body almost convulsing with the force. After about thirty seconds, the coughing began to slow down and decrease in intensity. I held Lindsey against me, her back against my chest, my arms wrapped around her. I silently thanked whoever or whatever had answered my prayers and brought her back to me.

"It's okay. We're out of the cave. We made it out of the cave." I cried as I rolled her back around and took her into my arms. I held her tight against my chest.

Stupid! Give her room to breathe! I thought to myself as I released my arms from around Lindsey. I moved back to give her room to breathe. Lindsey didn't say anything. She just stared at me with a confused look. I wondered if she had suffered any permanent injury. How long had she been unconscious? How long had she been without air? Had I managed to get her out of the cave only for her to have suffered brain damage from the lack of oxygen?

It couldn't be. She wasn't unconscious underwater for very long. It should have taken a lot longer to cause any permanent damage.

"How are you feeling? Can you talk?"

Lindsey opened her mouth. It looked like she was about to say something when another coughing fit ensued. I helped her sit up and held her, lightly patting her back until the coughing subsided. She tried again.

"I, I think I'm okay," Lindsey croaked, her voice low, deep, and raspy.

Then her eyes widened.

"Gary! Where's Gary??" Another coughing fit ensued.

I dropped my head. With the events that had occurred over the past half hour, I had completely forgotten about Gary. Not that we could have done anything differently. If we had breathed our tanks empty, Gary couldn't be alive.

"We never found him. We both ran out of air. Your tank emptied when we were about one hundred feet from the opening we came in. Fortunately…"

"Wait! Where are we? This isn't the cenote we entered."

"This is the other end of the cenote. The small pool on the north end where we could see the large opening to the cave. I saw the daylight coming from it and exited here instead. If it hadn't been for being right there when I took that last breath from your tank, we wouldn't have made it back to the surface."

Lindsey leaned back onto the rock she was lying on and closed her eyes. She hugged herself and rolled onto her side facing me. Her body started shaking again, but this time it wasn't a coughing fit that caused it. It was sobs of grief. I held her and also started to cry.

63

Gary

The movement to the left was another large fish. That didn't mean there wasn't a crocodile lurking in the shadows of this cenote. I nervously looked around as I followed the guideline the last few feet until I came to the end of it. The line was tied onto a small protrusion sticking out from the bottom of the mound.

I looked up. There was still a ceiling over me. The edge was only a few feet to my right, though. There was a lot more clearance between the mound and the ceiling. I continued swimming around the mound until I was completely out of the overhead environment and had a clear ascent to the surface. I swam toward the surface hoping I wasn't trapped in the middle of the jungle, but thankful I didn't have to go back the way I had come.

The cenote I was in looked like the one we had been entering the past few days. It had the same lush green bottom. It had the same old brown plants rising toward the surface from where they were anchored somewhere below the green carpet on the floor. It looked so familiar.

That wasn't the opening we had gone through into the cave. The opening I just came through was much bigger than the opening we entered more than three hours earlier. There was no mound at our entrance. Just a rocky opening about five feet wide by six feet tall. I looked back at where I had just come from. It definitely wasn't the same opening.

I scanned the cenote to make sure there wasn't a crocodile lying in wait. I still didn't see any. Movement to my right startled me. I turned my head and saw another fish, maybe the same one I saw as I swam out of the cave. I looked at my dive computer and saw the depth reading had been replaced by a dash. I was less than four feet from the surface. As I took my next breath, the air stopped coming halfway through. The gauge must have been wrong. Fortunately, my head broke through the surface at that moment, and I felt the heat of the day on it.

I quickly raised my head out of the water, spit out my regulator so I could finish my breath. I shook my head to clear my mask lens. I looked around. This was the cenote we had entered. Either that or a very similar looking one. I spun around. I saw our rental car parked near the edge of the cenote to my right. I was on the opposite side of the cenote from the opening we had been using. We entered the cave through a small opening directly across from where I just exited.

I turned around to look at the area where I came from. I dropped my mask back under the surface to look at the opening. I couldn't see it even from this short distance. The mound blocked the view and behind it was nothing but shadows and darkness. We had been swimming right by this opening the past three days without realizing there was another entrance to the cave beyond the shadows.

What I didn't understand was how I got to that opening from where we were in the cave. We had entered the cave to the right and continued to turn right as we made our way back to the tunnel we were in. This other opening was to the left. The only way I would have been able to get to that tunnel would have been if the tunnel I was in crossed under the cenote. I didn't have the maps memorized like Joey, but I definitely didn't remember a tunnel passing beneath the cenote.

Joey and Lindsey! They should have surfaced long ago! I frantically searched the perimeter of the cenote looking for any sign of them. I didn't see any tanks or dive equipment. The car was parked in the same spot under the trees.

I looked at my dive computer. The dive timer read three hours and twenty-four minutes. They should have surfaced more than an hour ago. Were they still in the cave looking for me? Were they trying to find me? What had I done?

64

Lindsey

I was thankful Joey and I had made it out alive. I was thankful to be alive. I was also devastated at the thought of Gary being lost in the cave. Lost and dead. I knew other people who had lost cave diving teammates during dives. I didn't know them well but knew them enough to know that they were never the same after their incidents. Losing a friend like that during an activity that's supposed to be fun and relaxing changed a person.

Cave diving wasn't without its risks. The purpose of cave diving training was to teach divers how to reduce the risks and how to deal with any issues that arose during a dive. We were taught how to plan dives so they were safe. We were told how to deal with issues such as team separation and losing awareness of the guideline. The problem was that once one thing went wrong, other issues were certain to follow if you didn't stop the process and mitigate the situation. I didn't know what issues Gary had encountered. I didn't know how bad it had gotten for him. All I knew was that we had gotten separated and never reunited.

Gary was dead.

I burst into tears. A huge relief that Joey and I were alive, but devastated that Gary was not. The feelings were so conflicting I didn't know how to deal with them. How could I be happy at anything with

Gary dead? As I continued to cry into Joey's shoulder, my mind began to clear from the confusion I had been feeling. I began to remember what had happened during those last moments before I lost consciousness. I was breathing into and out of my BC. I remembered my perception getting hazy. I remembered looking through a telescope. Then a feeling of euphoria came over me. I knew I was going to die, but I didn't care. I wasn't afraid. I was content. I was fine with the decision I had made.

What a strange feeling. I didn't know what to make of it. I never thought I would be content to know I was about to die. I didn't think I would welcome death, not at such a young age. Somehow, I hadn't died. Somehow Joey had been able to get us both out of the cave before I drowned. I never thought I would need to be rescued from a dive, especially from a cave dive. I had assisted others that had found themselves in trouble in a cave. I thought back to Alex and Emily and finding them in Eddy Spring a little more than a year earlier. I thought back to Jack Johnson trying to take credit for rescuing me and Emily.

I wondered what happened to Jack. After his incident in Jackson Blue, no one had heard from him again. He was sent to UAB Medical Center in Alabama for a series of surgeries and was never seen around the caves of Marianna, Florida again. I'm sure if Jack was here right now, he would have found some way to take credit for rescuing me and Joey. Why was I thinking about Jack at a moment like this?

I pushed back the tears, opened my eyes, and wiped my face. My forehead was sore. I touched it lightly. It felt tender. Then I remembered hitting my head on the ceiling where it dipped down. I felt the lump on my forehead. That was going to look lovely the next day.

I slowly pushed myself up into a sitting position. Joey helped. He was so helpful. I looked around the area where we had surfaced. I recognized it from the first day we had been here and walked this way to look at the big opening to the cave. I looked around the perimeter of the small pool of water we were in. We were alone. It was just me and Joey. I bent my knees so I could climb out of the water onto dry land. Joey held onto me.

"Take it easy, babe. You've just been through a lot."

"I just want to get out of the water, Joe. I need to get this hood and wetsuit off."

"Give me a minute to get my tanks off."

Joey quickly unclipped his tanks and let them drop onto the ledge he was standing on. He pulled himself up onto the edge of the cenote and flipped himself around so he was sitting on it with his legs dangling in the water. He then stood up and grabbed my arms. He pulled me up in one motion until I was standing on the ground next to him. I instantly felt dizzy and grabbed onto him.

The dizziness passed and I slowly pulled my hood off, careful to not have it press against the lump on my forehead too much, and let my hair drop down. It felt good to get the pressure of the hood off my head. I started to bend over toward the water.

"What are you doing?" Joey asked as he grabbed onto me.

"I just need to splash some water on my face."

Joey filled his hood with water and held it in front of me. I cupped my hands and he poured some water into them. I splashed the water on my face, rubbing the tear streaks from my cheeks.

I looked at Joey and saw he had also been crying. I wiped his face with my wet hands.

"Now what?" I asked.

65

Gary

As I was making my way to the place we had been using to get in and out of the water, I heard a splash behind me. I spun around as quickly as I could considering I still had my tanks clipped to my sides and fins on my feet. I was hoping to see Lindsey and Joey surfacing from the opening we had entered at the beginning of the dive. There was nothing there.

I pulled my mask and hood off so I could hear better. I heard another splash just as my hood cleared my ears. I didn't see anything in the part of the cenote that was in view. The sound was coming from the far end of the cenote. The end where the larger opening to the cave was located. The trees blocked my view of that end so I couldn't tell what was causing it. Was there a crocodile over there? Were there people over there cooling off in the water?

I turned back toward the edge of the cenote nearest me. I arrived at the wall and stood on a large boulder about four feet below the surface, my chest about even with the ground in front of me. I placed my hood, mask, and dive light on the hard, rocky surface in front of me and began unclipping my tanks from my harness. I pulled the stage tank off and slid it onto the ledge. I unclipped the sidemount tank on my right and almost dropped it when I heard someone coughing behind me. I pushed the tank up on the rock next to my stage tank and quickly unclipped my final tank. The coughing didn't stop. Someone was having a bad time. I hoisted the last tank up next to the other two. The coughing stopped almost as abruptly as it had started.

I pulled my fins off my feet and placed them on top of the tanks. I started to undo the belly strap on my wing, but my fingers didn't want to work properly. I heard more coughing. I decided I could leave the harness and BC on for the time being. I had to get out of the water to investigate. Could it be Lindsey and Joey?

I found the small foothold we had been using to climb out of the cenote and pulled myself up onto the edge of the shoreline next to my tanks. The coughing stopped again. I thought I heard people talking. It wasn't loud enough to make out what they were saying. I couldn't even tell if it was English or Spanish being spoken.

I stood up and began to run toward the sound. I ran from the hard rocky ground over the grass and into a muddy puddle caused by tire ruts. I felt my foot slipping as my other foot was coming up off the grass. My foot slid out from under me, and I went down. The back of my head slammed against the ground, hitting it hard. Fortunately, it was on the grass and not the rock. I lay there for a moment gathering my senses.

I pushed my upper body up and sat still for a moment, dazed from the fall. I felt a pain in my lower back. I had landed on top of my explorer reel. I reached back and unclipped it from the D ring it was attached to and brought it in front of me. There was no damage to it. I couldn't say the same for my back.

I decided to remove my harness before standing up. I forced myself to move slowly as I worked the bolt snaps and belt buckle holding the harness in place. I wanted to move faster but I couldn't. I finally got everything unclipped and began pulling the shoulder straps off. As I was slipping the first shoulder strap off, I heard what sounded like someone crying. I quickly shoved the harness off and pushed myself up. Leaving my harness in the mud puddle where I dropped it, I began running toward the sound of the crying. This time I was careful not to run through any puddles.

66

Joey

Lindsey and I sat down on the ledge, our legs dangling in the water. We held each other, both of us crying. We didn't know what we were going to do. Then I heard noise coming from the other end of the cenote. It sounded like something large being dropped. Could it be Gary? Could he have gotten out of the cave alive? Or was it a tourist group dropping a bicycle?

"C'mon. I hear someone on the other side of the cenote."

I pulled my legs up and scooted back. I pushed myself up. Once I was standing, I reached down for Lindsey and grabbed her under her arms. She pulled her feet in as I raised her up and into a standing position. The realization that I had almost lost her in the cave hit me again and I wrapped my arms around her, pulled her in tight and just held her. I heard more noise coming from beyond the trees.

"C'mon! That might be Gary."

I let go of Lindsey to head toward the sound.

"Wait. I feel dizzy. I think I'm going to…"

I caught Lindsey just as her legs gave way from under her. I kept her from hitting the ground. I carefully lowered her to a sitting position.

"I'm okay. I-I don't know what happened. I feel lightheaded."

"You've been through a lot. You lost consciousness. You almost died. We both almost died. Let's just sit here for a minute."

I heard more sounds. I wanted to run to the other side of the trees and see if it was Gary. I couldn't leave Lindsey alone, though. I needed to get her to a hospital and seen by a doctor.

I heard what sounded like someone grunting.

"Just sit here. Don't try to get up. I'm going to go check on the sounds we're hearing and grab some water from the car for you. Lie back and don't try to get up."

I helped Lindsey lie back on the ground. I folded my BC and placed it under her head with our hoods on top of it as a cushion.

"I'll be right back."

"Okay, but don't be long."

I took off running along the road and around the trees that were blocking our view of the other side of the cenote. Just as I rounded the last tree, I saw the back of a diver standing up from the mud pit that was on that end of the cenote. The bottom half of the wetsuit was covered in mud.

The diver turned toward me. It was Gary! I ran even faster as I watched him start to run in my direction. I watched Gary hit the next mud pit and fall backward into the first mud pit. I started to laugh.

Gary had made it out of the cave!

67

Gary

"Dammit!"

I was being so careful this time. I picked my head up and saw I had slipped in another mud pit. The water must have receded, but the area was still wet and slick. I fell back into the first mud pit, which cushioned the fall, but I was covered in mud from head to toe.

I picked my muddy head up and saw someone running toward me. It was Joey! He was running along the rocky dirt road coming from the other end of the cenote. He was also laughing.

"Slow down! This muddy road is slick as hell. This is the second time I fell in as many minutes!"

Joey heeded my warning and slowed his pace to a fast walk. He continued to laugh. I pushed myself off the ground and stood up, careful to avoid any more mud or puddles. Then I felt Joey's arms embrace me and hold me tight.

"Dude, what happened to you? Where did you go? We've been looking for you for more than an hour and a half!"

I looked at Joey, ashamed of what I had put them through. Embarrassed for myself.

"I'm so sorry, man!" I dropped my head in shame. "I headed down this tunnel I found. I came across some arrows that were pointing in the direction I was going. I was going to turn around, but I had blown the visibility out behind me so badly I didn't want to go back through it. You know how silt-outs freak me out. I decided to take my chance by going with the arrows. I just swam on. I kept going and before I knew it, I didn't have enough air to turn around and make it back the way I had come."

"Wait! What? What do you mean? Where did you exit the cave?"

"Right over there." I pointed to the opposite side of the cenote.

"There's an opening over there?"

"Yeah, we've been swimming past it for the last three days. You can't see it until you're practically on top of it. Even when I surfaced, I looked down into the water and couldn't tell it was an opening." I paused and looked around. "What happened to your forehead dude? Why is there a big ole goose egg there? And where's Lindsey?"

"Crap!" Joey took off running as he called back to me. "She's back near the main opening to the cave. We had some issues during our swim out and had to exit there instead. I'll tell you about the goose egg later."

I ran after Joey as he headed back to where Lindsey was lying on the ground.

"Linds, how are you feeling?" Joey yelled out as she came into view.

"Still a little woozy, but I think I'll be okay. Help me stand up again."

Joey and I each took one of Lindsey's arms and gently raised her up off the rocky ground to a standing position.

"Gary!! You're alive!!!"

I looked down sheepishly as Lindsey hugged me. I had really put them through a hard time. I might have almost gotten them killed all because of my desire to find some stupid virgin cave passage.

"Y'all are too." I mumbled.

Joey and I held onto Lindsey as she gathered her bearings. I wondered about what they had gone through. I wondered about what

I had put them through by swimming off without them.

We got Lindsey to the car. Joey started it so Lindsey could cool off in the air conditioning while I grabbed three bottles of water to keep all of us hydrated. I heard a truck pulling into the dirt lot and looked up. It was Jose, our dive guide from the first dive. He pulled in next to our car, shut off his truck and hopped out.

"Hey guys! I was just driving by on my way home from the marina and saw you here. How was your dive?"

68

Joey

While Lindsey sat in the car sipping water with the air conditioning keeping her cool, Gary and I filled Jose in on the dive. We didn't give him the whole story, just the highlights. We didn't want to be banned from diving the caves of Cozumel on our first trip there. All we told him was that we had gotten separated and did a much longer dive than planned while we looked for each other. All was well. We knew what we did wrong, and we were going to make sure not to get separated again.

We thought we had gotten away with it. Then the smile on Jose's face transformed to a look of concern.

"What's wrong with your girl?"

I turned around and saw Lindsey slumped back in the car. We had sat her sideways in the front passenger seat with her legs hanging out of the door opening. She had been sitting up with the vents blowing cool air on her while she sipped water. She was lying back over the center console. She was unconscious.

I ran to her and shook her shoulders.

"Lindsey! Linds! Wake up!"

No response. I felt for a pulse as I watched to see if she was still breathing. I saw her chest rise and fall. Her breathing was shallow, though. I couldn't feel a pulse on her wrist. I quickly moved my fingers up to her neck to feel for her carotid pulse. I found a faint one.

"Jose! Call 911!"

Jose was already on his phone talking to someone in rapid-fire Spanish. I understood one word – *emergencia*.

"Help me get her out of the car onto the ground!"

Gary ran around to the driver's door and positioned himself behind Lindsey. He slipped his hands beneath her shoulders as I grabbed her around the waist.

"On the count of three. One, two, three!"

We lifted Lindsey, and I backed up as Gary tried to crawl over the center console. Jose ended the call.

"The ambulance is on the way. There is one down the street near the Chankanaab road."

"Help us, Jose! Take her shoulders from Gary."

Jose stepped next to Lindsey and placed an arm across her upper back while Gary continued to support her head. I heard a siren in the distance. We got her onto the grassy area next to the car. A moment later, an ambulance came to a stop on the asphalt road. The passenger jumped out and ran to the back of the ambulance. The driver ran directly to us.

"¿Qué pasó?"

Jose responded. I had no idea what he was telling the woman. I wished I had told Jose the truth. I wished I had told him what had really happened in that cave. I wanted to tell him now, but I didn't know what he was saying and didn't want to interrupt him. I just wanted them to help Lindsey.

The man that had gotten out of the passenger side of the ambulance ran toward us pushing a gurney with a couple of bags of equipment on top of it. The dirt lot was so uneven he was having difficulty pushing it from the ambulance to Lindsey. Gary ran over to him and grabbed the front of the gurney. They lifted it and carried it the rest of the way.

The two medics began working on Lindsey. The man pulled out a football shaped device and used it to push air into Lindsey's lungs while the woman started an IV in Lindsey's arm. I flinched as I saw the needle puncture the soft skin in the crook of her elbow. I was used to seeing needles going into dogs and cats at the veterinary office where I worked, but it was different to see it happening to Lindsey.

With an IV in her arm and fluids dripping into her body, the medics rolled her onto a hard board and lifted her onto the gurney. They quickly strapped her down and raised the gurney. They half carried, half rolled the gurney across the fifty feet of pothole filled dirt lot between the grass and the ambulance. They slid the gurney into the back of the ambulance. I tried to climb in after them, but they pushed me away as they yelled something in Spanish. The woman slammed the doors shut and ran around to the driver's door. I stood there and watched them as they turned the ambulance around in the narrow road, trying to avoid the six-inch drop from the asphalt to the dirt lot.

I watched them take off up the road toward the hospital.

69

Joey

Once the ambulance had turned left onto the main highway and disappeared out of sight, I turned to Jose. The look on his face told me he knew we hadn't told him the entire truth about our dive. To his credit, he didn't ask for any more details.

"They are taking her to the international hospital. It's the hospital with a hyperbaric chamber. They will probably put her in the chamber, so you won't be able to see her for several hours."

"Do you think I'll have time to see her before they put her in the chamber? Can you tell me how to get to the hospital?"

"I'll do better. I'll take you." Jose turned to Gary. "Are you okay? Will you be okay here getting the tanks and the equipment if I bring Joe to the hospital?"

"Yeah, sure! Of course! Just tell me how to get to the hospital and I'll meet you there in about twenty to thirty minutes."

"Just go toward Mega Supermarket. Two streets more and turn right. The hospital is on the right side. Tall building. You can't miss it."

I climbed into Jose's truck, and we rushed off to the hospital. I hoped we would be able to get there before they put Lindsey in the chamber.

It took way too long. There were several cruise ships in port and the traffic, both vehicle and pedestrian, was super congested. I almost jumped out of Jose's truck to run to the hospital.

"You don't want to do that. We'll be through this in a couple of minutes then it will be better. This is only like this until we get to the cruise ships. Then no more."

I trusted him. But I fidgeted in the passenger seat. I should have fought harder to get into the ambulance with Lindsey. I should have insisted.

Jose was right. A couple of minutes later we drove past the cruise ship terminal and the street cleared of most of the traffic. Jose stepped on the accelerator, and we flew down the road. Whenever a motor scooter got in the way he hit his horn and maneuvered around them. I was glad Jose had kept me from jumping out. It was much farther than I remembered it being.

We were moving along quickly until we reached the traffic light in front of Margaritaville. I watched it turn red as we were approaching it.

"Almost there jefe. Less than a kilometer."

I could run that distance. I could be there sooner.

"Don't think about jumping out again. I'll still get you there faster than you can run."

He was right again. A minute later, the light turned green, and we took off down the road. Another minute and Jose turned right onto another street, and I saw the ambulance halfway up the block. The emergency lights were on, but the back doors were open. Lindsey had already been taken out and brought into the hospital.

"It's a good sign that the doors are still open. They just bring her in. After you see her, maybe you should get that knot on your head checked."

I jumped out of the truck before Jose brought it to a complete stop.

I ran toward the only doors I saw. The male medic was coming out of the door, and I rushed up to him.

"Where is she? Where did you bring her?"

He stared back with a look of confusion.

"¿Dónde?"

The medic pointed to a hallway inside the building. I ran through the door past him and in the direction he had pointed hoping they hadn't brought her straight to the chamber. Hoping I still had a minute to see her and hold her before they brought her in.

*　*　*

I did get to see Lindsey briefly before they whisked her away to the hyperbaric chamber. She had regained consciousness by that time. The doctors only let me see her for a minute. I hugged her and kissed her and told her I loved her. Then I watched them wheel her off for six hours in the chamber.

Jose walked up behind me just as I saw them wheel Lindsey around a corner down the hall.

"Did you see her? Is she okay?"

"She was awake. She said she felt weak. The doctors took her to the hyperbaric chamber."

Jose and I walked back to the waiting room. He sat down while I paced back and forth.

"You should sit. It will be a long six hours if you keep pacing like that. You will wear a hole in the floor."

I sat down for a minute. Then I stood back up.

"I'm too anxious about Lindsey. I can't sit still."

"I understand."

Jose looked at his phone for a couple of minutes.

"Do you want to tell me what really happened on your dive?"

I looked at Jose. I had to tell him the truth. Ban or no ban. He already knew too much not to suspect something. And he had been so helpful. I didn't know what we would have done if he hadn't stopped by on his way home.

Epilogue

Gary arrived at the hospital just as I was beginning to tell Jose what had happened. He sat down and listened to the details of our dive. When I finished telling them everything, they sat in front of me with their jaws dropped. They couldn't believe what they had just heard. Once the shock wore off, Gary told Jose and me what had happened to him. Jose knew about the tunnel that crossed under the cenote and came out into Shark Alley. He had made the connection only a year earlier. He had found it from the Shark Alley side. After Jose mentioned Shark Alley, we both remembered him telling us about it two days earlier. Gary finally understood why the visibility was hazy and why the current was going in the direction it was.

The doctor came out to give us an update. He told us Lindsey was doing okay. Then he disappeared and left us in the lobby.

"You don't have to wait with us, Jose. You can leave if you want."

"No, I wait. I don't have anything else going on."

So we waited.

The doctor came back out a couple of hours later.

"Senhorita Carter is doing fine. She is awake and talking to us. I don't think she had decompression illness. She is not showing any symptoms of it. But it was better to be precautionary and put her in the chamber. It does not hurt her. She will be done with her treatment in two more hours. Then we will watch her for an hour, and she can go home. But no more diving for her for at least two weeks. And only if she is feeling one hundred percent."

Two hours later a nurse came to get us and brought us back to see Lindsey. We sat with her until they discharged her. She apologized profusely for causing all this trouble. We all told her to shut up and just lie there and rest. And no more passing out!

Gary and I talked about what we were going to do the rest of the week. Lindsey insisted we dive. We were there to dive and there was no point in us not diving just because she couldn't dive. We just had to promise her that we wouldn't get separated from each other. We had to stay together even if it meant tying a rope between us.

"When you boys come out of that cave, your heads better be brown from swimming one right behind the other!"

Lindsey was well enough to make jokes. At least we thought it was a joke. We all laughed, but we were both afraid that she really meant it.

Jose told us he didn't have any clients the next couple of days and asked if he could join us.

"You most certainly can, Jose!" Lindsey cried out before we even had a chance to respond. "It will be your responsibility to keep them in line."

Jose grabbed his phone and scrolled through it for a second.

"Well, look at that. I just got a reservation for the next two days. Sorry!" There was a big smile on his face, and he winked at Gary and me.

Lindsey sat out the dives the next two days. She spent it lying back in a lounge chair by the pool, reading and enjoying the warm sun on her skin. Jose had to send Lindsey a message before each dive letting her know we were heading in and again after each dive letting her know everyone was safe and sound and out of the cave and no one had separated from the group. Jose, Gary, and I had to give a full report of our dives each afternoon when we returned to the house. Cave diving would never be the same for us.

Thanks for reading *Beyond Hope*!

Please take a moment to leave a review on Amazon. Reviews help provide more exposure to books. The more reviews a book has, the more likely Amazon will be to show it in search results. A simple statement is all that's needed to help boost exposure. But if you're so inclined, a more thorough review is always appreciated. Rob does read the reviews and uses suggestions to help improve his writing. You can find a link to the Amazon listing on the List of Works page at www.RobNeto.com/list-of-works

If you liked this book and want to see more by Rob Neto, please visit www.RobNeto.com for a list of his other books. Rob has drafts of several more books, including three other books beyond the fourth in the series, Beyond the End of the Line. This number will likely grow even more.

Be sure to check out Rob's new adventure series, *Beneath the Jungle of Cozumel*. The first book is due out in October 2024. In this series, Rob gives a factual account of the cave exploration he has done in Cozumel. You might even recognize some of the scenes from *Beyond Hope* in his first book, *Connecting the Crowns*.

Once you're on the website, make sure to subscribe to the monthly newsletter. Email addresses are not sold or distributed, and you will only receive one email a month to update you on Rob's books and alert you to any price specials he may have going on. You'll be the first to hear about new series, new books, and to see cover reveals.

See you in the next book!

ABOUT THE AUTHOR

Rob Neto is an avid cave diver who lives in the Florida panhandle just minutes away from some of his favorite caves. He is an active cave explorer and retired cave and technical diving instructor. He spent more than ten years teaching scuba diving in Arizona and Florida. He is also the author of the book Sidemount Diving The *Almost* Comprehensive Guide, the first comprehensive book about sidemount diving. With almost three hundred pages of information and photos, Sidemount Diving is on its 2nd edition and has been translated into Dutch, German and Spanish, and is currently being translated into more languages. Rob published his first novel, *Beyond the Grate*, in July 2023. *Beyond the Grate* was awarded a Silver Award in Suspense Thrillers by the Global Book Awards in September 2023 and has received numerous reviews on Amazon, GoodReads, and Facebook. Rob is already working on the fourth book in the Joey Simmons series, *Beyond the End of the Line*. Rob is also working on a new adventure series about his cave exploration in Cozumel. The title of the series is *Beneath the Jungle of Cozumel*. The first book, *Connecting the Crowns*, should hit bookshelves in October 2024.

Rob is married to his wonderful, supportive wife of almost twenty-two years and has a household of furry family members. At the time of this publication his family consisted of four dogs, one inside cat, and several outside cats.

Coming Soon!

Beyond the End of the Line

Another Joey Simmons and Lindsey Carter novel!

Beyond the End of the Line brings Joey and Lindsey back to the Florida underwater caves. Joey was bitten hard by the exploration bug in Mexico. After returning home to Florida, he made up his mind to focus his cave diving efforts on finding virgin passage in the Florida caves. His efforts paid off! Not only did Joey and Lindsey find virgin cave passage, but they found a whole new section beyond the end of the line of one of the most popular caves in North Florida. The problem was that another diver found their lead. This diver went to the new section and started leaving his own line and line markers everywhere. He even removed Joey and Lindsey's line markers and took credit for the find. Read *Beyond the End of the Line* to find out how Joey and Lindsey deal with this injustice.

1

Joey

"I can't believe someone scooped my lead! That's not cool! I've been working that area for months. I've surveyed and mapped it. I've spent more than a hundred hours exploring that section of the cave."

"Babe, calm down."

"I don't wanna fuckin' calm down! That was my lead! That was my section to explore. Whoever it was didn't just extend the end of my line by a couple hundred feet. There's hundreds of feet of lined tunnels back there now. Maybe thousands!"

"We'll get back there and survey it and make our own map and then continue to explore it."

"We don't have time for that. We have to get to the end of the line and just keep pushing. The survey will have to come later. If we try to survey the line that's already there, whoever put it there will keep pushing the end of the line farther and farther and we'll never get to put in more line."

"Yeah, you have a point. So we'll go back there next weekend and find the new end of the line. Whoever did this probably left a line arrow with his initials or his name on it. We'll know who it is then. But I don't know what difference that will make."

"It'll make a difference because I'm going to find that asshole and set him straight. That's my find! That's my exploration! He has no right being back there!"

"What are you going to do? What can you do? You can't kick someone's ass because they don't give a shit about cave diving etiquette."

"Why not?"

"Well, maybe because that could get you arrested for assault."

"He stole my lead!"

"That's not a crime, babe."

That's not what I wanted to hear. I stomped around the room looking for a way to get rid of the feelings I was having, a way to deal with my anger. I turned toward Lindsey, "Dammit! It's just so frustrating!"

"I know it is. We've worked hard on this. Especially you. You've put a lot of hours into this project."

I moved around the room again looking for something to hit. I was that mad. I didn't want to break anything, especially my hand. It wasn't worth it. But I had to get my frustration out somehow.

"Aaaaaaaaahhhhhhhhhhhh!!!!!"

"Feel better now?"

It was pissing me off that Lindsey was being so calm and rational about this. She had put in almost as much work as I had into this project. Why wasn't she as angry as I was?

"No, I don't. I won't feel better until I have the end of the line to claim as my own again. And I don't want to wait until next weekend to get it back."

"What are you going to do? We can't go back there tonight. We already did a three-hour dive today. And you're way too upset to be able to dive safely."

"I can control it. I just need to get back there and look around. I need to see how much passage has been lined. I need to see how far whoever did this has gotten."

"We'll find out in due course."

"But what if he goes back there during the week? What if while we're stuck at work, he's in the cave pushing more virgin passage? What if he's in the cave extending the end of the line hundreds or even thousands of feet?"

"What if he is doing that? You can't just stop going to work to go cave diving every day. Yeah, that would be nice, but it's not realistic. Besides, our light and scooter batteries aren't even charged."

"Dammit! I didn't think about that!" I paced around the room some more. "Who could it be? Who could have known we were working that area of the cave? I haven't told anyone. I haven't posted anything about it on social media. I've been careful not to go back there if anyone else was in the area."

"It wouldn't be too difficult to figure it out. We have safety tanks in the cave. And you've been leaving your line markers all over the place marking the lines that you've surveyed. All someone would have to do is come across some of those and they'd quickly figure out you were doing something back there."

"Dammit! That was stupid! I should have figured out another way to mark those lines."

"Well, hindsight babe. We can't change the past."

"I can change the future though. And I'm going to find out who did this and I'm calling him out on it."

"Let's cross that bridge when we get to it. Let's find out who this is first."

I grabbed a pillow off the couch and punched it. I punched it again. And again and again. It wasn't helping. I needed something more substantial. I needed to break something. Just then Lindsey took the last swig from her beer and set the bottle on the table. I quickly snatched it up, stood up, and looked around. Seeing nothing I could throw it against without causing major damage, I started walking toward the door.

"Where are you going? Why do you have my beer bottle?"

I yanked the door open and stepped outside, slamming the door shut behind me. I looked around the apartment complex. I couldn't see anyone around. I flung the beer bottle over the banister toward the sidewalk below with all the force I could muster up. It crashed on the edge of the sidewalk below and broke up into hundreds of little pieces all over the mulch landscape. It wasn't as satisfying as I had hoped. I should have gone down the steps and gotten closer to the sidewalk. Or better yet, I should have walked across the parking lot to the dumpster and slammed it against the side of the dumpster.

I turned around and stormed back into our apartment. Lindsey was sipping beer from a newly opened bottle.

"Do you feel better?"

"No!" I grabbed her bottle and gulped the beer down in one long swallow.

"Hey! That was my beer!"

I ignored Lindsey, turned around, and stormed back out of the room. This time I walked down the steps and across the parking lot to the dumpster. I flung the bottle as hard as I could into its side. The bottle shattered into thousands of pieces. I felt small bits of glass hitting my face and my bare arms and legs as it ricocheted back toward me.

Now I felt better.

2

5 hours earlier

What the fuck!?!?! I couldn't believe what I was seeing. I had just laid the line I was following farther into the cave the day before. This was virgin passage before that. And this was where I had stopped and turned around because the air in my scuba tanks had reached our agreed turn pressure.

I hadn't been ready to turn around and exit the cave. I still had knotted line on my reel. I was hoping to surface with an empty reel. The problem was I couldn't continue to push into the virgin passage safely. I didn't know what was beyond the end of the line and if something happened that delayed my exit, I might need the emergency air reserves in my tanks.

I learned that lesson the hard way a few months earlier in Mexico. I kept swimming farther into the cave, looking around the next corner, ignoring the pressure gauges on my tanks. I was lucky I got out of that cave alive. I swore that day that I would never push the limits again. Here I was really wanting to continue, but not being able to.

In cave diving, we planned our dives using the rule of thirds. We used one third of the air in our tanks to penetrate into the cave, one third to exit the cave, and one third was reserved for emergencies. I had breathed through the first third and had to tie off the line I was laying in this tunnel, no matter how much I wanted to go a little farther and see what was around the next corner only twenty feet ahead.

The marker with my initials on it was right where I left it three inches from the end of the line. I had left a loop dangling loose on the other side of the formation I had tied the line to so I could easily loop new line through it and continue to push the tunnel. That was how I claimed this lead. A loop at the end of the line with my marker right before it. Anyone who had the experience to be this far back in the cave should know that and respect it. At least that was my thought on the matter. Apparently, someone else didn't think so.

Someone else had come into this cave, back to this area of the cave, and back to this very spot, and scooped my lead. They had tied their own line into my loop and continued to line my lead. My passage. It just wasn't right!

My line marker and the loop were clear indicators that I was planning on returning to keep pushing the passage. Cave diving etiquette dictated that it should have been left alone. My line should not have been extended by anyone but me. Yet, here I was, looking at my line, and seeing someone else's line extending into the darkness and around the corner into the virgin cave tunnel I had found. This was bullshit!

I turned toward Lindsey and pointed to the atrocity I was looking at. She shrugged her shoulders like it was no big deal. Like it didn't bother her that someone had just come in and stolen a lead that we had worked hard to find. It didn't seem to faze her one bit.

I turned away from her and continued to follow the line. I had to see how far the tunnel had been pushed. I had to see what was around that next corner. I should have pushed that last twenty feet yesterday! Hopefully, whoever had done this hadn't put very much line in. How far could this person have gotten? Especially without knowing the cave back here.

We were about five thousand feet from the cave entrance. Almost a mile! It took us a little more than an hour to travel using our dive propulsion vehicles, or DPVs. We usually referred to them as scooters. If we were able to leave our jump lines in place it would take us less than an hour. But we didn't dare leave our jump lines in place. We didn't want someone to follow them and find the area where we had been working. Apparently, it didn't matter. They found it anyway. We might as well have left the lines in.

I thought back to the first time my cave diving instructor taught us about jumps and gaps and how to deal with them inside a submerged cave.

"I don't understand. Why aren't the lines all connected to each other? Why bother leaving gaps in them?" I asked Adam, my instructor.

"Think back to the dives you've been doing at the intro cave diver level and what your limitations have been," Adam replied.

"I could only breathe one-sixth of the air in my tanks before having to turn and exit the cave. I couldn't go deeper than one hundred feet. I had to stay on the main line in the cave. No navigational decisions."

"Exactly! And how many lines going off to side tunnels have you seen just here in Jackson Blue?"

I thought about it for a moment. The Horseshoe Circuit, Young's Siphon, Parallel Line, the Squirrel Tunnel. That was just in the first four hundred feet.

"Okay, I get your point. If the lines were left connected to the main line, intro cave divers would have to turn around long before they reached their turn pressure. But what about farther back in the cave? Beyond where intro cave divers might go? Why are there gaps back there?"

"Well, part of that is force of habit. We're so used to having gaps in the front of the cave that we continue to have them in the back. Although, once you start heading back farther into the cave, you'll notice there are a lot more intersecting lines. There are even some gold line Ts where white cave lines tie into the main passage gold line." Adam said referring to the places where the lines in the offshoot tunnels were tied into the line in the main tunnel. "As you get off the main tunnel and into the smaller side tunnels, you'll see even more intersecting lines. You'll still

see some jumps along the main tunnel simply because the rules state you have to mark all navigational decisions. A line intersection is a navigational decision and requires you to stop and place a line marker on the guideline leading out of the cave. Usually, if you're that far back, you're on a scooter and stopping isn't as convenient as when you're swimming."

"That makes sense."

"Another thing is exploration. Anyone doing exploration in a cave isn't going to want to mark the way to where they're exploring. Explorers will typically leave longer gaps to try to keep others from finding the path to where they're exploring."

Having these gaps in place, especially the longer ones, kept some divers out of the less traveled offshoot areas. They either didn't know about them, or they were simply too lazy to bother to run a jump line that far.

Except this time. This time someone had found the area I had been exploring. And that someone stole my lead. Cave diving etiquette dictated that if someone was working on an exploration project in a cave, that area was off limits to other cave divers as long as the exploration was ongoing.

I'd been working on this area for months and diving it every weekend with few exceptions so there was no reason to think my exploration wasn't ongoing.

Except I wasn't talking about it. I was so worried about someone hearing about my find and ignoring cave diving etiquette that I hadn't said anything about it. So did this person technically scoop my lead? If it wasn't common knowledge that I was exploring this cave, could it be considered bad form?

I didn't know and at the moment I didn't care. All I cared about was that my lead had been scooped and I had to find out how much line had been laid beyond the end of my line. I went around the corner twenty feet from the end of my line and the cave passage opened up even bigger. The tunnel must have tripled in size!

Not only was this going to be a fight to keep the end of the line, but now I had walls that were at least forty feet apart from each other in a dark cave. Finding new leads off of this main tunnel was going to be a lot more difficult.

I wished I hadn't left my scooter behind. It was slow going swimming along this line. I wanted to zoom over the line to get to the end of it so I could tie in the line from my own reel and take back the end of the line for myself.

I continued swimming as quickly as I could over the line, looking around occasionally to see if any leads off this tunnel popped out at me. I was more concerned about where this line went, though. How far had this thief gotten?

I looked at my dive computer display. I had already swum about ten minutes from the end of my line. Ten minutes! At a swim pace of fifty feet per minute, my usual, that meant five hundred feet. I was moving a little faster than that though. Maybe sixty to seventy feet per minute. So my end of line had been extended six to seven hundred feet.

So far. I wasn't at the end of this new line yet. And I didn't see the end in sight.

As I swept my light beam around the tunnel, I noticed a line heading to the right. The tunnel looked like it kept going straight beyond that. Had the thief decided to turn right for some reason? I sped up even more. A few seconds later I saw that the line continued straight and there was another line tied into it heading to the right. Whoever had done this had not only extended the end of my line but had also explored tunnels shooting off from this one.

How was I going to get all of this surveyed and continue my exploration? Fuck the survey! I just needed to find the end of the line and reclaim it as my own.

I noticed another light behind me. I looked back. It was Lindsey. I had forgotten she was with me. I reluctantly stopped and turned around, frustrated that she was preventing me from getting to the end of this line.

Lindsey pointed her index finger up and circled it around, the hand signal for turn around. What the hell? I shook my head no. She circled her finger again and then pointed at the pressure gauge on one of her tanks. I reflexively looked at my own pressure gauge. The needle was pointing at 2500 psi. That was our turn pressure. I had breathed through one third of my air.

3

Lindsey

I slowly walked up behind Joey in the parking lot of the apartment complex where we lived. I looked around but didn't see anyone else. Thankfully, no one had witnessed Joey's outburst. I had never seen him like this. He was normally quiet and reserved. Joey wasn't one to make a scene. This was very out of character for him.

"Joe? You okay?"

He slowly turned around to face me and raised his arms up. I instinctively jumped back. I don't know why but I thought he was going to hit me. He had never touched me in a bad way so there wasn't a reason for me to think that. Except I had also never witnessed him behaving this way. I wasn't quite sure what might happen next.

"Yeah, I guess."

He reached out for me, and I flinched again.

"What's up with that? Why are you jumping away from me?"

"I don't know, Joe. I'm not meaning to do it. I've just never seen you behave this way and it's a reflex."

"I'm not going to hurt you. I would never do that! I'm sorry I lost it. I don't know what came over me. I'm just so angry at what happened."

"I know, babe. I'm upset about it, too. But we'll deal with it. We'll find out who did this and deal with that person. That much I promise."